MISSING IN MANHATTAN

. . . is an intriguing collection of mystery and suspense tales by The Adams Round Table, bestselling authors who are devoted to nothing less than murder—and Manhattan!

═══════════════════

JUSTIN SCOTT   gives a female police officer a chance to show her stuff—on the streets of a deadly neighborhood—in "The Commissioner's Moll."

MICKEY FRIEDMAN   searches all over town for the lover who left in "Missing You."

JOYCE HARRINGTON   asks if a mother's marital advice could include murder in "Momma's Done a Flit."

WARREN MURPHY   investigates the murder of a mechanic with money to kill for when P.I. Devlin Tracy goes "Looking for Mister Green."

LUCY FREEMAN   analyzes the motives for murder when a New York shrink uncovers the secrets of five suspects in "The Great Taboo."

═══════════════════

The Ad_____ _____ _____ _____ erpart to the legend_____ _____ ___ ___l in 1982 by Mary ___ _____ _____ ___ the members m__ _____ _____ __ craft—plot murder ___ _____ _____ __ of the best-loved m____ ___ _____ _____. Collectively they have produced ___ ___ 100 novels, including bestsellers and Edgar Award–winners.

Also by the Authors of
THE ADAMS ROUND TABLE

MURDER IN MANHATTAN
A BODY IS FOUND

MISSING IN

MANHATTAN

The Adams Round Table

MARY HIGGINS CLARK
JUSTIN SCOTT • LUCY FREEMAN
JUDITH KELMAN • STANLEY COHEN
WARREN MURPHY • MICKEY FRIEDMAN
THOMAS CHASTAIN • JOYCE HARRINGTON
DOROTHY SALISBURY DAVIS

Created by Bill Adler

BERKLEY PRIME CRIME, NEW YORK

"Missing You" copyright © 1992 by Mickey Friedman
"Just Another New York Christmas Story" copyright © 1992 by Stanley Cohen
"Area Code 212" copyright © 1992 by Thomas Chastain
"Momma's Done a Flit" copyright © 1992 by Joyce Harrington
"To Forget Mary Ellen" copyright © 1992 by Dorothy Salisbury Davis
"The Absent Present" copyright © 1992 by Judith Kelman
"The Great Taboo" copyright © 1992 by Lucy Freeman
"Looking for Mister Green" copyright © 1992 by Warren Murphy
"The Commissioner's Moll" copyright © 1992 by Justin Scott
"Plumbing for Willy" copyright © 1992 by Mary Higgins Clark

MISSING IN MANHATTAN

A Berkley Prime Crime Book / published by arrangement with
Longmeadow Press

PRINTING HISTORY
Longmeadow Press edition published 1992
Berkley Prime Crime edition / March 1994

All rights reserved.
Copyright © 1992 by Bill Adler Books, Inc.
This book may not be reproduced in whole or in part,
by mimeograph or any other means, without permission.
For information address: Longmeadow Press,
201 High Ridge Road, Stamford, CT 06904.

ISBN: 0-425-14203-5

Berkley Prime Crime Books are published by The Berkley Publishing Group,
200 Madison Avenue, New York, New York 10016.
The name BERKLEY PRIME CRIME and
the BERKLEY PRIME CRIME design
are trademarks belonging to Berkley Publishing Corporation.

PRINTED IN THE UNITED STATES OF AMERICA

10 9 8 7 6 5 4 3 2 1

CONTENTS

INTRODUCTION   vii

MISSING YOU   1
  by Mickey Friedman

JUST ANOTHER NEW YORK
  CHRISTMAS STORY   33
  by Stanley Cohen

AREA CODE 212   60
  by Thomas Chastain

MOMMA'S DONE A FLIT   80
  by Joyce Harrington

TO FORGET MARY ELLEN   101
  by Dorothy Salisbury Davis

THE ABSENT PRESENT   121
  by Judith Kelman

THE GREAT TABOO   139
  by Lucy Freeman

LOOKING FOR MISTER GREEN   169
  by Warren Murphy

THE COMMISSIONER'S MOLL   193
  by Justin Scott

PLUMBING FOR WILLY   217
  by Mary Higgins Clark

INTRODUCTION

You might think that after seven years of monthly dinner meetings the members of The Adams Round Table would have engaged one another long enough. Not so. To be sure, we can almost anticipate one another's "pets and peeves." We can pretty well recognize one another's writing by its style, and most of us can say what most of us were last seen wearing at the round table. And while we rarely discuss politics or religion unless it bears on the fiction under consideration, we know our diverse affinities. No, the engagement at the round table comes from the reason for our meeting in the first place: it is in the ability of each of us to surprise. And that, at table or at typewriter, is the key to wonderland.

The Adams Round Table, founded by Mary Higgins Clark and Thomas Chastain, and named after the owner of the restaurant where we meet, gathers to discuss the craft of the mystery. And what, I ask, is craft if not the ability to surprise?

Fiction that does not surprise is not a story. It may be an elegant or an inept piece of writing, but it is not a story. But who among us at the table would not admit that to surprise, to spring the unexpected action with utter believability at the exact right moment, is the most difficult challenge a writer must face?

We are not likely to talk of surprises in our works in progress unless we doubt that they are indeed surprises or unless we fear they will not pass the test of credibility. For the writer in need, this is the moment when someone at the round table may endear him- or herself forever. He will ask the *right* question. It may pertain to any of the myriad elements of story, such as character, situation, locale, point of view, but it will illuminate the flaw. And almost always, when a writer discovers why something is wrong, he or she instinctively knows what will make it right.

Along with craft we talk of a medley of things. We celebrate one another's successes and help heal disappointments. We've all had them. We require an accounting of our work life, going around the table every month. We talk a lot about movies: it is hardly arguable that much is to be learned from that kindred craft. We share the advice of good editors; we share the experiences that fuel our fiction. We discuss murders of the day and trials in progress.

The subject of money sometimes enters the conversation. It is one of the most difficult things to keep out since we all write for money and all make it, but to be sure, in quite varying amounts. We discuss royalty rates, book returns, signings, publicity, gossip in the trade, and whether it's worthwhile to write a short story. Our consensus there is a resounding "Yes!" whether the gain is financial or in the flexing of our craft. Witness the ten stories in *Missing in Manhattan*.

They seem a kind of "Rainbow Coalition." Every story discovers someone or something to be missing, but except for that and the Manhattan locale, the stories go off in all directions.

Thomas Chastain's "Area Code 212" builds, call by call, entirely on dialogue: I am reminded of the radio suspense classic "Sorry, Wrong Number."

In Mary Higgins Clark's "Plumbing for Willy," Willy the plumber and Alvirah the cleaning lady win the $40 million lottery. Willy is kidnapped. Alvirah, afraid to go to the police lest it endanger Willy's life, plumbs his whereabouts on her own.

In "Just Another New York Christmas Story," Stanley Cohen gives us the tale of a missing Santa Claus who is found, you might say, in the Nick of time.

"To Forget Mary Ellen" by Dorothy Salisbury Davis is the story of a hit gone right, but terribly, terribly wrong.

In "The Great Taboo," Lucy Freeman's psychoanalyst, Dr. Ames, probes the cruel dark side of a man to learn who killed him.

Mickey Friedman's "Missing You" is the tale of a woman who knows the value of what she has lost and how far she would go to get it back.

"Momma's Done a Flit" is a grand romp by Joyce Harrington, but a romp with death.

In "The Absent Present," Judith Kelman gives us a little horror story of the twentieth reunion of the exclusive Parcher School for girls.

In Warren Murphy's "Looking for Mister Green," his P.I. Devlin Tracy thrusts through a maze of women's wiles to bring a killer to justice.

Justin Scott's "The Commissioner's Moll" tells of a perky young cop who wants to be a detective, not a chauffeur. To achieve both ends, the Commissioner partners with her on a case of her choice.

The eleventh member of the round table does not write stories, but many's the illumination contributed by playwright Frederick Knott, who perpetrated the surprise of surprises in *Dial M for Murder*.

Whitley Strieber, one of the original members, is not represented in this collection, but he has returned to the round table after a leave of absence when such stellar novels as "Communion" and "Unholy Fire" took him outside the province of the mystery.

So welcome to The Adams Round Table. Our next toast will be to you, our readers. Ciao!

—Dorothy Salisbury Davis
FOR THE ADAMS ROUND TABLE

Mickey
Friedman

MISSING
YOU

1

NATHANIEL WAS GONE WHEN COURTNEY CAME HOME FROM WORK. As
soon as she walked in, she noticed the open door to the hall
closet. His few clothes—faded jeans, a battered leather jacket,
an almost-new gray cashmere suit, an ancient tuxedo he'd said
he bought in a thrift shop—were no longer hanging there.

When Nathaniel moved in, Courtney had offered to make
room in the bedroom closet, shift some of her clothes. He
refused. "I'll leave my stuff here," he said with a teasing grin.
"Handy for a quick getaway."

He had, it seemed, gotten away.

Courtney put down her briefcase and searched the apartment. The rooms seemed even more barren and cheerless than
they had pre-Nathaniel. The place was on the tenth floor of a
high-rise on the far reaches of the Upper East Side. The traffic

on Second Avenue rattled the windows night and day, and the views were of windows in other buildings identical to her own, but the rent was reasonable. Some people even counted her lucky to have so much space. That's what Nathaniel had said when he first saw it: "Wow. Look at all the *room*."

Nathaniel had left no note, and he had left none of his possessions behind: not a used toothbrush, or the New York Mets mug he drank his breakfast coffee out of, or his Walkman. Neither—and she did hate herself for checking—had he taken anything of hers, even though there were a couple of valid credit cards in the desk drawer, as well as an envelope containing a hundred and fifty dollars in cash. Now she could admit, privately, that they'd been put there as a little test for Nathaniel.

So—he'd left what she could spare, and taken away the single thing she couldn't bear to lose, which was himself.

She had expected it, hadn't she? She hadn't imagined that they would stay together, maybe scrape up enough money to buy a place in the country, cheer each other along into old age?

In the first place, Nathaniel was fifteen years younger than Courtney, and old age never entered his mind. Courtney was looking at forty. She was looking at forty, and she'd just lost the best thing that had happened to her in the past—what? ten years? fifteen? Why not go on and say her whole life?

2

Most of the time, Courtney was cautious and sensible. She had a shrewd mind and an eye for detail. These qualities made her invaluable to her boss, Mr. Benson, a Wall Street executive. In their nearly two decades together, Courtney had heard Mr. Benson tell his callers, "Get in touch with my girl Courtney— she'll arrange it," and then, "Get in touch with Courtney, my good right hand," and, as the years slid by, "Get in touch with my right-hand woman—Courtney."

Prudent as she was, Courtney also had a buccaneering side. This part of her was fearless in Mr. Benson's behalf. Through sheer gall she could get him a table, and a good table at that, in any restaurant in New York City. She could get him tickets when the show was sold out. She could get him invited to parties.

The buccaneer Courtney had been ascendant when she met Nathaniel. The cautious Courtney would never have touched him.

Courtney and Nathaniel had been sitting next to each other on stools at a sushi bar across the street from Courtney's apartment building. As she often did, Courtney was having a solitary early dinner. She was never sure how it happened, but suddenly a piece of sushi flipped over and landed in her lap. Startled, she looked down. Red-gold salmon roe was oozing from its seaweed wrapping onto the skirt of her white wool suit.

"Oh, God, I don't believe I did it!" a voice said, and she turned to the stunning green-eyed young man beside her, whose awkwardly crossed chopsticks were dangling from his fingers. That was Nathaniel.

Later, when they'd shared Oriental food many times and she knew how expertly he handled chopsticks, she'd said, "You threw that sushi on purpose, so you could pick me up."

Nathaniel raised his eyebrows and smiled.

"You did," she insisted. She was positive.

Nathaniel said, "Do you want your fortune cookie? Or can I have it?"

Courtney didn't press the issue, because of the embarrassing question that would surely arise: Why would he do it? Courtney was—you could call her nice-looking. She kept in shape, had pleasant blue eyes, and spent money on good haircuts and blond streaks. Still, she couldn't kid herself that she was in the same league with Nathaniel, in either looks or style. If he'd wanted to pick her up, he probably wouldn't have had to throw sushi in her lap. So she said, "The cookie's all yours," and dropped the subject.

Nathaniel had told her he was "between apartments," camping out with friends. He moved in very soon. This was not typical of Courtney. She worked hard to afford an apartment she didn't have to share, and she valued her privacy. But Nathaniel was such fun to be with, so agreeable, so sensitive and inventive in bed, that she urged the move while he hesitated.

"Look. You don't have a place to live, right?" she said.

"Right." Nathaniel was standing in front of a picture window that looked out on a picture window across the courtyard. She saw him in silhouette—lanky body, hands in jeans pockets, tousled reddish-brown hair, androgynously sexy.

She swept her hand to display the expanse of the living room, to suggest the two bedrooms and two bathrooms beyond. "I've got *tons* of space here."

"I know."

"It wouldn't have to be for . . . long."

"Gotcha."

"Then for heaven's sake, why—"

The hands came out of the pockets and the arms spread wide. "I don't have any money, Courtney. I'm broke."

"So—"

"I couldn't help with the rent or anything."

"Nathaniel, I just . . . don't . . . *care.*"

Nathaniel moved in. After he did, Courtney had a brief interval of buyer's remorse. She knew nothing about Nathaniel and he seemed disinclined to enlighten her, turning aside the most innocuous questions. He didn't have a job, and for all she knew he never had. Suppose he was a criminal, a drug dealer? But because when she was with him she was happy, these fears bothered her only when Nathaniel wasn't around. They led to a shameful episode when, in his absence, she went through his possessions.

Nauseated with self-disgust, she investigated the pockets of his jackets, pawed through his underwear drawer. She found no address book, no letters, no papers. She took his canvas-sided suitcase from the back of the hall closet and unzipped it. It was empty except for a tee-shirt wrapped around an angular object which proved to be, not a box full of cocaine, but a book.

It was an innocuous–looking book in drab gray paper-covered boards. A bookplate was mounted on the inside cover, a woodcut of a galleon under sail and, in Gothic type, *From the Library of H. H. Marriner.* She looked at the title page. *A Shropshire Lad* by Housman. The publication date was in Roman numerals. She worked it out: 1896. Courtney remembered A. E. Housman from school. He had written a poem about cherry trees.

Crouching there holding *A Shropshire Lad*, Courtney felt her face reddening. How clever of her to have uncovered Nathaniel's dirty secret, that he kept a book of poetry in his suitcase. She closed *A Shropshire Lad* and put everything back as it had been. In those moments, she decided to take Nathaniel as he was, enjoy him, and not pry into his past.

Starting then, their time together was bliss. Nathaniel didn't help with the rent, but he helped in other ways. He proved to be a decent cook, specializing in pastas and gargantuan salads with unexpected ingredients. He bought fresh flowers every few days, and as early spring arrived Courtney came home to the scent of freesias or tuberoses. He went shopping with her and convinced her to buy an intricately patterned Bokhara carpet on sale at Bloomingdale's to make the sterile living room more homey. He did the cleaning and hauled the laundry down to the basement laundry room and brought it back warm, good-smelling, folded.

Sexually, they were passionately attuned. When Nathaniel breathed, "You're wonderful. Sensational," his voice sliding past her ear so faintly that she, half-dozing, barely heard it, she couldn't help but believe he felt something for her. Keeping her early vow, she didn't grasp or make demands. Everything she wanted or needed was given to her freely.

For a while.

In recent weeks, Courtney had gotten out of the habit of planning dinner. Now, abandoned, she stood in the refrigerator's glow, gazing at the nearly empty shelves. Nathaniel shopped every day, didn't keep a lot of food around. There was a bowl of leftover brown rice, covered with plastic wrap. Imported blackberry jam. A thirty-dollar bottle of Champagne.

Courtney had bought the Champagne. Nathaniel hardly drank at all. She had seen a display in a liquor store window and gone in on impulse, thinking she and Nathaniel might have something to celebrate sometime, or maybe they'd open it one night for a giggle. She took the bottle from the refrigerator, peeled off the aluminum wrapping around the top, untwisted the wire. The dull pop of the cork made her imagine a projectile lodging in the deep interior of her gut. She poured a tumbler full, not bothering with a Champagne flute—Nathaniel would have been horrified—and went to stand at the window in the dining area. In the evening gloom, she sipped and watched the ceaseless, growling traffic on Second Avenue.

She had known something was wrong in the past couple of days. Since he saw the card in the laundry room.

The previous Saturday, Courtney had had errands to do. Instead of going with her, Nathaniel decided to wash clothes while she was gone. Courtney had ridden down to the basement with him, because leaving Nathaniel, even for an hour to do Saturday errands, was always a wrench.

They had trundled the wire cart into the laundry room, with its steamy smell and groaning washers and dryers, to find all the washers already in use. Nathaniel rolled his eyes. "That's Saturday for you."

"Take it back upstairs and come with me."

"Nope." He steered the cart toward the clothes-folding table with an air of martyrdom. "I've gotten this far. I'll wait." There was a copy of the *Post* on the table, and he was reaching for it when she saw him stop cold. His eye seemed to have been caught by something on the bulletin board beside the table.

Courtney saw the color in Nathaniel's face drain to yellow. She could see every freckle on the bridge of his nose. "What is it?" she asked.

Nathaniel seemed reluctant to stop looking at the bulletin board, but he turned to her and said, "Nothing."

The bulletin board, a hodgepodge of scrawled notes, flyers, business cards, and posters, was where building residents and neighborhood businesses posted notices: used furniture or outgrown children's clothing for sale; animals needing new homes; tax accountancy or photocopying services; lost or stolen possessions. Courtney scanned it. "What on earth did you see?"

He squeezed her shoulder. "Nothing. Really." His color had come back a little. "No problem."

She didn't believe him, but what could she do? She waved good-bye and left.

And immediately returned, to watch him from the doorway.

She saw him reach out and remove a card from the board, where it had been secured with a pin. He half-turned in her direction as he studied it. She could discern no expression on his face, yet if she had to guess what he was feeling she would have said, without hesitation: dread.

After a while he seemed to sigh, his shoulders drooping. He

fastened the card to the board again, then leaned against the table, his head bent.

Courtney turned away. She went and did her errands. When she returned, she stopped in the laundry room. Nathaniel had already left. She had memorized the location of the card, and it was still on the board where he had replaced it. She took it down. It was an ordinary printed business card with a phone number in the lower left-hand corner:

Madame Sosostris
Clairvoyante

When she saw Nathaniel back in the apartment, she didn't mention the card, and neither did he. She studied him for changes. There might have been a new frantic note in his laugh, a wildness in his eyes, but for the most part he seemed the same as ever.

Courtney had put the card in her wallet. It was still there.

The Champagne tasted sour. She left the tumbler on the table and found her handbag, next to her briefcase on the floor by the front door. Back at the window, there was hardly enough light to make out the words and numbers on the card. She ran her thumb over the printing. Not engraved, not even thermographed. Flimsy stock. Cheap.

Madame Sosostris. A character in T. S. Eliot's poem, *The Waste Land*. Courtney hadn't looked up the reference. Maybe she should look it up now.

Maybe she should, but something kept her standing by the window, drinking the corrosive Champagne. A frantic chattering invaded her brain, an angry voice gabbling, *So what? So what? He left, didn't he? What do you care about the card? Let him go!*

She should let Nathaniel go. She wasn't going to demand explanations, beg him to come back. She had decided not to pry into his life, and she should stick to it. She had to keep her dignity.

She finished the tumbler of Champagne and poured another. It was dark now, the apartment illuminated only by the surreal yellow glow from the city outside. When she snapped on the ceiling fixture at last the other lights faded, replaced by her reflection in the windowpane.

Taking the Champagne with her, she went into the living room and pulled her old *Major Writers of America* text from the bottom bookshelf. The thin pages rustled under her fingers. She found *The Waste Land* and there, near the beginning, in the section entitled "The Burial of the Dead," was Madame Sosostris:

> *Madame Sosostris, famous clairvoyante,*
> *Had a bad cold, nevertheless*
> *Is known to be the wisest woman in Europe,*
> *With a wicked pack of cards. . . .*

Courtney felt dizzy. She blinked, tried to concentrate on the words. Madame Sosostris was reading Tarot cards.

> *Here is the man with three staves, and here the Wheel,*
> *And here is the one–eyed merchant, and this card,*
> *Which is blank, is something he carries on his back,*
> *Which I am forbidden to see.*

Courtney had had a Tarot reading once, at a street fair years ago. She associated it with the smell of Italian sausages frying in the next booth.

> *. . . I do not find*
> *The Hanged Man. Fear death by water.*
> *I see crowds of people, walking round in a ring.*

Courtney swallowed. Madame Sosostris's reading was threatening, full of menace. She remembered Nathaniel's pale face, the dread she believed he was feeling.

Drinking more of the sickening Champagne, she read the entire poem. By the time she reached the end her head was reeling. She put the textbook on the coffee table, slipped off her shoes, stretched out on the sofa, and passed out. Later she awoke, gagging and sweating. In the bathroom, she heaved until the spasms stopped, and sat on the cool tile floor with her head pressed against her bent knees.

3

Courtney didn't call the number on the card until the next afternoon.

Hung over and shaky, she had all she could do to get through the day. About three, though, an unexpected dead time came at the office. By then, Courtney had had a Coke, a tuna salad sandwich, quite a few painkillers, and was feeling a little better. Mr. Benson was out at a meeting. Her assistant was at the dentist. She took the card from her wallet, where she had replaced it, and dialed the number. A man answered. Courtney asked to speak to Madame Sosostris.

There was a long silence before the man said, "She isn't here." The man's voice was deep and nasal, with a New York edge. It was nothing like Nathaniel's.

"When will she be back?"

"Well"—another hesitation—"may I ask what it's about?"

Courtney tapped her desk with the eraser of her pencil. "I want to arrange a reading."

"A reading?"

"Yes, a reading. She's a psychic, isn't she?" Courtney never left herself vulnerable by sounding uncertain on the telephone.

"Right. She is. Actually, she's out of the country at the moment." The man seemed to be picking up steam as he went along. "I'm sorry," he added.

It took an excellent liar to fool Courtney, and apologies did not impress her. "That's a shame," she said. She moved in. "A friend of mine recommended her. Highly."

Another silence before the man said, "What's your friend's name?"

"Nathaniel Sawyer," said Courtney crisply. "When will Madame Sosostris be back?"

"Later in the week," he said slowly. "You can come Sunday at four. What's your name?"

"Courtney Pine."

"I see. Courtney Pine." He gave her an address in Greenwich Village, on Bank Street. He said, "Ring bell number three. The fee is a hundred dollars. Cash." He hung up.

In the several days until Sunday, Courtney had time to reconsider her visit to Bank Street. She kept thinking Nathaniel would call, even if only to explain why he'd taken off so abruptly. Even if only to apologize. When he didn't call, she told herself he didn't want to see her. She had worked up a fantasy about his being in danger to make his desertion more palatable.

Sunday was a sunny, mellow June day, a day when New York seemed almost benign. On the subway downtown, the faces of the riders had an unaccustomed dreaminess about them, or so Courtney imagined. She herself was perspiring with tension, and she climbed out on Twelfth Street blotting her face with a tissue. She put on her sunglasses and started for Bank Street.

The address she'd been given was a brownstone on a quiet, tree-shaded corner. The entrance to the building was in a recessed doorway. A row of five bells had slots for name placards next to each button. There was no name in the slot next to number three. Courtney pressed the button and waited, and in a minute the front door buzzed. She pushed it open and entered a shadowy hallway, where a staircase with a dark wood banister led upward.

The building was slightly shabby, the stair carpet frayed, the diamond-patterned wallpaper faded, but the atmosphere spoke more of a tight-fisted landlord than of squalor. Courtney gripped the banister rail. *Have you been in this place, Nathaniel?* Suppose he opened the door, was standing there when she knocked? But she didn't have to knock. The door with the tarnished brass numeral *3* stood ajar.

She pushed it open, and the smell of freesias wafted to her. A vase of them stood on a table next to the door. Her stomach lurched, and she pressed her handbag against her side. Stacks of books were piled on the floor of the narrow hall in front of her, pushed against the wall to allow for passage. Courtney stepped in and called, "Madame Sosostris?"

"Come in. In here," a voice answered. Courtney closed the door behind her and walked down the hall to double doors opening on a living room. She got an impression of musty Victorian elegance—a marble fireplace with a gilt-framed mirror above it, threadbare Oriental carpets, massive lamps with pleated silk shades—and books. Overfilled bookshelves lined the walls from floor to ceiling, and books were piled on the carpets, under the numerous occasional tables, and beside the overstuffed chairs.

Through gauzy curtains drawn over windows at one end of the room, Courtney could see green tops of trees in a back garden. A few feet in front of the window was a sofa where a woman reclined. When Courtney walked in, the woman raised her hand in a languid salute. Her blue-black hair was backlit by the window, and stood out around her head in tumbled, possibly artful, disarray. She wore a deep red kimono, a black chiffon scarf wound around her throat. An ivory-colored crocheted afghan was spread over her lower body. Her dangling earrings were heavy gold, set with red stones. "Forgive me," she said in a throaty voice. "I haven't been well. Not well at all." She spoke in a fretful tone, in an accent Courtney couldn't identify.

"Madame Sosostris?" said Courtney again. She had advanced several steps into the room. Her hands, she realized, were clasped together like a supplicant's.

"That is a name I use. No doubt you realize it is not my own," said Madame Sosostris. She beckoned Courtney. Her curving fingernails were painted red. "You want a reading," she said as Courtney approached. "You want to exhaust poor, ill Madame Sosostris, do you?"

"Well—"

"Yes, you do, or you would not have come here to disturb me. Stop there. Sit in that chair. You have been told the fee is one hundred dollars in cash. Have you brought it?"

"Yes."

"Very, very good. Put it there, on the table next to you."

Sitting where Madame Sosostris had decreed, in a brocade chair some five feet from the clairvoyant's sofa, Courtney opened her handbag and counted out five twenties. She put them under a heavy ashtray on the table beside her.

"So," Madame Sosostris said. Her dark eyes were heavily lined. She had a bony face, a prominent nose, a mouth painted glistening red. "So, so, so." Her voice trailed off, her eyes half-closed. Silence fell.

Waiting, Courtney looked around. Branches tossed in the sunny garden beyond the curtains. A door in the wall opposite the hallway stood half-open. Far away, a siren sounded.

Madame Sosostris said nothing.

After several minutes, Courtney cleared her throat. "Maybe I should tell you why I've come," she said.

Madame Sosostris's eyes flew open. "It isn't for you to tell me why you have come," she said. "Surely it is for me to tell you."

"All right," Courtney said. She laced her fingers in her lap and waited.

As if to show Courtney who was boss, Madame Sosostris let another interval pass before she began to speak. "Happy people do not seek my advice," she said. "It does not take extraordinary powers for me to know you are unhappy. But why? There are so many reasons for unhappiness. The world teems with them."

Courtney opened her mouth, and Madame Sosostris held up a hand. "Do not speak," she said.

Courtney pressed her lips together.

When Madame Sosostris began to talk again, it was in a hoarse, incantatory tone, almost a chant. Running the words together in a rush, she said a number of things about Courtney that were indisputably true, if general and vague. Courtney was a loner. She had been a shy, sad child. She had dealt with many disappointments. Courtney was prosperous and intelligent, but something was missing in her life.

Missing.

Madame Sosostris sat up straighter. "Yes, I see loss," she said with more inflection. "You have suffered a painful, a terrible loss."

"Yes," Courtney said, the word lurching out of her.

She had forgotten she wasn't supposed to say anything. This time Madame Sosostris didn't chide her. She nodded and said, "And now you want to recover what you lost. You have become a searcher, scrabbling in corners, hoping for one more glimpse of your treasure, unwilling to realize—" Madame Sosostris stopped. She hid her mouth with the tips of her fingers. "I don't know if you will want to hear what I will tell you," she said.

"Go ahead."

"You are better off without your treasure," Madame Sosostris said. "You do not believe me now, but you must accept it.

Your treasure would surely have blighted your life. You must let it go." She wagged an admonitory finger. "Your loss is your gain. A paradox, but it is true." She bent her head for a moment and then said, "Do you have questions for me?"

"Yes, I do." Courtney leaned forward. "My . . . treasure. The thing I've lost. What if I'm afraid it's in danger? That it may . . . come to harm?"

Madame Sosostris sighed. "Your treasure has moved beyond your reach. What happens to it, whether harm or good fortune, is no longer your concern. I will tell you this, however. Your lost treasure is better off without you, as you are better off without it. You may take comfort from that, if you will."

Courtney was tired of fencing. "Do you know Nathaniel? Did you do a reading for him? Did you . . . give him a book?"

Madame Sosostris looked blank. "Nathaniel?"

"The young man—the young man I—"

Madame Sosostris shook her head. "I see many people. Young men, old men, young women, old women. If I kept them and their needs in my head, my brain would be like a hive of bees. If this Nathaniel was one of my clients I have forgotten him, just as I will forget you. Certainly I never gave him a book."

"He had your card. I saw him take it—"

"Many people throughout the world have my card, my dear," she snapped. She added, in a softer tone, "Your pain is intense. I feel it. Let it go. Let it go." Her head bowed forward, and her eyes closed.

"Well, thanks," said Courtney with asperity. She eyed her hundred dollars under the ashtray. And yet, even though she wasn't impressed with Madame Sosostris, perhaps the psychic had given reasonable advice. *Your treasure has moved beyond your reach. What happens to it . . . is no longer your concern.*

Still, it wasn't going to be easy to forget Nathaniel.

Courtney stood. Madame Sosostris opened her eyes, lolled back against the sofa cushion. "Godspeed," she said in a husky whisper. She did not get up to escort Courtney out.

As Courtney opened the apartment door she heard a male voice in the living room say, "All right?"

The only answer was a sibilant *"Shhhh!"*
Courtney let herself out and went down the stairs.

4

In the weeks that followed, several things happened: Courtney's assistant quit, and she had to hire a new one; she spent a
week in bed with a feverish summer cold; a former lover called
to announce his impending divorce and his interest in seeing
Courtney again. The new assistant and the cold worked out all
right. The former lover? Courtney saw him a couple of times,
but she couldn't get interested.

She thought about Nathaniel a lot.

Although she tried to ignore it, the notion that Nathaniel had
been in danger continued to bother her. She considered going
to the police, but balked at the thought of the interview: You
say he took all his possessions with him? Have you checked
with his friends and family? You think he might be in trouble
because of something you read in a *poem*?

You see, officer, I miss him so much. I can't believe he'd
take off without—

Excuse me, lady. Next!

Lyrical June gave way to July. The sidewalks baked. The
humid air smelled like exhaust fumes with an overlay of
garbage and urine. Shouts, screams, and car alarms echoed
through the simmering evenings. By August, everybody who
counted had escaped to the country, to rusticate until after
Labor Day.

The rusticators didn't include Courtney. She was still at her
post, still hurting like hell, reading the *Times* at her desk on
slow mornings while Mr. Benson spent a good part of the week
in Sag Harbor.

Although activity winds down, it never quite halts in New
York. Even in the depths of August, a small theater company
will open a show. And since so little is happening, the *Times*
might run a photo along with the review. And because
Courtney's boss was in Sag Harbor, Courtney might have time
to notice the photo.

Which is how she happened to rediscover Madame Sosostris.

The play was Oscar Wilde's *The Importance of Being Earnest*, which had opened for a limited run at a tiny theater downtown. The *Times* review was illustrated with a photograph of a scene between the hero, Algernon, and the elderly Lady Bracknell. Courtney had spread the paper on her desk, and her coffee mug was placed so it half-obscured the picture. She picked up the mug to take a swallow, and there was Madame Sosostris.

She wasn't Lady Bracknell. She was Algernon.

Courtney did not know how she made the imaginative leap that told her the indolent psychic and the jaunty, straw-hatted man in the striped jacket were the same person. She knew immediately. She didn't have to sketch tangled tresses on the picture, or outline the dark eyes, or paint the lips. Madame Sosostris was unquestionably this youngish male actor, this—she checked the photo caption—David Del Valle.

Courtney picked up the phone. Despite the *Times* notice, the box office at the Bare Bones Theater did not seem to be mobbed with requests for tickets to *The Importance of Being Earnest*. They would be glad to hold one for the evening performance.

The night was meltingly, outrageously hot. After a hellish ride in a taxi without air conditioning, she arrived at the theater, a converted warehouse on Mercer Street in SoHo, to find a number of people gathered on the sidewalk in front of the entrance, fanning themselves with programs. When she went in to claim her ticket, she realized the theater wasn't air conditioned either.

Ticket in hand, plucking the front of her dress to promote air circulation, she strolled over to inspect the bulletin board where black-and-white glossies of the cast were displayed next to a blowup of the *Times* review.

There he was. David Del Valle, alias Madame Sosostris. In this incarnation he had black curls falling over his brow, but the eyes, nose, and mouth were definitely the same. *Your loss is your gain.* Thank you so much, Mr. Del Valle.

With time to spare, Courtney inspected the layout of the Bare Bones Theater. The place lived up to its name. The bathrooms were little more than tacked-together plywood stalls. Around the corner from them hung a curtain, blocking the hallway. She could see light behind it, and hear a low babble of voices. A furtive peek told her she had, as she suspected, located a communal cast dressing room. She went back the way she had come and found her seat.

Courtney had once seen *The Importance of Being Ernest,* and as best she remembered she had enjoyed it. She didn't enjoy it this time. Even without the constant, desperate rustle of people fanning, she would have had trouble concentrating. Peripherally, though, she noticed that the actors were very good. Especially David Del Valle, who was as convincing as Algernon as he had been as Madame Sosostris. When at last the curtain fell—metaphorically, since there was no curtain—David Del Valle received the biggest ovation when he took his bow. He responded by grinning and blowing a kiss to the audience, then bounding offstage only to be coaxed back one last time. Then the house lights came up and the overheated audience staggered out to get some air.

Courtney was the first one up the aisle. At the cast dressing room, she pulled the curtain aside. Immediately, a young man in a white tee-shirt, his blond hair slicked back, stepped in front of her and said, "Sorry. Private."

"Will Mr. Del Valle be coming out this way?"

"Could be. You a friend of his?"

She waved her program: "I was hoping to get his autograph."

The man smiled. Over his shoulder he yelled, "Hey, Dave! You got fans out here!"

"In a minute!" a voice replied. Courtney moved back down the hall. A few other people arrived and also stood waiting.

David Del Valle emerged from behind the curtain wearing black jeans, black high-top sneakers, round glasses with black wire rims, and a Shakespeare in the Park tee-shirt. Some of the people hanging around spoke to him, and he smiled, shook hands, patted backs. Courtney was standing by the entrance to the lobby. When he reached her she held out her program and said, "May I have your autograph?"

He flashed the grin she'd seen onstage, said, "Sure thing. You got a pen?" and took the program.

Courtney handed him a ballpoint. "How will you sign? David Del Valle? Algernon? or Madame Sosostris?"

David Del Valle's hands fell to his sides. For the first time, he looked directly at Courtney. "Oh, shit," he said. "Shit, shit, shit." He dropped the program and pen and shoved past her into the lobby.

Courtney was right behind him. "Wait a minute. I want to talk to you."

He shook his head and kept walking.

"You owe me an explanation!" she cried. Heads swiveled at the concession stand, where people were clustered drinking lemonade.

At the front entrance he turned and said, "It was a job, all right? That's all I've got to say." He pushed through the glass doors and started down Mercer Street at a brisk jog.

"A job? Who hired you?" Courtney was wearing sandals with a moderately high heel. She ran after him. Except for a small group lingering in front of the theater, Mercer Street was deserted, only half-illuminated by streetlights. A hot breeze whirled a mini-tornado of trash—a foam cup, gum wrappers, a crumpled napkin—along the sidewalk. She speeded up. "Tell me!" she yelled.

David Del Valle turned. Walking backward, he made a hushing gesture. "Shut up, for God's sake!"

Her breath catching in her chest, Courtney said, "If you don't tell me, I'll come back tomorrow night. And the night after. And the night after—"

"Oh, Jesus God." Still walking backward, he said, "It was a job. He said it was a joke."

"Who said? *Who?*" She was only a few yards from him now, stumbling forward in the accursed sandals.

He shook his head. "I can't say any more."

Courtney stopped walking. *"Listen to me!"* she shrieked. "My life has been screwed up, and I want to know why!" She buried her face in her hands and felt her shoulders start to heave. She thought: I'm not doing this.

"I'm an actor!" cried David Del Valle, sounding almost as anguished as Courtney. "That's all I am, an actor! Your quarrel is with Bobbo, not with me!"

Courtney took her hands away from her face. She blinked through a teary haze. "Who's Bobbo?"

"Bobbo Steig, all right? Take it up with him. That's all I've got to say." He turned and pounded down Mercer Street.

"Who's Bobbo Steig?" Courtney called after him. She wasn't surprised when he didn't stop or answer.

5

Courtney had to walk all the way to Sixth Avenue before she found a taxi. When she did she told the driver to take her to Bank Street.

On Bank Street, the streetlights cast leaf shadows on the pavement, and the townhouses looked sturdy and placid. Courtney could see light in the window of the third-floor apartment where she had had her meeting with Madame Sosostris. She climbed the front steps and scanned the row of doorbells. Now, there was a card in the slot next to number three:

Robert Steig
Old and Rare Books

She pushed the button and waited. After a few minutes, a static-obscured voice came out of the speaker, asking who it was.

"It's Courtney Pine. I'm looking for Nathaniel."

"He isn't here."

She leaned in the doorway. Even in the heat, the shaped stone was chilly against her shoulder. "Is that Robert Steig?"

"Yes."

"I have to talk to you, Mr. Steig."

"Call me tomorrow."

"If you don't talk to me I'll call the police tomorrow and report Nathaniel missing."

No answer, but the front door buzzed.

The man awaiting her in the open doorway of apartment number three was in his fifties and paunchy, with lank salt-and-pepper hair and deep circles under his eyes. He wore a knit shirt and rumpled khaki shorts, and was barefoot. His legs were white and thin, with knobby knees and prominent blue veins. When Courtney got close to him, she smelled liquor. "Mr. Steig?" she said.

He nodded. "What's all this about?" he asked, but the question was without heat.

"I expect you know," said Courtney. "Surely David Del Valle has called you by now."

"He has, as a matter of fact." He stepped back, and with mock courtliness bowed to invite her in. She walked past him, down the hall still lined with piles of books, to the living room. The sofa where Madame Sosostris had reclined was littered with newspapers, and a glass and a bottle of Scotch sat on a side table. "Have a seat," Steig said, and Courtney was sure, now, that it was Robert Steig she had spoken with when she called to make the appointment with Madame Sosostris.

She didn't sit down. She wouldn't accept even that much hospitality. She stood next to the table where she had left her hundred dollars. A book, bound in brown leather, lay where the ashtray had been. *Leaves of Grass,* by Walt Whitman. She ran her fingers over the cover. Steig lingered by the double doors, watching her.

"You know why I'm here," she said.

He grimaced. "I know you're a persistent woman. You should have taken good old Madame Sosostris's advice and let well enough alone."

"Were you listening?"

"Naturally."

"Why did you set up that stupid charade?"

Steig rubbed the back of his neck. Overgrown locks of his hair shadowed his face. "I don't expect you to believe me, but I did it to spare your feelings and end a difficult situation gracefully."

Courtney shook her head. "To *spare* my feelings? You mean Nathaniel—"

"To put it plainly, Nathaniel doesn't want to see you. Or hear from you. I thought if we sugarcoated the message via psychic mumbo-jumbo you'd accept it and go on about your business."

Courtney was quivering, but she kept her voice steady. "What do you know about what Nathaniel wants?"

Steig chuckled. "I'm the expert on what Nathaniel wants. He lived with me for the past ten years."

I shouldn't have come, Courtney thought. I can't stand here and listen to this man. To avoid looking at him, she picked up *Leaves of Grass* and opened it. There was a bookplate on the inside cover—a galleon in full sail, *From the library of H. H. Marriner.*

"I took him in off the street when he was fifteen years old," Steig was saying. "And so you don't misunderstand, when I say we lived together I mean we were a couple. Lovers. If you don't believe me, ask anybody. Ask David Del Valle."

Courtney closed *Leaves of Grass* and replaced it on the table. She would not show weakness to Robert Steig. "So why did he leave you?"

"We quarreled. The reasons are unimportant." A muscle jumped in Steig's cheek. "Nathaniel took off. I tracked him down. He came back."

"What about the card? Madame Sosostris?"

"A private joke. *The Waste Land* is one of Nathaniel's favorite poems. Juvenile, but there's no accounting for tastes. When I found out where he was, I had the card printed and tacked it up in the laundry room. I know Nathaniel. I knew he'd be there doing somebody's laundry. The card was to tell him I'd found him. He called, so I came and got him."

Courtney was burning, scalding. Nathaniel and Bobbo, together again. And Courtney? Where did that leave Courtney? She was burning, yet in a frosty voice, as if she didn't believe a word of it, she said, "I'd like to see Nathaniel. Hear the story from him."

"That won't be possible."

"I don't care how much he doesn't want to see me. I insist on—"

"It's impossible because he's in California. As a getting-back-together present, I stood him to six months in Hollywood. He always believed he could make a go of it in movies. I think his chances are slim to none, but it seemed a good time to let him get it out of his system."

Courtney faced Robert Steig. "Then have him call me."

He shook his head. "I already told you—"

"Have him call me, or I keep looking for him. I won't give up just because you tell me to."

"Ms. Pine—"

"Have him call me." She swept past him out of the room.

In the taxi going uptown, Courtney tried to take in what Steig had told her. She was not terribly shocked at the revelation of Nathaniel's homosexuality, or bisexuality, or whatever it was. The possibility had been in her mind from the beginning, and she had been scrupulous about protection when they made love.

That part of Steig's story she believed. Why didn't she believe the rest?

Courtney moved restlessly on the cab's lumpy seat. She didn't believe Nathaniel had called Steig, or had wanted to go back to him. Maybe she was trying to salvage her pride, but she had seen Nathaniel's face when he looked at that card. And she knew, dammit, she *knew*—that he had been afraid.

Courtney did not buy Steig's assertion that Nathaniel "always believed he could make a go of it in movies." Nathaniel had never expressed such an ambition to her: He didn't even enjoy *going* to movies. If Steig had told her he had sent Nathaniel to Paris for cooking lessons at Cordon Bleu because he had always wanted to be a chef, or that he had sent Nathaniel to a Mets farm team because he had always wanted to be a major league pitcher, it wouldn't have strained Courtney's credulity quite so much. But the movies? She could almost hear Nathaniel laughing at the notion, those whoops of laughter that deepened his dimples and crinkled the corners of his eyes, and—

Tears began rolling down Courtney's face. They were still falling when she got out of the taxi on Ninety-third Street.

6

The next day was Saturday. Courtney woke up late, bleary and headachy. Although the air-conditioner was doing its job, churning mournfully and keeping the temperature a stale seventy-five or so, she could tell it was hot again by looking out the window at the abbreviated clothing and underwater-slow movements of people on the street below.

She made iced coffee and toasted a bagel, thinking about Robert Steig. Thinking about Nathaniel.

Courtney's envy of Robert Steig had formed into a piercing ache in her chest. She heard Steig's voice: *I know Nathaniel. I knew he'd be doing somebody's laundry.* How could Courtney be so sure Nathaniel didn't want to be a movie star? She hadn't even known *The Waste Land* was his favorite poem.

She swallowed, trying to force the pain away. Nathaniel had owned only one book that she knew about—the edition of *A Shropshire Lad* she'd found in his suitcase. That book had had the same bookplate, *From the library of H. H. Marriner,* as the *Leaves of Grass* she'd seen in Steig's apartment last night.

Who in the hell, Courtney began to wonder, was H. H. Marriner? And what were Nathaniel and Robert Steig doing with H. H. Marriner's books?

There was only one Marriner listed in the Manhattan white pages. Celia Marriner, on Park Avenue. Courtney left the directory open and went to get dressed. She needed to pull herself together in order to make this call.

She made her face up, donned a crisp cotton sundress, brushed her hair a hundred strokes. When she was sure she could sound confident, not like some slob sitting in her nightgown with a half-eaten bagel in front of her, she dialed the number.

A recording informed her that Celia Marriner's line had been disconnected.

Instead of flinging the phone across the room, Courtney slammed down the receiver, crossed her arms tightly over the front of her dress, and stared out the window at a plastic bag wallowing past in the wind. When she was calmer, she hauled the Yellow Pages out of the drawer, turned to the listings for "Book Dealers—Used & Rare," and started phoning. She didn't allow herself to stop and demand why she was doing this. Deep down, she knew she was doing it because she couldn't think of anything else to do.

The exercise had begun in frustration, and so it continued. Many used and rare book dealers were closed on Saturday. Those she reached displayed reticence, indifference, and even outright hostility to her inquiries. She claimed to be searching for an 1896 edition—which would be the first edition, a dealer informed her in a surly tone—of A. E. Housman's *A Shropshire Lad.* She had heard there was one in the library of somebody called H. H. Marriner.

Most of the people she reached seemed to think she was crazy; a few had copies of various editions of *A Shropshire Lad* they wanted to sell her; nobody admitted to knowing, or knowing of, H. H. Marriner.

Until she got to the W's. The listing for Charles Wykes wasn't even in boldface, and he sounded a hundred years old. At the name H. H. Marriner he rasped out a phlegmy laugh and said, "My word, young lady. Horace Marriner has been dead forty years or more."

"Has he? I was wondering—"

"Hold on a sec."

She heard the receiver thump down, and a sound of shuffling papers. This went on for several minutes, until Wykes got back on the line and said, "He passed away in 1954, to be precise."

Uncertain how to respond, Courtney said, "I'm sorry to hear that."

Wykes seemed uninterested in condolences. "We did sell him a few things," he went on. "My God, looking at my records, Horace practically *stole* a copy of Thomas Paine's *Common Sense* from me. I was young then. Eager for a sale."

"Mr. Wykes—"

"And look at the price I gave him on a first edition of *Huckleberry Finn*! What was I thinking of?"

"Mr. Wykes, do you know what happened to Mr. Marriner's library?"

"Why, I would imagine his widow inherited it. Dear Celia. She wasn't a collector herself."

"I'm afraid Celia's phone—"

"Celia and Horace had a daughter, too. Jane, her name was. Little Jane. She married a Rybold, if I'm not mistaken."

Jane Rybold, Courtney wrote on the phone pad. She extricated herself from Charles Wykes's burgeoning reminiscences and went back to the white pages, where she found four Rybolds listed, none of them Jane.

Jane was not difficult to locate. She proved to be married to one of the listed Rybolds, and she answered the phone herself when Courtney called. She had a pleasant manner, an upper-class New York accent, and a soothing willingness to listen as Courtney struggled to explain why she wanted to know what had happened to the library of H. H. Marriner. "You see, I had—have—a friend. A good friend, named Nathaniel Sawyer—"

"Nathaniel!" Jane Rybold broke in. "Is Nathaniel back in town? You tell him how naughty he is for not getting in touch with me. And for standing me up. I haven't forgiven him for that."

Courtney felt faint. She pressed a hand against her sweating forehead. "Mrs. Rybold, do you think I could possibly—see you? Sometime soon? To have a talk?"

Any friend of Nathaniel's, apparently, was a friend of Jane Rybold's. If Courtney was free, perhaps she could come for tea at four-thirty? She gave an address in the East Seventies. No, no apartment number. Jane and her family, Courtney deduced, had an entire house to themselves.

For her interview with Jane Rybold, Courtney changed into her linen suit and her double strand of coral beads. She wore panty hose, even though the temperature was pressing one hundred. The address she'd been given turned out to be a superb limestone town house. It was probably too small to be called a mansion, but the word came to mind. A maid ushered her through cool, high-ceilinged rooms to french doors opening on a jewel-like garden. The supple branches of weeping cherry trees stirred in the warm wind, and yellow roses nodded on trellises. There, a woman wearing grass-stained trousers, a voluminous untucked blue work shirt, gardening clogs, and a straw sun hat was kneeling in the dirt of a flower border. When Courtney appeared, she looked up and said, "You must be Courtney Pine."

As they settled at a wrought-iron table under an umbrella and were served tea, Courtney studied Jane Rybold. H. H. Marriner's daughter was obviously well into her fifties, and doing nothing to disguise it. She was scarecrow-thin, with light blue eyes, delicate skin crisscrossed by tiny lines, straight brown hair shot through with silver. Her fingernails had dirt under them.

Courtney wasn't sure what to make of Jane Rybold, and so she was shocked when Jane leaned back and said, "Tell me. How is our darling Nathaniel?" to hear herself answer, "I don't know, Mrs. Rybold. I'm worried."

Courtney began talking about Nathaniel, and once she was started she couldn't stop. It was a long time before she gave Jane Rybold a chance to say anything at all.

At last she came to a halt and drank a swallow of her cooled tea. Jane looked thoughtful. She said, "The books created a problem, I expect. I always thought they would, but Mother—" She shrugged. "You know how old people are. She had her ideas."

"Your mother is Celia Marriner?"

"Was." Jane pressed her lips together. "She died—oh, it must be six or seven months ago, now." Courtney started to speak, and Jane shook her head. "It wasn't unexpected. She had gotten terribly frail. Her last days were relatively happy, thanks to Nathaniel."

"Mrs. Rybold, if you could tell me—"

Jane Rybold nodded. Her eyes moved past Courtney, unfocused in memory. "A year or so ago, Mother hired Bobbo Steig to catalogue my father's library. Bobbo is a book dealer in a small, private way. Mother had met him somewhere, they knew some of the same people. Father had left his collection in a bit of an unorganized mess. Neither Mother nor I had the inclination or, quite frankly, the interest to do anything about it all this time. As she became weak and ill, though, she began to want to put her house in order. Apparently people do get that inclination, toward . . . the end."

A breeze stirred the lace borders of the crumpled napkins on the table. Jane bit her lip. "Bobbo began spending time at my mother's house working on the collection, and once in a while Nathaniel would come there to meet him. Mother and I got to know them quite well. Nathaniel was the loveliest—the loveliest young man." Jane's eyes reddened. She said, "Those days were like a gift."

Courtney stared at the fluttering napkins and thought: I know. *I know.*

Jane continued, "Nathaniel started coming over especially to visit Mother. While Bobbo worked on the books Nathaniel ran errands, he read to her, he watched soap operas with her. They had such fun together!"

The maid came and cleared away the tea things. "Thank you, Dolores," Jane said, her voice hoarse. She shaded her eyes. "God, the pachysandra is taking over that corner, isn't it?"

Courtney didn't know what pachysandra was. She looked in the direction Jane Rybold indicated and said, "It certainly is."

After a moment Jane went on, "So anyway, everything was lovely. Bobbo was somewhat obsessed with the library. He raved on about it until the rest of us were completely bored with it all. One day, impulsively, my mother gave Nathaniel a first edition of *A Shropshire Lad*. Just picked it off the shelf and gave it to him. I thought Bobbo was going to faint.

"After that, Bobbo kept calling mother into the library and haranguing her about the books. Naturally, she would rather have been watching "As the World Turns" with Nathaniel. Bobbo also began to drop hints that the collection should be in the hands of a person who would really appreciate it, obviously meaning himself. I think most of it went past Mother. She would simply agree with him, tell him he was absolutely right. Then, one afternoon, she and Nathaniel were gossiping over a cup of coffee and she had a heart attack and died. Quite honestly, although it was tough on Nathaniel, it seemed as good a way to go as any."

Jane Rybold's eyes filled with tears again, and she blotted them with the back of her hand. "If there is a good way to go," she said.

Courtney waited. When Jane didn't speak again she said, "Were you there when it happened?"

Jane shook her head. "Normally I would've been, but that day I had another appointment. In fact, only Bobbo and Nathaniel were there with Mother. The nurse had the afternoon off, and the maid was called away for a family emergency." She frowned. "Why?"

"I don't know why." After a moment Courtney asked, "What about the books?"

"I'm sure what my mother did seemed perfectly logical to her," said Jane dryly. "She left my father's entire library to Nathaniel."

Courtney pressed a hand to her mouth to stifle an inappropriate, semi-hysterical giggle. "Oh my God."

"Precisely."

The garden was filled with the lemon-colored light of approaching evening. Courtney said, "Mrs. Rybold, when I called today you said something about Nathaniel standing you up."

Jane took off her straw hat and shook back her hair. "That's right. It was strange. I saw quite a lot of him after Mother's death. For one thing, I wanted to empty the Park Avenue house as soon as possible, and there were the logistics of moving the library to Bank Street. We were in the midst of it all when Nathaniel called one day. He sounded upset. He said he wanted to see me and talk to me. Of course I said I would be glad to see him, and we set up an appointment to meet here. He never showed up. When I called to inquire, Bobbo was very apologetic. He said Nathaniel had been terribly depressed about Mother's death, and finally Bobbo had insisted on sending him out to California for a while. Nathaniel had sent apologies and love to me, and he'd be in touch when he got back."

Courtney picked up her bag. "When exactly was this, Mrs. Rybold?"

"Sometime in March, I suppose."

"I see." Sometime in March. Nathaniel had not been in California sometime in March. He had been at a sushi bar on the Upper East Side, flipping a sushi into Courtney's lap. He had been looking for a place to hide.

7

Courtney walked the twenty-some blocks home. She took off her jacket and slung it over her shoulder and pushed forward through the heavy air. *Oh Nathaniel, Nathaniel*, she chanted noiselessly, *Nathaniel, Nathaniel* until she had left the stately world of limestone mansions and returned to her own less imposing neighborhood of soulless high-rises.

Nathaniel, Nathaniel. It was Saturday evening. The restaurants were full of early drinkers. Courtney floated, her attention unmoored.

He had needed a place to go. Why had he chosen Courtney? People who live on charm must have an instinct for singling out those who'll respond to them. Drop a sushi, find a haven. Imagine the nerve it would take to do such a thing.

Courtney had reached her building, set in the middle of a concrete plaza furnished with benches nobody ever sat on. In the lobby the doorman's station was, as usual, empty. The doorman was having some legal problem that called for extended appearances in court. She took the elevator up to ten and walked down the hall.

She had unlocked the door, was pushing it open, when Robert Steig emerged from the stairwell. She saw him surge toward her, half-turned to try to ward him off, but he threw himself at her and propelled them both into her apartment. She stumbled against the wall and dropped her jacket. Steig had a gun in one hand, a blue gym bag in the other. He pointed the gun at her and said, "Don't say a word."

Into Courtney's mind came a picture of herself forty-five minutes ago, sitting in Jane Rybold's beautiful garden.

Steig was unshaven, his eyes red-rimmed. He said, "We're going into your bedroom. Pick up your jacket and let's go."

Black spots danced in front of Courtney's eyes. She picked up her jacket.

In the bedroom, Steig said, "Close the blinds."

Courtney closed them. The room plunged into shadow. "Take off your clothes," said Steig.

Courtney tried to shake her head, but her neck felt stiff. "Why?"

"Because I said so." Steig moved toward her. "Go on."

"No," Courtney whispered.

"You have to. That's how it's done. You wouldn't lie down in your suit, would you? With your stockings on? Go on. Strip."

Courtney fumbled with the button of her skirt. She said, "I've just come from talking with Jane Rybold. She told me about the books."

Steig nodded, blinking rapidly. "The stuff they had. And neither Celia nor Jane gave so much as a damn."

"Did Nathaniel give a damn?"

Steig snorted. "Nathaniel would rather have had a chocolate chip cookie than a first edition of *Paradise Lost*." The gun was shaking. His hand was shaking. "Get on with it," he said. He put the gym bag on the bed and unzipped it.

Courtney peeled off her panty hose. She took off her necklace and dropped it on the dresser. She pulled her silk shell over her head and left it, inside out, beside the necklace. She said, "Don't do this."

"That's what Nathaniel said. He couldn't believe it. He couldn't believe I wouldn't weaken if he begged. I'd always given him everything he wanted. The stock market crash kicked a hole in my trust fund, I lost a hell of a lot of money then, but still, if Nathaniel wanted a new sweater, or a trip to St. Barts, or—" Steig cleared his throat with a sobbing sound. "Did I tell you I found him on the street?"

"When he was fifteen. Yes." Courtney was starting to tremble. She said, "So he begged, and you killed him anyway."

"He wouldn't shut up about Celia Marriner. I told him she was taking Quinidine, maybe she took a few extra. All he had to do was shut up about it."

"He guessed you'd killed her."

"She was taking Quinidine anyway. What was the problem? A few extra in the coffee. Nathaniel acted like I was some . . . *monster*. He was going to tell Jane. Why'd he get so righteous all of a sudden? He'd never been that way before."

"I guess you never confessed to murder before."

"Take off everything. Strip! Take it off!"

Courtney slipped off her bra and stepped out of her underpants. Steig's eyes flickered over her without interest. She wasn't even sure he saw her. He said, "You've got a robe somewhere. Put it on."

Courtney got her flowered robe from the hook on the bathroom door. She was filled with such pain for Nathaniel she could hardly stand upright. "I have to know," she said. "Was it death by water? Like in *The Waste Land*?"

"After a fashion," Steig said. "I took him out to the pier. One shot in the back of the head, and I rolled him into the Hudson. No identification on him. As far as anybody who cares is concerned, he's in California. He's going to stay out there."

"I see." Courtney's knees gave. She sat down on the edge of the bed.

"Perfect. Right where I want you," Steig said. He took a bottle of vodka out of the gym bag and set it on the bedside table. Next to it, he put a Ziploc baggie filled with small red pills. He said, "You're very unhappy, aren't you, Courtney Pine?"

Courtney nodded. "I miss Nathaniel," she whispered.

His face twisted. "Take my word for it, we all miss Nathaniel." He stepped into the bathroom and came out with a glass. "Pour some vodka in here. And start on the pills."

"So I'm killing myself," Courtney said. At the edge of her mind was the thought, *Why not?*

"You're sad. So sad about Nathaniel."

"Sad about Nathaniel," Courtney repeated. She poured a glassful of vodka. She thought, *Why not? If this can happen, why not?* She took a swallow of the liquor, closed her eyes as it went down.

When she looked at Steig again he was watching her intently, his mouth half-open. She took another swallow. She said, "Nathaniel loved you."

Steig's face contorted. "Shut up."

She thought, *I don't care.* "He did. He talked about this wonderful man who knew all about books."

"Take a pill. Go on!"

Courtney swallowed one of the red pills. "He said there was a man who took him in, and fed him, and clothed him, and he would never be able to repay this man . . ." It hardly seemed possible, but Courtney felt woozy already. She settled against the pillow, ready for a nice long chat, a nice, long spun-out lie about the good things Nathaniel had told her about Robert Steig. She drank more vodka. "He said this guy was handsome, too, and—"

"I told you to be quiet!" Tears were streaming down Steig's face.

Courtney reached into the baggie. "Looks like you could use a pill. What are they? Seconal?"

"He called me a cold-blooded murderer," Steig rasped.

"When I came here, he refused to go with me. I had to hold the gun on him while he packed."

"Well, that was Nathaniel. Bull-headed." Courtney stared at the pills in the palm of her hand. How many would it take, she wondered. "He was crazy about you, though."

"Nathaniel!" Steig bent forward, shuddering with grief.

Courtney, thinking, *Well, I'd better do this now that I have the opportunity,* rolled sideways off the bed, came up beside him, and grabbed for the gun. Steig pulled back, she clung to his wrist, they whirled around the room together. The gun went off with a deafening explosion, the bullet going Courtney had no idea where. When it went off again, a second later, she felt Steig's body contract and knew he was hit.

He crumpled to the floor, leaving Courtney holding the gun. He curled up, whimpering, looking up at her with pain-glazed eyes. He gasped, "Is it true—Nathaniel said—"

"Don't be ridiculous. He hated your guts, you son of a bitch," Courtney said.

8

The man came up to Courtney with a piece of paper in his hand. He held it out to her. "This is yours, ma'am?"

Courtney was moving. She was leaving New York. The man handing her the paper was one of the movers, a pleasant fellow who didn't speak much English. "Thanks," she said, taking it from him. With any luck, they'd be out of here by noon.

Courtney was going back to her hometown, a middle-sized city in the Midwest. She didn't exactly have a job, but she thought she'd find something. Mr. Benson had done everything he could to get her to stay, but when he couldn't convince her he'd augmented her severance with a handsome bonus. The day they'd said their final good-byes he'd had tears in his eyes.

Courtney would have to come back and testify at Robert Steig's trial, but she wasn't going to stay around on Steig's account.

The folded paper in her hand had a *C* scrawled on it with a black felt-tip pen. "Where did you find this?" she asked the mover.

The mover pointed across the living room, where two of his cohorts were rolling up the Bokhara rug and the sisal mat beneath it. "Was there. Between carpet and mat." The man made a little bow and went back to work.

Courtney stared at the paper a while before she unfolded it. The message inside was brief: *I love you.* The signature was a shaky *N.*

Stanley Cohen

JUST ANOTHER NEW YORK CHRISTMAS STORY

December 23, mid-morning

COLD. BONE-CRACKING COLD. COLD? OH, JESUS, MARY, AND JOseph, too cold for any human being to be standing in one spot. Even for ten minutes. All day? Forget it. But there he was. And he was there for all day.

He'd just have to take it. For the first year after nine years in the corps, he got to pick the spot he wanted. Right in front of Macy's. And he intended to hold on to it. No question one of the best spots. Year after year, one of the biggies for payoff. And even close to home. When he'd heard that the big guy who'd had it wasn't around this year, he'd made his demands on the basis of seniority and gotten it. But this day he wasn't so sure he liked it. The wind blowing down Thirty-fourth Street was a wind tunnel. Gusting probably forty-fifty miles an hour, the wind-chill probably forty below. Hell! More like fifty. If you're moving, out fighting it maybe five-ten minutes, that's one thing. But standing still? All day? It could freeze the balls off a brass monkey.

He knew he should have listened to Murphy. She was always right. He could still hear her talking in his ear. "Francis, didn't you hear the forecast? What's the matter with you? You want to freeze? Wear everything you own out there today." So what did he answer? "Sweetheart, you don't know how warm that red suit can be out there. I'm tellin' ya. Red velvet, or whatever the hell it is. It can be roasting. I'm wearing my longies and a flannel shirt." And then he'd added, "Besides, I've got the pillow." That'd just made her madder. "Francis, the pillow's on your belly, not your back."

She'd finally just dropped it with a "You're gonna be sorry, Francis." And she was really pissed. Something he didn't need right through this stretch. Not with all her talk about what her daughter in Jersey wanted. That was scary. He didn't know what he'd do if Murphy left him. She was about all he had in the world.

An old lady came by and stuffed a dollar bill into the slot in his chimney and he gave her one of his best "Merry Christmas's" and got a big grin and that reminded him of how much he loved being in the corps.

He especially loved the kids. The little ones. He'd never had his own. He remembered once a whole busload got off right in front of him and every one of those soapy-smelling kids had to hug Santa. Now that was a payoff! But not the big kids. Not those bastards. "Hey, Santa, straighten your beard. There's kids around." Or "Hey, Shrimp, you're losing your tumtum. Pull it back up there." Or, "Why ain't you somewhere making toys for my kid brother?"

But the little kids . . . huggin' 'em, talkin' to 'em, posin' for pictures . . . how could there be any better kind o' work? And he was good at it. He had one o' the best Ho-Ho-Ho's in the corps. Even if he was the smallest Santa they had. One hell of a voice for such a scrawny little Santa. Ask any of the others.

And it was a good job for a person with time on his hands. He liked to think of himself as one of the temporarily jobless. Which he had been for some years now. He didn't like to think about how many. And damn good pay. Thirty-five bucks a day plus fifteen percent of anything over a hundred. At least from

Thanksgiving to Christmas, he didn't have to think about Murphy carrying him. He looked across the street at the clock. Just past eleven-thirty. It was about as warm as it was going to get all day. Come late afternoon and he was going to see some real cold.

Then he caught the eye of a man stepping from a long grey limousine. This man was no loser. Homburg, overcoat with a fur collar, silk scarf, shined shoes, the whole megillah. And a very fancy-shmancy brass and alligator-skin briefcase. You didn't see too many briefcases like that one. And the man was coming straight at him with a smile.

"Merry Christmas."

"Here you are, Santa," the man said, holding out a bill between his second and third gloved fingers.

Franny eyed it quickly and grinned. It had the number *100* in its corners. "Merry Christmas, Chief. You just made me my deductible, and that makes my day."

"My pleasure, Santa. It's the least I could do. I just closed a deal that made *my* day. And many thousands more of these, I might add. Literally."

"Well, all the best to ya, friend, and a very merry Christmas," Franny beamed as he kept stabbing at the quarter-inch slot in his padlocked chimney. But he wasn't missing the slot. He knew exactly what he was doing. The second he saw the number in the corner of that bill, something happened in his head, and he knew he had to do what he had to do. As soon as Mr. Homburg moved on, he deftly relaxed the lengthwise crease in the bill and folded it in half the other way, burying it in a pants-pocket inside his Santa suit. And he did the whole thing with just one of his frozen hands in its too-thin glove. He glanced around to see who might have been watching. He couldn't find anybody staring at him cross-eyed, and if somebody'd noticed, they would have been.

He looked across at the clock again. Almost twelve noon. The relief man would be coming soon to give him his lunch break. He had his lunch in his canvas shoulder bag with his smokes, and he could go into Macy's, have a smoke with some coffee, and warm up a little.

Actually, he didn't feel all that cold anymore. Money in your pocket tends to keep you from feeling the cold. He had very definite plans for that bill, and what the hell, he could pay it back. He was a working man. Right? Right. The last thing he'd do was steal from his own collections. Right? Right. He'd put it back after payday.

December 23, early evening

As soon as the van came by and picked up his chimney to take it to headquarters and empty it, Franny started walking with deliberate steps toward the destination he had been thinking about throughout the bitter cold day. A couple of short blocks and he was there. It was also only a couple of blocks from where he lived. He could have grabbed a subway down to Houston Street to the Rehabilitation Center for a hot meal with the rest of the Santas, but Murphy said she was putting up something special for him to eat before she left for her job.

He stood in front of McAnn's Bar and stared at the door for a long time. Should he go in? Of all the doors on God's earth he was forbidden to pass through, this was the most forbidden. Not because it was McAnn's, but because it was a bar. Any bar. He'd been struggling with it all afternoon, standing there, freezing his ass off, and now came the moment of truth. Did he break the pledge? Did he fall off? He yanked the beard and mustache and stuffed them into his shoulder bag. Then he pulled the door open and stepped into the enveloping warmth.

He tried to walk as if he knew what the hell he was doing, but he was shaking like a leaf in a windstorm. How long had it been? He wasn't sure, exactly. A few months, anyway, since before signing up with the corps for another year. It *had* to be that way with them. You *had* to be clean. Most of the Santas were "recovering alcoholics." Homeless. Living at the rehab center on Houston Street. Going regularly to the meetings. He'd gotten special permission to stay at the hotel with Murphy because of his years of service. He'd moved out of the Center when Murphy'd agreed to take him in.

He looked around and decided he had to stay. He had to have a couple. Just a couple. A little something to give him a mild glow. Just a bit of a buzz, a quick pick-me-up, a little help in thinking about how he would present his case to Murphy to keep her from moving to Jersey without him.

If they found out, they'd strip him of his red suit and whiskers. And the job. And the money. But what the hell, they wouldn't find out. They only did random testing and they'd had him pee in the bottle and breathe in the gadget just two days ago. They wouldn't check him again for a while. And even if they did, he'd be clean by morning.

He hoisted himself onto a stool and fumbled in that pants pocket inside his Santa suit for what was left of the C-note. The stupid pillow was always in the way of something. He finally withdrew a fifty and a couple of singles. He laid the fifty on the bar in front of him and smoothed it out. The singles went back.

The bartender came over. "Hello there, Santa. What can I get ya?" He had a friendly smile.

Franny began to tremble. It wasn't too late. He could always have a cup of coffee and get the hell out of there before he blew the game. Yeah! Why didn't he do that? He'd promised Murphy. *Promised* her.

"What'll it be, Santa?"

It was no use. "Bar Scotch, neat."

The bartender studied him. "You're sure, now?"

"You see my money, don'cha? Start me a tab."

After looking at the fifty, the bartender set the shot-glass in front of him and poured the drink. He poured it past the white line, right up to the rim.

Franny listened to the barely audible bubbling sound of the liquor passing through the little chrome nozzle atop the bottle. Of all the wondrous sounds the universe had to offer, that was at least among his top ten, and he hadn't heard it in a while. He picked up the glass, and as he watched the bartender start a tab, he nodded, breathed a "Merry Christmas," and took a sip, then a bit more, maybe half the shot. As the delicious heat rocketed to the farthest limits of his body and his soul, all the months of restraint and meetings and pledges and promises to Murphy went down the tube. He was back.

He looked around. Now back, it felt good to be back, and the scene was to his liking. The place wasn't empty and it wasn't crowded. He didn't like drinking in empty bars or in the middle of a noisy crowd. He thought about what he'd say to Murphy, and then reminded himself that by the time he got back to their room, she'd have left for work. So what did he have to worry about? He'd have slept it off before he'd have to face her.

He looked at the man next to him and felt a sudden pang of fear. The man was large, but lean, with dark hair and eyes, and a dark, thick mustache. A big-ass mustache. Like a walrus, or something. He and a partner, both big men in heavy mackinaws and stocking caps, were nursing drafts, and the man was studying him, looking first at his face, half-shaven under the silly Santa hat, and then at the fifty-dollar bill on the bar. Once he'd made eye contact, he could tell the man was going to make conversation.

"Hey, Santa, looks like the Christmas business is pretty good," the man said, smiling.

Franny didn't want to deal with this. The man scared him. Franny picked up his glass and drained it. Then he nodded at the bartender and pointed at his empty glass. He watched the bartender refill it.

"Cat got your tongue, Santa?" the man said, a trace of annoyance in his voice.

The bartender turned on an over-the-bar TV to a Rangers game just about to get under way.

"So let's go, Santa. Talk to me. How's business?" the man said, becoming more annoyed.

"You talkin' to me? I'm just one o' the collectors for V.O.A."

"V.O.A.? What's V.O.A.?"

"Volunteers of America. You know, those red brick chimneys they got out there with a Santa by each one?"

"So what do you do? Collect one for them and one for yourself?"

"Hey, are you crazy? Those things are padlocked. We don't ever touch that money."

"Yeah?" The man chuckled. "Looks to me like you're doin' pretty well," he said, nodding at the fifty on the bar.

"Oh, they pay me a little something, but not very much." Franny was frightened of the man. He'd picked the wrong bar on the wrong night.

"So I see," said the man. "They pay you in fifties. Right?"

His partner grabbed his sleeve to get his attention. Franny did not see the partner wink at the man, nod at Franny, and smile a smile of total communication. "Let's watch the game for a while," his partner said.

Franny picked up his glass and took about half. Jesus, it tasted great. For sure he wasn't cold anymore. Then he thought about the present he'd gotten Murphy in Macy's. It was the kind of thing he knew she'd like to have, really like to have, but could never buy for herself. But, what the hell, that's what Christmas was about. Right? Right. Comes Christmas you don't think about practical stuff. Dream wishes. That kind o' stuff. Right? Right.

He hoped she'd like the particular one he'd picked out. He didn't know one from another. It was the only one he could ever remember hearing about. And it was expensive stuff! How could they charge so damn much for such a little-ass bottle? Nearly half his C-note. The saleslady wrapped it real nice for him.

He patted the side of his canvas bag where he had the gift-wrapped perfume, and as he did, he glanced at Mr. Mustache next to him to find the guy had taken his eyes off the hockey game to watch him pat his bag. This sent another shiver of absolute fear up his back.

"Whatcha got in your bag, there, Santa? Toys for tots?" Mr. Mustache asked with a grin.

Franny tried to think of something. A quick answer. A good solid counterpunch. But he couldn't think of anything decent, so he finally said, "Just my smokes. And the brown bag from my lunch." And with that, he unbuckled the bag, reached in, and took out what was left of his cigarettes, which turned out to be a crumpled, empty pack. He wadded it up and laid it on the bar and asked the bartender to get him another pack of Camels. "Just put it on my tab," he instructed. He liked saying that. Made him feel like somebody of means. Then he drained his glass. When the bartender returned with his cigarettes, he pointed at the glass.

As he watched the amber liquid being poured and listened to that haunting little bubbly sound, he went back to thinking about Murphy. How was he going to keep her from skipping out on him and moving to Jersey to live with her married daughter and child? And that S.O.B. husband of hers.

"What kinda life are you gonna have in Jersey? What? You

gonna be happy baby-sitting and cleaning that dinky little house o' hers?"

"It's better than living in one room in a hotel for the homeless and cleaning offices at night, Francis. And it ain't dinky. It's a nice little house."

"And what about putting up with that rotten husband o' hers? You're gonna have to watch the way he treats her, the bastard. Cardozo. What the hell kinda good Irish Catholic name is Cardozo? She'd be a lot better off coming to live with us, Chrissakes."

"He'll treat her a lot better with me around, Francis. I guess you know that . . . He really doesn't treat her all that bad. Matter fact, he takes pretty good care of her. Gets her anything she wants."

"When he's not knockin' her around. And what about me, Murphy?"

"What can I tell you, Francis? You're just not invited."

"I mean, what *about* me? You're gonna be sleepin' on a couch there. You're sleepin' in a double bed now. If you know what I mean. And you know what I mean."

"That's a problem for me. I have to admit."

Yeah, that's a problem for her, all right. Some things he did pretty well, and this was one department where he delivered the goods. 'Course, when you don't do nothing for a living, at least you're rested.

"I do care about you, Francis. A lot. But I'm sick and tired of living in that smelly hotel and working nights. Maybe if we could make things a little better for ourselves. If you could get some kind of job. A regular job . . ."

Job? What kind of job? What? What did he know how to do? Other than being Santa Claus.

"Maybe if I could get on at the hospital, I could learn to do brain surgery."

"How about being an orderly?"

"What? And carry around bedpans all day?"

"As long as you washed your hands before you came home."

He wondered what she'd left him to eat back in the room. She could work miracles with that little hotplate. A scrap of cheap meat, a couple of potatoes, a carrot or two, and it was a banquet. A stick-to-your-ribs feast. Soups. Eggs. Something great out o' nothing. The hotel rules said no cooking in the rooms. That's a joke. The smells in those hallways? It was like a Chinese restaurant in the barrio.

Franny picked up his glass, brought it to his lips, breathed "Merry Christmas," and downed it. He was drinking them in wholes, now, not halves. He needed the impact of that full belt. He savored the shock waves of the drink for a moment with his eyes closed and then glanced to his side. Mr. Mustache was watching hockey with one eye and him with the other.

December 23, mid-evening

Franny had held off for what seemed to him to be an eternity, at least an hour, well, maybe a half-hour, anyway, because he couldn't figure out where he was going to put any more. But it was definitely time for another, so he motioned to the bartender.

"Don't you think you've had about enough there, Santa?"

"Me? I'm just fine. Getcha bottle there and fill me up. Still got a lotta stuff to think about. Need all the help I can get." *Still got a lotta stuff* . . . Even Franny could hear that he couldn't get it out. One long slur.

"I think you've had about enough, old-timer."

"One more."

"Well, if you're gonna take any more, you're gonna have to add to your deposit there on the bar. You've about drunk that all up."

"Then, do it. I got plenty money. Plenty money."

"On second thought, forget it. I'm not serving you anymore. Want me to go out there and get you a taxi?"

"Taxi? What the hell do I need with a taxi? I just live around the corner . . . right around here, somewhere."

The bartender picked up the tab and the fifty, rang it up, put two dollars and change on the bar. "You take it easy, old-timer."

"Old-timer, shit!" He smiled. "But, Merry Christmas to you anyway, pal." He tapped his knuckles on the bar next to the money and slid off the stool. He moved uncertainly toward the door, pushed it open, and made his way through it. He did not see Mr. Mustache and his friend pick up their change off the bar.

Once outside he found the cold bracing and pleasant, something he badly needed. The bartender was right. He didn't need any more. No place to put it. The old hollow leg was full. He stood, weaving just slightly, trying to get his bearings, and then trudged toward Sixth Avenue. He tripped and fell, skidding on his palms on the frozen sidewalk and, with considerable effort, struggled back to his feet, rubbing his hands on his Santa suit. To the corner, turn right, a couple blocks and then cross Sixth. Or cross Sixth and then a couple blocks.

When he got to the corner, the light was just turning green and traffic was sparse, so he crossed and then turned right. Greeley Square. Just two blocks and home to the hotel. He moved along in that direction, Merry Christmas-ing anybody he passed.

He came to an alley between buildings and was suddenly lifted off the ground by his upper arms and carried, running, into the alley. He twisted his head around and there it was. The black mustache! "Hey! Hey! What the hell is this? Put me down! Put me down!"

"We're gonna put you down," the mustache said.

The other one had a silly giggle. "Hih, hih, hih, yeah, Santa, we just thought we'd let you put a little something under our tree, first. Where've you got all those fifties, Santa?"

"I ain't got no money, guys. I swear. Two bucks."

Mr. Mustache slapped Franny ferociously. "Don't fuck with us, Santa. Where's your money?"

"I ain't got no money! I'm tellin' ya."

Another brutal slap that turned Franny's head sideways. Then a fist to the body that landed just above the pillow, knocking all the wind out of him, blacking him out momentarily.

"Where's your money, Santa?"

He hardly heard the question.

"Where's your money, Santa, or do we have to break you in half?"

Franny struggled to get the words out. There was no air in

his body for speaking. "No matter what you bastards do," he breathed, "I got no money. No money, you bastards."

A crushing fist to the temple and Franny dropped like wet laundry.

"Jeez, you really gave him a shot," said the other one.

"I got sick and tired of his mouth. Let's find his money and get the hell out of here." He jerked Franny's limp body out flat, opened the big white belt, and ripped open his Santa coat, looking for pockets. The Santa suit had none, inside or out. He looked in the pocket of the plaid flannel shirt. Nothing. He yanked the pillow out of the way, rummaged through Franny's pants pockets, and found the two singles and change, a rusty old pocket knife, a wilted, half-used book of matches, and a ragged wallet that was empty. Annoyed, he tossed Franny's body around to see if there was someplace else he hadn't checked.

"What about his bag, there?" the other one said.

The flap was unbuckled on the bag. He didn't find anything of value. The Santa's beard and mustache with elastic straps, a folded brown bag, the Camels, and a *Daily News* Franny had picked up. "Nothing."

"Guess he wasn't lyin'," the other one said.

"Let's get outa here."

"Poor sumbitch gonna freeze left here like that."

"Guess that's *his* problem, isn't it?"

They walked back to Sixth Avenue, leaving Franny out of sight from the street, only a few yards in, but obscured by a pile of empty drums.

December 23, late evening

Nicky Varrone was walking up Sixth Avenue, heading back toward Forty-fifth Street where he lived and thinking about how cold it was, when he saw the chauffeured grey Cadillac move west across Sixth and then stop in front of an office building. He'd been hanging out at this little restaurant on Twenty-sixth where there was a young beauty working as a waitress, and she really rang his bell. Unfortunately, she wasn't having any part of him, and he was a little down. His problem was, he decided, that he didn't have anything. If he had real bread, he'd be Mr. Big with the ladies.

Nicky watched from a distance as the chauffeur opened the back door and allowed his passenger, some hotshot-looking type with a fancy hat, to get out and walk to the door of the building. Now, *there* was money. Why, hell, even the man's chauffeur probably drew three times what he was making. But what the hell were they doing showing up there at near midnight?

A night watchman opened the door and the man entered, signaling to his driver to come with him, and as the door closed behind them, Nicky decided he had to see the car up close, so he walked over and began admiring it, inside and out. Some piece of machinery. One of those thirty-footers. Hell, you could almost set up a table and four chairs in the back of that car.

A briefcase lay on the backseat, light glinting off the hardware. Had to be brass, of course, but Christ, it looked like gold. Rich-looking case. Was it alligator? Looked like the kind of case that could be filled with money. Neatly banded bundles of high denomination bills. What if it was?

Nicky looked into the lobby of the building. The night watchman had apparently gone somewhere with the man and his driver. Nobody in sight. The street was quiet . . . Then his heart suddenly began to pound. What the hell, he'd done worse. He was going for that briefcase.

The case was on the side toward the street. He looked in the lobby again and then walked around to the street side of the car. As soon as he touched the door handle, a voice came from the car: "Please do not come near the automobile." He jumped back and then smiled. One of those high-tech alarm systems. Nevertheless, he was still going for the case.

He peered into the lobby once more and then up and down the street. Quiet. The car door had been locked when he'd touched it; he'd have to find something to take out the window. He looked around and found just the ticket. A few yards away the curb was busted and he could lift out a section of it. A big solid chunk of concrete. After glancing around, he picked it up. Heavier than he expected, but he could handle it.

He checked the lobby again, and as soon as he put the concrete through the window, the car's alarm began screaming.

He reached in, grabbed the briefcase, and was off. He didn't look back. He sprinted to Sixth and headed north, running with the briefcase under his arm. There were few people walking and they paid him little attention. This was New York. Still, he knew he looked conspicuous, so he slowed to a walk and tried to look natural. But he found that he couldn't, so he started running again. He still didn't dare look back. After running another block, he dashed into the middle of Sixth Avenue, dodging the light traffic, and crossed, continuing north on the opposite side.

He felt that he had to get out of sight, so when he came to an alley between two buildings, he plunged into it, deciding to take his chances. He didn't want to surprise anybody. Only crazy people went into alleys in New York, day or night, but this was special circumstances. He hadn't gone very far before he came to something that reminded him once again that, hell, nothing surprises you in New York. Nothing! Here was a man in a Santa suit, half-undressed, lying there asleep. Asleep? Sleeping one off? In a Santa suit? At that temperature?

He kept plunging ahead, figuring if he could make it to Fifth, he was home free. Then he stopped, out of breath, and turned around. He just stood there, looking toward Sixth, to catch his breath and to see if he was in fact being chased. He waited motionless for several minutes. Dead still. He squatted on his haunches and waited another minute or so. Poor Santa back there would be dead before morning. A piece of ice. He stood up and started walking slowly back toward Sixth.

When he reached the Santa, he said, "Man, what the hell're you doing here? You're gonna freeze."

The Santa, in a state of near unconsciousness, managed, "Think I already have."

"How'd you get here?"

"Did I get hit by a truck? No, coupla, musta been longshoremen, I think. Big bastards . . ."

Nicky spotted some weatherbeaten corrugated boxes. He put the briefcase in one of them, squashed the box flat, and stuffed it behind the empty drums. Then he bent down and easily picked up the scrawny little Santa.

"Put me down, dammit! Leave me. I was just beginning to feel good." Then he went limp and quiet.

Nicky walked out of the alley carrying the little Santa, who now seemed totally unconscious. A canvas bag dangled from the Santa's shoulder. Nicky found a grate with warm air rising from it. He placed the Santa down on the grate. He yanked the pillow dangling from the belt around his waist and put it under his head, noting the bruises and swelling. He pulled the Santa's clothes together as best he could. Then he went to a refuse basket and lifted out a thick *New York Times*. He blanketed the Santa with it, tucking edges under.

When the wind began to loosen and blow away the sheets of newspaper, Nicky went back into the alley and picked out another corrugated box. Returning to the street, he split open one side, and wrapped it around the newspapers over Santa, tucking it under. The little Santa's feet protruded from the end of the box. "Best I can do for you, Santa," Nicky said. "The cops'll come pick you up. They won't leave you here long."

No answer.

Nicky headed back to the alley.

December 23, around 11:30 P.M.

"Nine-one-one. Where is the emergency?"

"I want to report a missing person. My, uh, husband."

"Your name, please?"

"Bridget Murphy."

"Where are you located?"

"The Martinique Hotel."

"At Sixth and Thirty-second. Right?"

"You know the lovely place?"

"Deed I do, Mrs. Murphy. Mrs. Murphy, a missing persons call is not considered an emergency call to be responded to by the nine-one-one switchboard. You need to contact your local precinct. Call Midtown South at 555-9811. They'll take the call."

"Can you connect me? I don't have a quarter."

"Just dial Operator and give her the number. She'll connect you. Tell her I told you to call. That number again is 555-9811."

"If she doesn't connect me, I'm calling you back."

"She'll handle it, Mrs. Murphy."

Murphy dialed Operator and asked for the number, saying it was an emergency.

"Midtown South. How may I help you?"

"I need help. My husband is missing."

"Hold on. I'll connect you with the detectives' squad room."

"Detective McGonigal here. How may I help you?"

"D'ya say McGonigal? Good."

"Good? Why good? Do we know each other?"

"My name's Murphy. That clear it up?"

"Well, sure an' it does, Mrs. Murphy. How c'n I help ye?"

"McGonigal, my husband is missing."

"For how long has he been missing, Mrs. Murphy?"

"He should have been home by seven o'clock."

"Mrs. Murphy, we don't normally consider a person missing until he's been missing twenty-four hours. Now there are three exceptions, but they wouldn't seem to apply here."

"What are the three exceptions?"

"A small child, a mentally incompetent, or an EDP. That's an emotionally disturbed person. Any of those apply?"

"He's never late home, McGonigal. Something's got to have happened to him. I know."

"Have you been home all evening? Could he have tried to call?"

"We don't have a phone, but if he'd tried to call, they'd have called me from security. Been home all evening." She felt safe in this lie because the pot on the hotplate was still untouched and there were no dishes in the bathroom sink. "McGonigal, you gotta help me. Don't give me no song and dance."

"We'll put it out and see what it brings in, Mrs. Murphy. Okay? Where are you calling from?"

"The Martinique Hotel. You know it?"

"We know every hotel in this precinct, Mrs. Murphy. Be assured. And especially the Martinique. We've been in the Martinique, my partner and I, more than a few times over the years. Tell me, the kids still play stickball in the hallways?"

"That should be the worst that goes on in those hallways."

"I'm aware. Mrs. Murphy, what's your husband's name?"

"Francis Gilhooley."

"I thought you said he was your husband."

"Don't start with me."

"Can you give me a description of him?"

"About five-foot-four, maybe a hundred 'n' twenty, twenty-five, mixed brown and gray hair, and beautiful blue eyes."

"How old?"

"I'd say between forty-five and fifty, fifty-five."

"Don't you know?"

"He says forty-five. He said that last year, too."

"When did you last see him, Mrs. Murphy?"

"When he left for work this morning."

"And where does he work?"

"In front of Macy's."

"Doing what?"

"Collecting money. He's a Santa Claus. How about that?"

"Oh! So we're looking for Old St. Nick. And a wee one at that. White belt or black belt, Mrs. Murphy? V.O.A. or Salvation Army? See? I know a couple things, too."

"White belt. They pick up his chimney at around six-thirty and he always comes straight home. I'm sure something's happened to him."

"Mrs. Murphy, what are the chances he just decided to go with a couple o' the other Santas and down a few and talk it over?"

"They're absolutely forbidden to touch a drop. They even test the men. One trace and they're outa there. Through. You should know that, McGonigal. And the same thing applies here with me, I might add. He goes off the wagon, he's out the door."

"Now that you mention it, I did know that about the Santas and the juice. We'll get on it, Mrs. Murphy. We'll see if we can't find that blue-eyed little Santa of yours. But listen. If he shows up, you get back to us and let us know. Okay? I'll be here all night. Okay?"

"Something's happened to him, McGonigal. I'm positive. And I'm counting on you. Y'hear me?"

December 24, 12:45 A.M.

The Sector C (South Charlie) NYPD prowl car moved slowly north on the Avenue of the Americas (Sixth Avenue), approaching 34th Street and Herald Square. Officer Al Aliem

Shabeez sat on the passenger side, his head back on the seat, his hat pulled down as if to shade his eyes, when actually the hat was simply a bit too small. His partner, Officer Vinnie D'Amico, looked left, watching the quiet traffic coming down Broadway as he drove. They were enjoying the lull, knowing full well that it could get to be a very busy night before this graveyard tour was over.

Suddenly Shabeez did a double-take and sat bolt upright as he looked back at something to his right they'd just passed. "I could swear I just saw a pair of feet."

"A pair of feet?"

"Sticking out of a box back there on the sidewalk."

"Somebody threw away a perfectly good pair of feet? Gimme a break, Shabeez. Next thing you'll be telling me, Muslims have perfect night vision."

"Back there, just before Thirty-fourth. Vinnie, humor me. Okay? Go around the block and let's take another look. If I'm right, he's gonna freeze."

When they came back around, it was clear there was a body in the box on the subway grate, and the occasional pedestrians were walking quite wide to avoid it.

"Looks like Santa fell off his sled," D'Amico said as they peeled back the box.

"I think he had himself a private party and decided he'd sleep it off here," Shabeez said. "Let's get him up and moving before he freezes stiffer than he already is."

They attempted to get the little Santa to his feet and quickly surmised that they were wasting their time. This one was more than just preserved in alcohol, judging from the battered face. "We're gonna need a bus for this one," D'Amico said. He walked quickly over to the car and the radio. "South Charlie to Central K."

"South Charlie proceed."

"Central, we need a bus. Unconscious male on the street. Broadway, a hundred feet south of Thirty-fourth, east side of the street . . ."

December 24, 1:10 A.M.

"South Charlie to Central K."

"South Charlie proceed."

"One unconscious male en route to Bellevue. Dressed in a Santa suit. No identification possible at the scene."

"Ten-four. Resume patrol, Charlie."

Inside the ambulance, E.M.T. Wong Lee determined that the unidentified male in the Santa suit had blood pressure and clear respiratory function.

December 24, 1:20 A.M.

Nicky Varrone sat on the side of his bed, looking at the briefcase. He was glad his mother had been long asleep when he got home so he didn't have to explain the case. Fancy leather. Not alligator, though. Something else. He looked at the business card in the matching leather card-holder attached to the handle. Mr. Ramon Henriquez, President. Peerless International Textiles Importers. West Twenty-ninth Street. Big bucks in that case?

How to get it open. He didn't want to bust it apart. No use messing it up. Nice case like that? No keyholes to try and pick with a bent hairpin, either. Each catch had a three-digit combination lock. He tried several random combinations, which of course didn't work, and finally concluded that what he had was time. The thing to do was start at 001 and go up one number at a time until it opened.

It was boring but he stuck with it, annoyed that the son of a bitch couldn't have used a low number. The lock opened when he got to 975. He set the other lock on 975, but it didn't open, either. Smooth operator, Señor Henriquez. Back to 001 and up. The second catch opened at 579. With a deep breath and a tremor of intense anticipation he lifted the top of the case . . .

Papers! Letters. To Henriquez, from Henriquez. Folders of papers. Contracts. Shit! He thumbed through the papers. Boring stuff. A small cloth label sewn into the case caught his eye. Genuine Ostrich Leather. Too bad for the poor fucking ostrich. He slammed the case shut and tossed it across the floor.

He threw himself back on his bed. Well, at least he had himself a nice briefcase. Not that he knew what he'd ever do with it. Maybe when *he* got to be president of something, like Henriquez. From where he was in Shipping, he had a ways to go.

He thought about the little Santa. What if he'd saved the man's life? If it turned out that way, what the hell, he would hardly say the evening had been a total waste. He'd have to check the *Daily News* for the next couple of days. Maybe it'd get a mention. Then again, maybe it wouldn't. This *was* New York.

December 24, 1:30 A.M.

McGonigal looked through the directory and then dialed.

"Police Headquarters."

"This is Detective Harry McGonigal calling from Midtown South. I dialed Missing Persons. None of them in right now, I guess."

"Not for a while. Try first thing tomorrow."

"I'll get whoever's catching here tomorrow to give 'em a call first thing in the morning. Thanks."

"Don't mention it."

December 24, 2:20 A.M.

The E.R. at Bellevue was a zoo when the ambulance carrying the little Santa arrived. The doctor in charge, on being advised that the little Santa had good blood pressure and normal respiratory function, along with a truly remarkable level of alcohol concentration in his blood (determined from a single whiff of his breath), advised his staff to treat his hands and feet for acute exposure and place him in the recovery room. "We'll admit him when he wakes up and can explain himself." The doctor then turned to consider the next patient, who was bleeding from a stab wound in the lower abdomen, in fact, very low in the abdomen.

December 24, 8:30 A.M.

Home from her night's work, Bridget entered the phone booth in the lobby of the Martinique, dialed Operator, and was set to raise some hell if she got an argument when she requested Midtown South. The call was put through and she asked for McGonigal.

"He went home. He's on nights."

She patiently explained who she was and why she was calling.

"There's a note here, Mrs. Murphy, now that you mention it. McGonigal left a note. We'll call Headquarters right now and check with Missing Persons and see if we can't get them right on it. We'll get back to you as soon as we know something. Okay?"

Murphy went up to their room and fell onto their bed.

December 24, early afternoon

Nicky waited until his mother had left for the grocery before dialing the number.

"Peerless International."

"I'd like to speak to Mister—I guess it's—is it Henriquez?"

"That's close enough. He's left for the day. As has most everyone else. Christmas Eve. Half-day."

"We had that today, too. What are *you* still doing there?"

"Somebody's got to sit here on the stupid phone till five."

"Too bad. You sound pretty cute. You married?"

"Yes, I am."

"Too bad, again. Listen. I'm calling because I found something that belongs to Mr. Henriquez."

"Is it his briefcase?"

"Yes, it is."

"Please hold."

"Do you have Mr. Henriquez's briefcase?" Another voice. It sounded like an older woman, like a tough old broad.

"Yes, I do. I found it."

"Is it still intact?"

"It's still locked, if that's what you mean. I'm hoping there should be some kind of reward for it. It's a nice-looking case."

"I'm sure he'd be interested in getting it back. Give me your name and phone number. I'll see if I can reach him and get back to you momentarily."

The phone rang in what seemed to Nicky like a minute or less.

"Mr. Varrone?"

"Yes, ma'am."

"Can you take the briefcase to Mr. Henriquez at his home? It's on Fifth Avenue. Central Park East? Ten-eleven."

"Sure. Any apartment number, or anything like that?"

"Just ask the doorman. Ten-eleven Fifth Avenue. When do you expect to be there?"

"About an hour or so okay?"

"He'll be expecting you."

December 24, around three P.M.

Nicky knew he was uptown when he entered the lobby. This was the real thing. Polished brass everywhere, *clean* Oriental rugs, marble floors, classy-looking furniture. The doorman's uniform looked brand-new.

The doorman made a brief phone call and then led him to an elevator, pressing the button for the eighth floor. When the elevator door opened again, Nicky was not in a corridor but in the foyer of the biggest, fanciest layout he'd ever seen. Large picture windows overlooked Central Park. He gazed around tentatively, the briefcase in his hand.

"Come in, young man," the man on the sofa said to him. He was heavily built but not fat, a large head and full face, lots of streaked gray hair swept straight back. Another man in the room, apparently the driver, walked toward the door as if to make sure Nicky couldn't cut and run.

"Mr. Henriquez?"

"Yes. Come in. You have my briefcase, I see. Good. Good. Let me have it."

Nicky walked over and handed it to him.

Henriquez quickly set the locks and opened the case. He looked relieved as he riffled through the contents and everything was apparently there. "Where did you find this, young man?"

"I happened to spot it in an alley. Sort of over behind a bunch of old steel drums. Couldn't figure out what it was doing there. Brought it out, saw your card on it, and decided I should give you a call. Figured you might give me a reward."

"An alley where?"

"Over off Sixth Avenue."

"What were you doing in an alley in the middle of the night?

Only a stupid fool would go in an alley in this city in the middle of the night."

"Not last night. This morning. I sometimes cut through there on the way to work." Nicky was pleased with himself for coming up with that one. A question and answer he hadn't even thought about on the trip over.

"Well," Henriquez said, and his expression suddenly hardened, "thank you for returning it. And now, get the hell out of here."

"Huh?"

"I said, get out! Go! Before I call the police!"

"But, sir, don't you think I should get some kind of reward for bringing it back?"

"Just be glad you're not going to jail. Your story doesn't hold, young man. *You* must have taken the briefcase. If someone else had taken it, they wouldn't have left it intact. They'd have broken it open to see what was inside before discarding it. You obviously broke into the car to get it, very patiently opened it, and when you found nothing of value, at least not to you, you decided to go for the reward. Fortunately. Because the contents happen to be very valuable to me."

"Wait, sir," Nicky protested. "Really. I cut through that alley this morning, taking a shortcut to work, because I was running a little late. I wouldn't've even seen the briefcase except it was stuck behind some drums right where I found this little guy in a Santa suit about to freeze to death. I brought him out and I think I may have saved his life. This is no shit."

Henriquez chuckled. "Now I'm sure I've heard it all. The children of the world will be eternally grateful that you've saved the life of Santa Claus. You and I have both had encounters with him during the last day or two, and I think mine made out a little better than yours. Thank you again for returning the briefcase, and now get out of here. Roger, show him to the elevator."

December 24, 3:30 P.M.

It took Marvella Robinson three calls to finally get the number of Security at the Martinique Hotel. She called and it rang a dozen or so times before somebody finally picked it up.

"Yeah?"

"Is this the Martinique Hotel?"

"Yeah."

"Who's this?"

"Security."

"I'm calling from Bellevue Hospital. I need to reach Bridget Murphy in room 1213."

"I'll look around here'n see'f I can find somebody to send up there. I can't leave the desk here."

"This is important."

"May be. But so's this. Somebody's got to be here'n this office. The other man didn't come in today."

"Who's this I'm talking to?"

"There's 'nother man comin' on at four. Maybe when he shows up, we can get a message up there."

"Don't you have some kind of intercom?"

"We did when it was workin'."

"Jesus H. Christ! What'd you say your name was?"

"My name's Abraham LaFontant, not that that'll do anything for ya."

"Well, Abraham, do you think you can get a message to Bridget Murphy as soon as possible? Room 1213? Tell her to get in touch with me right away. Right away, now. My name's Marvella Robinson, and I'm at Bellevue Hospital, the number's 555-4141, and I'm at extension 2114. D'you get all of that?"

"Call Miz Robinson at Bellevue. Say, what time d'you get off from there?"

"In time to go home to my husband. Jesus! Abraham, will • you please get Bridget Murphy back to me? Her man's here in one of our wards. Now will you please do what I'm telling you?"

"Call Miz Robinson at Bellevue. Okay?"

"Marvella Robinson. Marvella Robinson. Don't let me down, now, Abraham. You hear me?"

"I'll get on it as soon as I can." As he hung up, his replacement, Slick O'Reilly, a little silver-haired man, came walking in, and almost before they'd so much as exchanged greetings, a skinny twelve-year-old with some lady's expensive-looking pocketbook clutched in his hand came running into the lobby, chased by a uniformed cop. LaFontant and O'Reilly watched the excitement and then Lafontant left. His shift was up.

Christmas Eve, a few minutes before midnight

"Midtown South. How may I help you?"

"Detective McGonigal, please. Is he there?"

"Hold on."

"Detective McGonigal here. How may I help you?"

"McGonigal?"

"That you, Bridget Murphy? I was just thinking about you."

"Thinking about me's one thing. Doing something's another. Did you do anything?"

"Absolutely. Missing Persons got it and is working on it."

"When're they gonna have something?"

"When they find him. They'll find him, Mrs. Murphy. I doubt he's left the city."

"McGonigal, I'm worried sick something's happened to 'im."

"I wish I could tell you more. Sit tight and hope for the best. What else can I tell ya?"

"It's Christmas, McGonigal. And I've gotta go clean offices all night, worrying about him."

"No fun working all night Christmas Eve, is it? I don't like it either, I can assure ya. I got a wife and family."

"At least none of 'em's missing. You better have some good news for me tomorrow."

"I hope we will. What else can I tell ya?"

Christmas morning, around five A.M.

"Detective McGonigal, here. How may I help you?"

"McGonigal, this is Sergeant Gotti over at the Borough office. I need some help. You got somebody who can cover the phone there for you for a little while?"

"I'm catching here alone right now, sir, but I can probably get one o' the guys downstairs to come up for a while. Whaddaya need, sir?"

"Sorry to have to bother you, but I can't seem to find a warm body on the East Side at the moment to handle this. Run over to Bellevue and get a statement from a shooting victim. He's in the E.R. right now, but he should be able to talk by the time you get there. The victim's name is Walker. Cas Walker."

"I'll take care of it, sir."

Christmas morning, around seven A.M.

McGonigal walked out of Bellevue and was about to get into his car when something caught his eye. He went over to it to take a closer look. In one of a long line of clear plastic garbage bags waiting for pickup was a red Santa's hat. McGonigal went back into the hospital.

Christmas day, around noon

Bridget Murphy entered the ward at Bellevue and saw Francis in the far corner of the room. He was propped up in bed, his hands and feet in loose bandages. As she started toward him, she noticed that the other beds were also occupied, all with older men, all surrounded by family. Too bad. She'd have to keep her voice down.

When she reached his bedside, she saw the side of his face and wanted to cry. But there was no way she could allow herself to do that. Not with the things she had to say. He was looking at her with his crazy, disarming smile. It wasn't going to be easy.

"Hello, love," he said.

"You all right?"

"'Course I'm all right. Whaddaya think? Mild concussion, one broken rib, a little frostbite. Day or two, I'll be outa here'n as hot after my sweetie as ever."

"Francis, I'm afraid we're going to have to have a talk."

"Not now, sweetie. It's Christmas."

"Now!" She glanced around at the other people in the ward. She didn't want to attract attention. "What happened to you?"

His wacky smile. "Tellya the truth, I'm not sure I hardly remember. It's all kinda hazy."

"I'll tell you what happened. You tested positive is what happened. Very, very positive."

The smile. "Good thing, too. That stuff's like antifreeze. Otherwise, I might not be here now."

"If you'd come straight home like you were going to do and not gotten yourself stupid drunk, you wouldn't be here, either. Where'd you get the money, anyway?"

"I'm gonna pay it back."

"I figured. Francis, I came here to tell you something. I've decided to move to Jersey and live with Kathy."

"You can't do that, sweetie. What kinda life are you gonna have living with them? You know you'll hate it. And what about me, who loves ya?"

"You're on your own, Francis. I'm sorry. But I'm not tying myself to no Irish suicide. I've had it. I warned you last time. Remember?"

"Murphy, this time's different."

"Different? Why is this time any different? Would you like to tell me why it's different?"

"Look at me. Look what I been through this time. Don't you think it's different? I was nearly all finished out there. No more, Murphy. Not after this."

"It's no use, Francis. I've made up my mind."

"Wait. Got a Christmas present for ya. It's in my bag, hanging here on the bed. You'll have to dig it out." He held up his bandaged hands.

"You got me a present?"

"Wait'll you see. Something I think you'll really like. I wanted to get you something you would want but wouldn't ever buy for yourself. That's what Christmas is for. Right?"

She went into the bag and felt around, searching among the whiskers, and newspaper. She finally came up with the tiny package. "This is for me?" She had to smile just a little. The package was beautifully wrapped.

"Open it."

She opened it and found a tiny bottle of real perfume. Not cologne or toilet water or any of those. Real perfume. "Francis!"

"Hope it's one you like. You know me. I don't know shit about stuff like that."

"Francis, it's lovely. I'm sure I'll like it." How could she not smile? "Thank you." She leaned over to kiss the good side of his forehead, and when she did, he quickly tilted his head back and caught her smack on the mouth.

"So whaddaya say, Murphy? One more chance? C'mon. You gotta. Never again this business. Okay? I'll get a job. Somewhere. They'd probably take me on at McDonald's. They always got signs in the window. I'll work nights. When you work . . . Whaddaya say, Murphy?"

"You rotten little bastard." But she could feel the water forming in her eyes. And she could feel her lips bending into a smile. And she could see his face lighting up. "I'll give it a little more thought, Francis. Okay?" What the hell . . .

Thomas Chastain

AREA CODE 212

"Hello. You have reached Five-Five-Five-Two-One-Three-Eight. I'm sorry I can't come to the phone right now. If you leave your name, a message, and the time you called, I'll get back to you as soon as I can. Wait for the beep. 'Bye."

"Jacklyn, it's your mother. Where are you? I've been calling you all evening. It's nine-thirty now. Call me!"

"Hello."

"Jacklyn! Oh, thank God you're there. I've been calling—"

"I just got in, Mother. I haven't unpacked or anyth—"

"You were supposed to be home hours ago. I was worried."

"I know. I know."

"What happened?"

"The bus broke down just as we were leaving the hospital grounds. We had to wait for them to send another bus. And then the traffic on the thruway was simply unbelievable."

"I fixed a casserole especially for you. I've been waiting to bring it over—"

"Thanks, Mother. But I'm really not hungry."

"I could still bring it."

"Mother! It's late. And I told you I'm not hungry. The drive down took so long we stopped along the way. I had a hamburger. All I want to do now is have a hot bath and go to bed."

"Jacklyn, I have to know: Dr. Frescher did think it was all right for you to leave the hospital?"

"*Of course!* You don't think I just walked out on my own? There's no way they'd let me get away with that. Besides, I told you yesterday when I phoned you that I was being released today."

"What I meant was, did Dr. Frescher think it's all right for you to be on your own now?"

"If it'll relieve your mind any, Mother, Dr. Frescher arranged with a shrink here in the city to see me twice a week. Dr. Lewistein."

"Is he any good? And I wish you wouldn't use that word, 'shrink.' It's so vulgar, dear."

"Whatever, Mother. Dr. Frescher says he's one of the best. I start seeing him next week."

"You *are* still on medication, aren't—"

"Yes, yes. I *wish* you wouldn't—"

"Now, don't get upset, dear. It's natural that I should be concerned. You have to remember that you aren't the only one who's been through a trying time."

"I do know that."

"And if I ask you questions it's that I care about your welfare. Now that your father's gone you're all I have. If I ask questions, it's because I love you."

"I love you, too, Mother. But I'm very, very, very tired and I want to go to bed. We'll talk tomorrow morning."

"Get a good night's sleep. And remember I love you."

"I love you, too. 'Bye."

"Hello."

"Jackie, it's Caddy."

"Candace, hi!"

"Wow, is it good to hear your voice again! Welcome back. Are you in the middle of anything?"

"Would you believe I just got up a little while ago? And no, I'm not busy. It's great to hear from you, Caddy."

"I spoke with your mother yesterday. She told me you'd be home last night. The gang has really missed you."

"I missed all of you. And it was so sweet of you to send me all those cards and letters. Sweet of all of you. It meant much to me."

"We wanted you to know you had our support."

"The message came through loud and clear. I hope all of you know how much it meant."

"So, how's everything?"

"Not bad, all things considered. Which takes in a lot of territory, under the circumstances."

"You're feeling okay now, huh?"

"As they say, like my old self. Come to think of it, I don't know whether that's good or bad."

"I always did like your sense of humor. But seriously, Jackie, I want you to know something. We all think you've been incredibly brave."

"You're sweet, Caddy. However, I think a more appropriate phrase to describe my old self is incredibly stupid."

"It's good to hear you say that, Jackie! We all think, though, for what it's worth, that David is the one who's incredibly stupid."

"It really doesn't matter, honestly. It's a closed chapter, finished and done with."

"Boy, am I glad to hear you say that! Oh, listen, Fran told me to be sure and tell you she'll call you later in the week. She had to fly up with her mother to Boston. They have to make some arrangements about Fran's Aunt Margaret. She's suffering from Alzheimer's disease. Poor thing. But Fran said to tell you she'll phone you no later than Friday."

"Fine."

"One more thing. The gang wants to have a welcome home dinner for you. Is Friday night okay? Fran will be back by then."

"My social calendar's not exactly filled these days. Friday night's fine."

"Fran'll give you all the details when she calls. I'm glad you're back—see you then. 'Bye."

" 'Bye, Caddy."

"Hello."

"How's my big girl today? Did you sleep well?"

"Like a baby, Mother."

"Good, because I have a nice surprise planned for us. You're going to get ready and meet me for lunch at twelve-thirty at the Plaza. Then we're going to do the stores, outfit you with a new wardrobe. I just received a big dividend check in the mail and you and I are going to spend it. Bergdorf's, Bendel's, Bloomie's, here we come!"

"Sounds like fun. I could use some fun *and* a new wardrobe. But I have plenty of money of my own. Begrudgingly or not, David's alimony checks have been arriving right on time. I have to say that for him."

"Darling, when you and I spoke last night I didn't want to ask you so soon about something that's still troubling me."

"Ask me anything you want, Mother. Dr. Frescher explained to me that a lot of problems I had in the past were because in crisis I was very good at concealing my true feelings from people. He said I'd become expert at it; it was second nature to me. The best thing Dr. Frescher did for me was make it clear that I must not flinch from talking openly, honestly, about everything connected with my 'episode.' "

"What it is is that there's no chance you'll suddenly disappear again, will you? The ten days you were missing, when we didn't know whether you were dead or alive, was sheer hell for me. I don't think I could go through it another time."

"I'm not going anywhere."

"And you won't do anything harmful to yourself again? Take too many pills . . . accidentally?"

"I did not overdose accidentally. I overdosed on purpose. I just finished telling you Dr. Frescher was insistent that I must talk about it all openly, honestly. That's what he and I did when I was in the hospital. That's how I finally came to understand that what happened between David and me wasn't all that terrible; that David's leaving me, divorcing me after only six months, wasn't a rejection of *me*. David just didn't want to be married. Not to anyone. Once I understood that I could accept it."

"If I can just believe you won't—"

"Listen to me carefully, Mother, to set your mind at ease. Dr. Frescher made me see that what I did, running away, hiding, taking the pills, I did to hurt David because of what I *thought* he had done to me. I was suffering from a damaged ego in psychiatric terms. Dr. Frescher made me see that what I did to myself was what I really wanted to do to David. In situations like mine, Dr. Frescher said, when one person actually commits suicide, what they really want to do is murder the other person, only they can't bring themselves to do it. Dr. Frescher says that what I did is classic behavior in such cases. Only mine didn't go that far."

"Thank God."

"Yes. Now will you stop worrying?"

"I feel so much better, Jacklyn. I'm glad we had this talk. You get ready now. I'll see you at the Plaza at twelve-thirty. 'Bye."

"'Bye."

"Hello."

"Jacklyn?"

"This is she."

"I'll bet you'll never guess who this is. Robert . . . Are you there? Robert Whitter."

"Oh, yes. Sure, Robert. Hi."

"Caddy told me you were back home. I've been calling you all afternoon."

"I was out shopping with my mother. I just got in. I was making myself a cup of tea."

"It's been a long time since we talked. About what—eleven months or so?"

"I expect it's been about that long."

"Listen, Jacklyn, I heard about your divorce. I meant to call then. But I heard you were away for a while."

"Yes."

"Well, now you're back."

"So I am."

"The reason I'm calling—and look, you have every reason to say no—is that I'd like for us to get back together again."

"Robert, didn't you tell me when you suggested we stop dating months and months ago that you'd met someone else? What was her name, Julia?"

"Uh, yeah. Julia. It didn't work out, though. We split. I can see I was wrong to break up with you. I thought now that you were free again, well, maybe we could get back together."

"I, ah, don't think that would be a good idea."

"Maybe just have drinks? Or dinner? Or something?"

"I really don't think so. I'm trying to let some of the past stay the past."

"Maybe we could just meet, take a walk, have a talk?"

"I think not."

"Come on, Jacklyn, we had a lot of fun together, didn't we? Why can't we—"

"Robert, I don't like to be rude but my tea water's boiling. I have to run. Good-bye."

"Hello."

"John, John Powwer?"

"Yes. Who is this?"

"John, it's Jacklyn—Jacklyn Harlar."

"Jackie! It's terrific to hear your voice again. What a surprise! How are you?"

"I'm fine. And you?"

"No complaints."

"You never were one for complaining much, in all the years I've known you."

"The eternal optimist, that's me."

"John, you know I've been divorced, don't you? And that I've been away . . . a while?"

"Yes, I heard. I don't see many of the people we both knew, but somebody told me. I wanted to get in touch with you, only I wasn't sure—well, whether you'd want to hear from me."

"Of course I would! You know, you were right about David; you warned me not to marry him. I should have listened. Looking back, I've thought how you've always been right about so many things. The trouble was I didn't always listen. If

I had, things would have been different. For me. For us, you and me."

"I've thought about it, too, Jackie. But I think that you were already too . . . involved . . . smitten with David by the time I met you. You know?"

"Yes. I have thought about that. You did know, though, didn't you—even when I told you I was going to marry David—that you were special to me. That . . . that . . . that . . . well, that I loved you?"

"You were kind, Jackie, if that's what you're worrying about. I understood that you *cared* about me—"

"Loved you!"

"All right, loved me, even if it wasn't the same kind of love you had for David. You were never unkind to me—"

"That's not what I mean. What I'm trying to say—listen, let me just talk for a minute. I've been home for two days and you know what I did yesterday? I went to the Frick Museum. By myself. You remember, where we used to go. Did you know I always thought of it as our place? I sat on the stone bench by the fountain at the indoor pool. You remember how we both always thought it was so restful, so calming there. Remember how when I'd get all upset about something and call you and you'd suggest we meet at the Frick? And we'd sit there and talk and afterwards I'd be calmed down—"

"Jackie—"

"No, wait. Let me finish. Yesterday, when I was there, thinking back over so much, I suddenly realized, saw, that *you* were the one I really loved all along. I just didn't—"

"Jackie, stop, please! Jackie, I'm married now. I've been married for a couple of months . . . Jackie? Jackie, are you there? Jackie . . . ?"

"I . . . don't know what to say. I'm . . . sorry for sounding so foolish just now."

"Please don't feel foolish. I want to see you. I want you to meet my wife, Carol. No one you ever knew. I want us to be friends. I want us, you and I, to always be friends. And you and Carol to be friends. Okay?"

"Yes . . . I want that, too. You're . . . a special person, John."

"So are you. Is it all right if I call you and we'll set a date so you can meet Carol?"

"I want to, yes."

"We're going to leave tomorrow on vacation for ten days. I'll call you as soon as we get back."

"I'll look forward to it."

"You take care of yourself, Jackie. I say that with much love."

"Thank you, John. You, too. 'Bye."

"Good-bye."

"Jacklyn?"

"Yes. This is she."

"This is Dr. Frescher."

"Dr. Frescher! Hi!"

"The reason I'm calling is I made a notation on my calendar that you were to see Dr. Lewistein today."

"I just got back from my session."

"Good! I wanted to check and see how it went. If you liked him."

"I do. He's such a warm man. I like his sense of humor, too. He makes you feel that while he *knows, believes,* the troubles you experience in life are real, nothing is as terrible as you think it is."

"I take it then that you were comfortable with him?"

"Absolutely. He reminds me of you."

"That's a compliment. Tell me, now that you've been back for a few days, how are you doing? What have you been doing? Has it been much of an adjustment for you to make?"

"It felt very strange at first, coming back to the city. I felt like I had been away for a long, long, time. Not a few months, but years. Everything that had been so familiar looked different to me, changed. The streets, the buildings, even the rooms in my apartment, the furniture, going into the stores; my mother took me shopping one day. And then after a few days back it wasn't like that at all. You know what it reminded me of?"

"Tell me. What?"

"You know how it sometimes happens with people you've known for maybe most of your life and then they go away for years and years and when you finally see them again for the first time you think you don't recognize anything about them? They're like strangers you never knew. But as you go on seeing them again, gradually, so you hardly notice it, you see them, hear them, just as they were before, when you first knew them. That's the way it is now with me being back."

"Yes, I do know. That's exactly the way it always is; the familiar that becomes strange becomes familiar again."

"Exactly."

"How about the people you've seen or heard from since you've been back home? How did that go?"

"Everyone seems to be glad, seems to have missed me. My friends are giving me a dinner party Friday night. As for a couple of other people, it's been fifty-fifty."

"How do you mean?"

"There was this one person who called. We used to date, but he wanted to break it off. Now he calls and says he'd like to get together again. I told him, no thanks. Then there was someone I broke off with a long time ago when I knew I was going to marry David. John Powwer. Well, I called John to tell him I'd like for us to start over again—and guess what? He's married."

"And how did that make you feel?"

"I guess I wished it could have been different. But I could accept it. After all, I rejected him. I decided that the two instances evened out, I guess."

"Jacklyn, I think you've made great progress. I'm pleased."

"Dr. Frescher?"

"Yes?"

"I want to thank you again for your patience, for all the help you gave me."

"You're more than welcome. I do want a promise from you, though."

"What's that?"

"If you ever need to talk to me, you'll call."

"I will. I promise."

"Take care."

"You, too."

"Jacklyn Harlar?"

"This is Jacklyn."

"My name is Jerry Keenan. You don't know me but Candace Shayler suggested I call you. You know; Caddy."

"Yes. Caddy's a friend of mine."

"Yeah, she said. Anyhow, the reason I'm calling is Caddy told me that she and some of your other friends are having a dinner for you Friday night. Caddy invited me and so did Fran Millin before she went to Boston. Caddy thought maybe you'd let me take you to the dinner since I'm going alone and she said you were, too. She thought it would be good for us to get together. I like the idea. What do you think?"

"Um. Tell you what, Jerry. I just got in from doing some grocery shopping. Let me put the stuff up and I'll call you right back. Give me your phone number. Are you going to be there for a few minutes?"

"I am. My number's Five-Five-Five-Five-Seven-Nine-Nine."

"Call you right back."

"Caddy?"

"Yes—oh hi, Jackie."

"What's all this about my going to the dinner with Jerry Keenan?"

"He called you, huh?"

"Just now. I told him I'd call him back. Are you trying to play matchmaker?"

"It occurred to me that you and Jerry would get along swell. He'll like you. And I'm real positive you'll like him. He's a neat guy. He's a researcher for *Discover Magazine.* Very quiet, very bright, *very* good-looking."

"In that case, why doesn't he have a date for the dinner if he's all that attractive?"

"He and his girlfriend just broke up."

"There's a lot of that going around. Maybe somebody put something in the drinking water."

"You're funny, Jackie. Anyway, Fran met him first. She introduced him to the rest of us and everybody likes him. Before Fran went away she told me she thought you and Jerry ought to meet."

"How old is he?"

"Twenty-eight, a year older than you. No problem there,

huh? Call him back and tell him yes. What have you got to lose?"

"I guess you're right. I'll call him."

"Great! See you Friday."

"Hello?"

"Jerry, this is Jacklyn Harlar. Thank you for calling me. The answer is, yes, let's go to the dinner together Friday."

"Thank *you*. But don't hang up for a minute. Now that we have the dinner settled there's something else I want to ask you."

"What's that?"

"Now please don't misunderstand what I'm going to ask you next, but you see I have these two tickets for the Frank Sinatra concert at Radio City Music Hall tonight. The concert's sold out, but I ordered the tickets well in advance and now I have no one to take with me. I hate to go alone and waste a ticket, besides. If you'll go with me we can have dinner first at Rockefeller Center, you know, down under, and then walk around to the theatre. This way, too, we won't be total strangers when we meet the others at dinner tomorrow night. How about it?"

"Well—let me think—oh, why not."

"Fantastic! Six-thirty okay? At the American Festival Cafe. You know on the—"

"I know where it is. I go ice skating at Rockefeller Center in the winter. But how'll we recognize one another?"

"I'll tell the maitre d' I'm expecting you. Ask for me. Anyway, I'll know you. Fran showed me a picture of you taken with her. I'll recognize you."

"I should be able to make it by six-thirty. I do have to stop by my mother's apartment first. I'll try not to be too late, though."

"See you then."

"What . . . ?"

"Jacklyn, it's your mother."

"Uh, hello."

"It's ten-thirty in the morning. Aren't you awake yet?"

"I guess I am now."

"For heaven's sake, what time did you get to bed last night?"

"About one A.M. I think it was. I got home earlier than that, but I read for a while."

"How was your evening?"

"It was nice. Seeing Frank Sinatra in person was exciting."

"And how was the young man, what's-his-name?"

"Jerry Keenan. He was nice, too, pleasant."

"I take it you weren't that impressed with him."

"No, no, it wasn't that. He's a very nice person."

"And do you think he liked you?"

"Oh, *yes*! He made that quite clear. I think he'd like us to become a 'thing.' But it's just not going to happen. He's not my type. I didn't feel any attraction to him. Or whatever."

"I'm sure you know best, dear. But you are going to the dinner with him tonight?"

"Of course. As I said, he's a very nice person."

"The reason I called you early is to remind you I'll be out the rest of the day in case you tried to phone me. This is my day to do volunteer work for the City-Meals-On-Wheels group. Before I left I wanted to tell you to have a good time tonight, enjoy yourself."

"Thanks, mother. I'll tell you all about it tomorrow. 'Bye, now."

"Hello?"

"Jackie! Is it really you?"

"Oh, Fran, how are you?"

"Super! Lordy, Lordy, Lordy, I've missed you! I can't want to see you tonight."

"You better believe I missed you, too, Fran."

"I've had no one to talk to."

"That wasn't exactly *my* problem. For three months all I've done is talk, talk, talk. To the shrink, Dr. Frescher. But of course that wasn't the same as talking to you."

"We have a lot of catching up to do. And we will."

"Caddy told me about your aunt in Boston. How is she?"

"She has Alzheimer's disease. It's so sad. I mean to totally lose your memory is like everything that ever happened to you before, since you were born, has been wiped out. The whole history of your life is gone forever for you and you're still physically here. It's . . . devastating to see."

"Do you know I just got goose pimples while you were talking, Fran? Listening to what you were saying, I was thinking it was the *exact* opposite of what I've been through; having to remember everything that ever happened to me before, since I was born. Even stuff that's supposed to be lurking in my subconscious mind and maybe affecting my behavior."

"Yes, but that was to help you, wasn't it? Seems to me it would be a relief to get it all out of your head."

"It is and it isn't. It is a relief to talk about some of the things that happened to you that you thought were so bad. You find out through help with analyzing them that they weren't so terrible after all. What isn't so wonderful is that there are a whole lot of unpleasant memories you dredge up from the past where what happened was your fault. You don't get rid of them by just talking about them, you know? You're stuck with them. They'll always be there forever in your mind and you have to live with them as constructively as you can . . . Whew! I didn't mean to go into all this, please forgive me, Fran."

"Listen to me, Jackie! We've always been best friends, haven't we? I always share with you everything that's on my mind, don't I?"

"Yes."

"So—"

"You're right."

"While we're on the subject of the recent past, being in therapy did help you, didn't it?"

"If you mean as far as David is concerned, absolutely!"

"Caddy said that's what you told her, too."

"I'll tell you what I also told her. David is a closed chapter, finished and done with, in my life."

"It doesn't bother you to talk about him, to hear about him?"

"Why should it?"

"I was hoping you'd say that. There's something you have to know before the dinner tonight. About David. I don't want you taken by surprise, to find yourself in an awkward situation."

"Don't tell me David's going to be there!"

"No, no. That's not it. It's that David is engaged to be married again. The wedding's in two weeks. Nobody knows the girl. If I didn't tell you, I was afraid someone else at dinner might mention it . . . Jackie? Jackie . . . ?"

"Sorry, Fran. I thought there was someone at the door. I heard what you said about David. You know what my response is? I have to tell it to you in terms of a story Jerry, Jerry Keenan, told me last night about a writer friend of his. This friend had his first published work printed on the Op-Ed page of the *New York Times* recently. A humorous article. The day the piece appeared the writer got on a bus and happened to sit next to a woman who was reading his article and smiling. He was so pleased, he leaned over and said, 'I wrote that article.' And the woman looked back at him and said, 'So *what*?' The poor writer got off the bus at the next stop. Does that tell you how I feel about your news of David?"

"God, Jackie, that's funny! *So what*? Don't ever lose your sense of humor, promise? Jerry's bringing you to the dinner tonight, right?"

"Yes. He's picking me up at six-thirty."

"I can't wait to see you."

"You, too, Fran."

"Jacklyn, good morning. I thought you'd call me and tell me how you made out at the dinner last night."

"I was going to, Mother. I've been puttering around the apartment all morning, changing some of the furniture around. I was going to call you when I finished."

"Well, did you enjoy yourself? Was everyone glad to see you again?"

"They were, they really were. It was fun catching up with all that's been going on; who's doing what with whom and why or why not."

"And your new friend—Jerry, isn't it?"

"He was nice as could be."

"I'm not trying to tell you what to do, but I wouldn't be too quick to drop him if I were you. It's good to have someone with you when you go out to parties and whatnot."

"I'm aware of that."

"Your voice sounds a little husky. You're not catching a cold, are you?"

"No. It's just that I haven't been talking to anyone this

morning. I'm perfectly fine. Actually, what I thought I'd do today is go to the health club and work out."

"That sounds like a good idea. If you want to drop by later, give me a call."

"I think I could use a little time by myself, straightening up the apartment, stuff like that, you know?"

"Of course."

"I'll call you soon, though."

"All right, dear. Talk to you then."

"Sixteenth Precinct. Sergeant Mallory."

"Yes. I—I—can I talk to someone about a man who's been following me?"

"Give me your name and address."

"I'm Jacklyn Harlar. My address is Six-eleven East Seventy-ninth Street, first floor."

"You say a man has been following you—"

"He's right outside my building now. I'm afraid—well, he's going to do something to me."

"Hang on. I'll let you talk to Lieutenant Graines."

"Look, can't you send—? Hello? Hello?"

"Lieutenant Graines. You have a report about a man following you?"

"And he's right outside my apartment now. I'm afraid—"

"Jacklyn Harlar, right? Six-eleven East Seventy-ninth Street, first floor, right?"

"Yes—"

"We'll have a patrol car there in the next few minutes. Meanwhile, keep your door locked."

"Thanks . . ."

"Jacklyn, it's Mother. Call me please, dear."

"Jackie, hi. I've been trying to reach you. Oh, you know, it's Caddy."

"Jackie, it's Jerry Keenan. I'd like to see you again. You said you liked Italian food. Can we have dinner Saturday night and see a movie? Let me know, please."

* * *

"Jackie, it's Fran. Where are you? Call me, please!"

"Sixteenth Precinct."

"Let me speak to Lieutenant Graines, please. It's urgent!"

"Lieutenant Graines. Can I help you?"

"Lieutenant, this is Jacklyn Harlar—"

"Oh, yes, Ms. Harlar—"

"The man who's been following me. He's outside my apartment again. I'm frightened! Can you send someone?"

"Ms. Harlar, the last time you called and we sent a patrol there was no one there outside your apartment—"

"He ran away. But now he's back. I'm scared to death!"

"All right. I'll dispatch a car. Hang on a minute, though . . . Okay, the patrol car's on the way. Now, Ms. Harlar, according to the reports I've received from the patrolmen who have come to your apartment before, you say you don't know who the man is—"

"Oh, but now I do. I saw him clearly tonight for the first time. It's my ex-husband, David Harlar."

"I see. David Harlar, your ex-husband."

"Yes. I'm positive. Can't you do something to stop him?"

"I'll tell you what, Ms. Harlar. If the patrolmen don't find him there tonight, you come into the precinct tomorrow and talk to me. Okay?"

"Yes, all right . . ."

"Jacklyn, it's your mother. If you're there, pick up the phone! If you're not, call me, do you hear?"

"Jackie! It's Fran. Call me, call me, will you?"

"This is Dr. Lewistein's office calling. Dr. Lewistein asked me to remind you that you missed your appointment for today and that you will be billed for the time. Please call the office for your next appointment."

"Jackie, this is Jerry Keenan. I would like to hear from you. 'Bye."

*   *   *

"Jacklyn, this is Dr. Frescher calling. Will you please—"

"Hello, Dr. Frescher, this is Jacklyn."

"Oh, Jacklyn, you're there. Dr. Lewistein called me. He says you missed your last session and you haven't called him back for another appointment. He's worried that something might have happened to you."

"No. I'm perfectly fine. I've just been busy."

"Are you sure you don't have a problem?"

"No . . . Well, yes, I do."

"Do you want to talk to me about it?"

"I don't know."

"Come on, Jacklyn. If you have a problem, tell me. Talk to me."

"Well, I don't know how to tell you. It's going to sound crazy. I'm afraid you'll think I'm crazy after all I went through before. I'm sure the police think I'm crazy—"

"The *police*! Tell me what's going on."

"All right, okay, I'll try. It started several nights ago. I thought someone was following me. Then I thought, well, it was just my imagination. But I caught glimpses of him, this person, outside my apartment, looking like he was trying to make up his mind about breaking in on me—"

"And?"

"I called the police. They sent a patrol car, but he ran away each time, I guess, when he spotted them. The last time I saw him outside I recognized him. It was David."

"David? David Harlar? Your ex-husband?"

"Yes. And the night I recognized him outside I called the police but he got away again before they could get to him. So, the next day, when the police suggested it, I went to the station house to talk to them. And you know what they told me?"

"What?"

"That there was nothing they could do. Even if it was David. Even if he was following me. Even if he was standing outside my apartment, there was nothing they could do unless he actually threatened me and I had proof. They did say I could go to court and file a complaint against David, but that I should have some kind of proof, more than just my word for what was going on. The truth is I think the police believe I was just making the whole thing up, or that I was crazy. I didn't do anything about filing a complaint because I thought the court would probably believe the same thing. Boy! If there's one thing I *don't* want it's for people to start thinking I'm crazy."

"I don't think you're crazy, at all, Jacklyn. But why in the world would David want to harm you? *He* was the one who wanted the divorce."

"Yes. But I can tell you why David might want to do something to me. You don't know this but, you see, David's planning to marry again. Now do you understand?"

"I'm not sure."

"Don't you see? David has to pay me alimony every month! Don't you think he'd like to have me out of the way?"

"I can see . . . where you might think that—"

"Of course. That's what it is. But nobody believes me."

"I believe you. And now I'm going to tell you what I think you should do. I think you should make arrangements with your mother to move in with her temporarily. In that way you won't feel as threatened by David as you are living alone. And then I want you to see Dr. Lewistein as soon as you can make an appointment. Tell him everything you've told me. Then he can talk to the police and see that something is done. I want you to do those two things right away. Do you understand?"

"Yes."

"Good. Meanwhile, I'll speak with Dr. Lewistein and after you and he talk, you and I will talk again. Now, call your mother right now and do as I have suggested."

"Yes, but before I call Mother, I'm going to call David and tell him to stop bothering me."

"If that's what you want to do, all right, but under no circumstances are you to meet him anywhere."

"No, I won't."

"Good. Call me if you need me. And take care."

"I'll be perfectly fine, Dr. Frescher. Thank you again."

"Hello."

"David, is that you?"

"Yes, this is David Harlar. Who is this?"

"David, this is Jacklyn."

"Oh . . . Jacklyn, I'm right in the middle of a—"

"This'll only take a second. I'm cleaning out the apartment. I'm thinking of moving. And I came across your gun, you know, that revolver you bought right after we were married? You must have forgotten and left it here when you moved out."

"I guess I did, come to think of it."

"I don't want it around. I want to get rid of it, and I don't think a revolver is something you just throw in the trash. Especially since it's licensed to you and somebody might find it and later it could cause you a lot of trouble."

"Can't you send it to me by messenger or something?"

"A gun, a revolver? Don't you think that's risky? Anyway, I don't want to give it to some messenger."

"Then what do you want me to do about it?"

"I want you to pick it up yourself."

"I guess I could do that. I'll call you tomorrow—"

"No. I want it out of the apartment tonight."

"Tonight? But I'll be here in the office until about eight."

"You can pick it up on your way home. I'll wait here for you. You should be here about—what, eight-thirty?"

"All right, all right, I'll be there. Around eight-thirty."

"Thank you so much, David."

"Sixteenth Precinct. Sergeant Herbert."

"Listen closely!"

"Can you speak up, please?"

"I can't. I can't. This is Jacklyn Harlar. Six-eleven East Seventy-ninth Street, first floor. He's—my ex-husband's in the next room. He has a gun. He's going to kill me! Send someone! Hurry! Hurry! Hurry . . ."

"Sixteenth Precinct. Sergeant Herbert."

"Yeah, hello, Sarge. This is Patrolman Anders. I got a homicide. Put me through to Lieutenant Graines."

"Hang on."

"Lieutenant Graines."

"Lieutenant Graines, Patrolman Anders. We've got a shooting, a homicide. I'm at the scene right now, the apartment of Jacklyn Harlar, you remember her, we were here before, Six-eleven East Seventy-ninth Street, first—"

"I remember, yeah. What? Fill me in on the details of the shooting."

"You're going to love this one. We get here to the building and you know what? We run smack into this guy busting out the door to her first-floor apartment. He says his ex-wife is dead inside, shot to death. He says she called him to pick up a gun he'd left behind when he moved out. He's got the gun in his coat pocket when we grab him. He says he got here, she went into the bedroom to get the gun, and when she came out she walked right over to him and as he started to take the gun, she turned it on herself and fired two bullets into her chest. He says when he saw she was dead, he panicked. He grabbed up the gun and because it was licensed to him, he was afraid nobody would believe he hadn't shot her. He ran out the door and right into our arms. Did you ever hear such a ridiculous story? We got an open-and-shut case against him."

"I agree, Anders. I'll notify the medical examiner. We'll be right there."

"Lieutenant?"

"Yeah, Anders."

"Isn't it weird? Every time she called us we all thought she was some kind of kook, looking to spook her ex-husband. And she was telling the truth all along. It just shows you."

"For what it's worth, I hope it would please her that the son-of-a-bitch won't get away with what he did. See you shortly."

"The number you have reached, Five-Five-Five-Two-One-Three-Eight has been disconnected . . ."

Joyce Harrington

MOMMA'S DONE A FLIT

"IF YOU MUST THROW DISHES, DARLING, BE SURE TO THROW THEM INTO the sink. The mess won't be so hard to clean up."

That was my mother's advice to me when I told her I was getting married. She was recovering from her third marriage, but through them all, I had never noticed her following her own advice. She threw everything, from Wedgwood to Woolworth. And the husbands left. My own father left after nineteen years of shattered china and smashed hopes. The others weren't so patient.

"I won't be throwing any dishes," I told her. "Or anything else." But I smiled as I said it to let her know I considered it a family joke. We were having lunch in her new apartment and the plates that held our curried chicken salad were new, too. "This is delicious," I added. "How about giving me the recipe?"

"Of course," she said, grinning impishly. "Take the elevator to the ground floor, cross Third Avenue, enter the deli with the yellow awning, and speak to Franz."

"I should have known," I said, grinning back at her. "Mom, you'll never change."

"Any reason why I should?"

I could think of at least three, but the most important one was that I wanted my father at my wedding and I didn't want any trouble. It wasn't that my mother set out to create difficulties. It was just that trouble trailed along in her wake like scavenger gulls after a garbage scow. No. I take that back. My mother's nothing at all like a garbage scow. She's a sleek racing yacht, magnificent in full sail on the high seas, but restless and discontented in port.

And I'm a sturdy little tugboat, plain and reliable, happy to stick close to shore doing my unglamorous but necessary duty. Until just a few weeks ago, I taught music at a public school in Brooklyn. Budget cuts put an end to that.

"I'll sing, of course," she was saying. "One of my old standards. How about 'Wedding Bells in June'?"

"That's about a wedding that didn't happen," I reminded her. I know all of my mother's old songs by heart. My father wrote a lot of them, but he never wrote the one that was supposed to blast her to the top of the charts.

You've probably heard of her, though. She turns up from time to time in one of those "What ever happened to . . . ?" newspaper features. Glory Rhodes. That's my mom.

"Well, I don't think I'm up to 'Ave Maria' or 'O Promise Me' but don't worry, I'll think of something."

"Don't *you* worry," I told her. "All you have to do is be the beautiful mother of the bride. And be nice to Daddy."

"He has to be there, I suppose?"

"Yes. He does," I said firmly. "I've already asked him."

"You asked him before you asked me?"

"You were busy," I told her. "I couldn't get a date with you until today."

She sighed. "Oh, Penny. If you only knew. Busy isn't the word. I'm out there every day, seeing managers, promoters, sleazy characters who own nightclubs in Staten Island, for God's sake! But no matter how hard I try, I can't even get a gig singing lullabies to senior citizens. Peggy Lee still sings. Ella never stopped. But nobody wants to hear from Glory Rhodes.''

I'd heard that song before, but it was heartbreakingly true. "Mom," I said, "you don't have to do that anymore. Adolph left you pretty well fixed. Even if you never sing again, you won't starve."

Adolph Springer, her third husband, had made a fortune in running shoes and he was wearing a pair of them when he dashed off in pursuit of a girl he'd met at the New York City Marathon.

She gazed at me pityingly. "I don't expect you to understand, Penny. It's not a question of money. If no one wants to hear me sing, I might as well be dead."

"Don't say that, Mom. You'll sing at my wedding. I won't get married unless you do." My sincerity was highly questionable, and she knew it.

"Well, I don't know," she hedged. "People might think it was tacky."

"Since when do you care what people think?"

"I'm only thinking of you."

"I insist," I told her. Wedding insurance. If she sang, she'd be less likely to try other ways of stealing the show.

"Well, all right, then," she said graciously. "I'll start rehearsing for it this afternoon. Maybe I should do two numbers, with a third in reserve for an encore."

"Mom, it's a wedding, not a floor show. Relax."

"You're right," she said, settling down to dessert, a chocolate mousse cake that deserved to be called sinful.

No matter how much or what she ate, she never gained an ounce, while calories seemed to attach themselves to me by osmosis. I'm not fat, exactly. Just round. And short. An eternal disappointment to my tall, slender, glamorous, beautiful, bubble-headed mother.

"Ask me about Mitchell," I prompted her.

"Mitchell who?" she asked.

"Mitch," I said, with just a tiny note of exasperation creeping into my voice. "My beloved, my intended, the man I've been living with for the past three years."

"Oh, him," she said dismissively. "The flatfoot."

"He's not a flatfoot," I flared. "He's a detective. And your slang is out-of-date."

She brushed my indignation aside. "What about him?"

"He's quit the force and opened his own detective agency. We've just rented an office. No clients yet, but it won't take long. Mitch has a lot of contacts."

"Is there money in that?" she asked.

"There will be," I assured her. "I've lost my job and I'm . . ."

"Hallelujah!" she interrupted. "Now if you'd just listen to me and get yourself a new hairdo, lose a little weight, and pay some attention to your clothes, I could introduce you to the right people and pretty soon you could be doing club dates. I hate to see all those singing lessons going to waste."

". . . I'm going to be working with Mitch," I plowed ahead. "I know enough about it already to take on a few easy assignments. Women are very good at undercover work. Especially plain, ordinary women like me. No one ever looks at us."

"Oh, baby," she moaned. "No daughter of *mine* could ever be plain and ordinary. You just never learned how to make the most of your assets." She eyed my straight brown hair. "Not blond, I think. A mass of flaming red curls. That would do it. We could get you a pair of green contact lenses. Oh, Penny! A whole new you!" She beamed at me, delighted with her creation.

"Mom. This *is* a whole new me. Remember? Mrs. Mitchell Crane? Penelope Crane, private investigator? Haven't you been listening?"

"Oh, I heard you," she sulked. "Does this mean you'll be packing a gun and trailing dope addicts and murderers?"

"Don't be silly. And of course I have a gun. Mitch taught me how to use it." I opened my shoulder bag to give her a glimpse of my brand new Beretta Minx. "Cute, isn't it? But this'll be safer than teaching in Brooklyn. Most of our work will be for corporations. Security consultations, tracking down embezzlers, industrial espionage, that sort of thing."

"Oh. Well, I'm relieved. But it sounds boring. At least let me treat you to a day at Elizabeth Arden. So you'll look scrumptious for your wedding."

"Maybe I will," I said. "On one condition."

"What's that?" she asked.

"That you go with me."

"Oh!" she shrieked. "What fun! The two of us together. Just like . . . just like . . ." She groped for a word. She knew I wouldn't go for the little sister ploy. Finally, she settled for "best friends."

"And you are my best friend, Penny," she added wistfully. "All the ones I thought were my friends, I never see them anymore. Would you believe that one of them lives right in this building and hasn't even invited me for cocktails? You're the only one who ever calls me up, except, of course, for . . . whoops! I wasn't going to tell you about him."

"Him? Who him?" Now she had me. And she knew it. She was smirking and otherwise behaving like a brat.

"Well, it's supposed to be a big secret. But if I can't tell my own daughter, then I might as well forget the whole thing. His name is"—she leaned closer and whispered hoarsely across the table—"Peter."

"Peter," I repeated stupidly.

"Peter." She beamed at me. "And he's absolutely gorgeous. Smart as a whip. And he loves me. At last I've found someone who isn't intimidated by fame."

"You mean he's famous and not knocked out about it?"

"No, child." She smiled her superior "I am a star and you're not" smile. "He's warm and kind and gentle and not in the least upset when people ask me for my autograph."

I knew that the only autographs my mother had signed in the last ten years had been on her American Express card. "Peter, huh? Warm and kind and gentle, huh? How old is he?"

I don't know what made me ask her that. Probably helping Mitch get set up in his private detective business. It's made me suspicious of everybody.

My mother turned coy. "Old enough," she simpered. And then she delivered her thunderbolt. "I think we should make it a double wedding. Wouldn't that be fun?"

"No!" I said, before I could think of a way to take the sting out of it. "I mean, it wouldn't be right. You ought to have your wedding all to yourself. After all, when Glory Rhodes gets married, that's news."

And believe it or not, she shook her head. "No, Penny dear. I'm through with all that. From now on, my private life is

strictly private. I think that's what jinxed all my other mar-
riages. Everything I did was so public. When I married your
father, there were pictures in *Life* magazine. And then what's
his name, the one in the middle . . ."

"Henderson Blackwell Crump," I murmured.

"Crumpie, of course. Never marry a banker, dear. They have
no sense of humor and they take all their money away with
them when they leave. We had one of those priggy little
announcements in the *New York Times* and a spread in *Town
and Country*. But Peter doesn't want any of that. Just a quiet
little wedding with only our immediate family in attendance.
Just like you and Marshall . . ."

"Mitchell," I corrected her, but she breezed right past me.

". . . so why shouldn't we have our quiet little ceremonies
together? I'm sure Peter wouldn't mind."

"Well, that's very decent of Peter," I muttered. But my
sarcasm was wasted. She was spinning some dream wedding in
her mind, and I was getting lost in the shuffling off of reality.

"I guess I'll be going. I promised Mitch I'd help him get the
office in shape this afternoon. Thanks for lunch."

"Oh, don't go yet." She glided out of her chair and around
the table before I could even shove my own chair back. "I need
your advice on something. It's about these dishes. Like them?"

"They're very pretty," I said. And, indeed, they were. Very
Art Deco. Black with a pink geometric border and a single
stylized flower right in the center. They weren't precisely my
cup of tea, but then I didn't have to live with them.

"Good," she said. "I'll go right over to Bloomingdale's and
sign us both up with the Bridal Registry. Then, if either one of
us ever gets an overwhelming desire to fling a plate, we can
borrow from each other to fill out the blanks."

"Mom, don't bother," I told her. "Mitch and I have dishes.
We don't need any more." But she wasn't listening.

"I'm so glad you're getting married at last. I was beginning
to think you were going to be an old maid." She hugged me
and I hugged her back.

And then I left.

All the way downtown on the bus, I wondered about this
Peter who'd walked into my mother's life. Warm and kind and

gentle sounded wonderful, until you take into consideration that she'd said exactly the same thing about Crumpie and Adolph. I don't know what she said about my father when she married him. And the way she'd hedged about Peter's age made me nervous.

Oh, I know it's okay nowadays for young men to marry older women, but my mother! I know perfectly well how old I am. I know my mother was no teenager when I was born. She had to be somewhere past her half-century mark. Well past. There was an ugly word for guys like Peter. But I put the idea aside. If he made her happy, why not? It'd be a miracle if he did, though. None of the others had brought it off.

Mitch was waiting for me at the office. In his jeans and sweatshirt, he looked more like a moving man than a private detective. But maybe that's because he was trying to wedge a file cabinet into the space between my desk and the wall. I dropped my bag on the desk and put my shoulder to the other side of the cabinet. Together, we eased it into place.

"Thanks," he said, and planted a nice, warm, sweaty kiss on my cheek. "It was such a bargain, I couldn't pass it up. It's just what we needed. How'd it go?"

"Just about as I expected," I told him. "With one big surprise. She's getting married, too."

"What! I thought she just got divorced."

"Exactly. I should have expected it. That's what always happened before. I don't think she's been without a husband for more than two minutes since she reached the age of consent. She's planning to sing at our wedding."

"And you're not happy about it." One nice thing about Mitch, he can always read my moods and make me feel better about whatever's bothering me.

"No, I'm not. I'm tired of being her straight man. I don't want our wedding turned into a showcase for Glory Rhodes."

"Why don't you threaten to sing at hers?"

"What!" I laughed. I had to. The idea was ridiculous, and I told him so. "She'd never go for it."

"Why not?" he asked. "I've heard you sing. You're good."

"I'm good in the shower. Not so good without the water to drown me out."

"I don't mind if she sings at our wedding. If it keeps her out of trouble, why not?"

I was about to tell him exactly why not, when the phone rang. We stared at each other. The phone had been installed only the day before. It was Saturday. Nobody knew we were in business yet. Who could be calling?

The phone kept on ringing.

We both dived for it and I got there first. "Crane Investigations," I announced, with a proud grin at Mitch.

"Baby, is that you? Penny?"

"M-mom?" I stammered. "What's the matter?" She sounded strange. Not her usual bubbling, overbearing self.

"Is Marshall there?" she whispered.

"Mitchell," I said automatically. "Yes, he's here. What's up?"

"Let me talk to him. Please."

"Mom, if this is one of your hysterical fits, I'll hang up on you this minute. Tell me what's the matter."

"Penny!" she shrieked. "For God's sake, let me talk to Mitchell. It's important!"

I handed the phone to Mitch with my hand over the mouthpiece. "It's her," I muttered. "She wants to talk to you."

He took the phone and calmly said, "Hello, Ms. Rhodes. What can I do for you?"

He listened for a while, nodding and then beginning to look serious. All I could hear was my mother's voice clacking away like a roulette wheel.

At last, he said, "Have you called the police yet?"

He listened some more. By this time, I had my head next to his and I heard her say, "No. I can't. I know how this looks."

"All right," he said. "Sit tight. We'll be there in twenty minutes. Don't touch anything."

"I already did," she moaned. "I touched his face. Please hurry. I'm frightened."

"Lock the door," said Mitch. "Don't let anyone in until we get there." And then he hung up.

"What?" I mouthed, not daring to imagine what had happened.

"It's your mother's boyfriend. He's dead. Let's go."

*   *   *

The cabby made good time, but still it seemed like years before we pulled up in front of the glossy new apartment building on Third Avenue. The doorman recognized me and picked up the house phone as we hurried past him to the elevator.

Three other people were waiting and they all had to get off before we reached the twenty-second floor. Mitch held my hand all the way, and I could feel my own sweat making his palm slippery. My teeth were clenched so hard my jaw ached.

"Take it easy," he murmured after the last of the other passengers left the car.

"I can't," I gritted back at him. "I'm afraid . . ."

But the door slid open before I could say what I was afraid of. I'm not sure I knew.

I broke away from him and ran down the corridor toward my mother's apartment. He was close behind me, but I got there first. The door was slightly ajar. I pushed it all the way open and hollered, "Mom! We're here!"

No answer. The living room looked just as I had left it only two or three hours earlier. The Art Deco dishes were still on the table in the dining alcove, the remains of chocolate mousse cake congealing on her plate. But my mother was nowhere in sight.

"I'll check the bedroom," Mitch said behind me as he closed and locked the door. "You look in the kitchen."

The kitchen was state-of-the-art built-in everything, but there wasn't anywhere for a fully grown former cabaret singer to hide. And why should she be hiding? The doorman would have told her who was on the way up.

She wasn't in the bathroom either. Or in the coat closet in the foyer.

Finally, I took a deep breath and followed Mitch into the bedroom. He was bent over a fully clothed male human person sprawled across the apricot satin coverlet on the king-sized bed. A whole lot of the apricot satin had turned a dull rusty red. The potpourri bowl on my mother's dressing table was fighting a losing battle with a thick gamy scent that lodged in my throat.

I turned away quickly and went to the walk-in closet, the last place in the apartment where she could be hiding. I envisioned her scrunched down in a corner, shrouded by the chiffon and spangles of her work clothes. But she wasn't there.

"She's done a flit," I said from inside the closet, swallowing hard against the growing conviction that my mother had finally come unwrapped. I could smell her perfume—White Shoulders. She never used anything else. Her clothes were loaded with it. But there was just a hint of another perfume, Opium or something like that. Well, maybe she'd changed to suit Peter Perfect.

"I'll have to call the police," Mitch said. "I'll try to get Harry."

That brought me out of the closet and, reluctantly, to a closer look at what was lying on my mother's bed. "He's really dead, isn't he?" It was a stupid question—the gash across his throat would have felled an ox—but I couldn't help wishing that the young man would suddenly sit up and shout "April Fool!" But it wasn't April, and the only fool was me for wishing the impossible.

Harry Blaine had been Mitch's boss and rabbi in the NYPD. We still counted him as a friend. It turned out he was also a longtime fan of Glory Rhodes. Once his men had set to work in the bedroom, he stood as if hypnotized, staring at the dozens of portraits of her that lined the walls of the foyer. "I saw her years ago," he said. "At the old Copacabana. I was just a kid with a phony I.D., but I felt as if she was singing just for me. I think I fell in love a little. I have all her records at home."

"She'd love to hear that," I told him. "But first we have to find her. Do you think whoever did that"—I jerked my head toward the bedroom—"do you think he could have . . . taken her somewhere?"

Harry tore himself away from the pictures and studied my anxious face. "Maybe," he said. "And maybe she just took herself somewhere. And what makes you think it was a he? Did she say anything about some other guy in her life?"

"No. You mean a jealous rival? No, nothing like that. All she could talk about was Peter. That *is* Peter in there, isn't it?"

Mitchell interrupted. "When she called, all she said was, 'He's dead.' Over and over. We just assumed she meant Peter." He turned to me. "Did she mention his last name?"

I shook my head. "No. Just 'warm and kind and gentle and gorgeous.' One of the doormen might know. They have to announce visitors."

"Good idea," said Harry. "We'll be talking to all of them. Did she have any friends, anybody she might go to if she was upset or scared?"

"Not since she got unfamous. She was complaining about that at lunch today. Said I was her only friend. What about her address book?"

"We'll be checking that, too. If she didn't take it with her." Harry sighed deeply, like an adolescent in the throes of hopeless love.

"You think she did it, don't you?" I demanded.

Harry's face softened. "I don't think anything, Penny," he said. "Yet. But I'm like you. I don't want it to be her, but I have to consider it. That's what you're doing, aren't you?"

I didn't want to cry, but that's exactly what happened. I slobbered all over Mitch's shoulder for about two of the longest minutes of my life. Then I mopped up and was ready to face facts. If there were any to face.

Harry had gone into the bedroom where all the action was, and as soon as I was finished blubbering, Mitch followed him.

The picture gallery in the foyer had overflowed onto the fireplace mantel. Normally, I didn't spend much time gazing at my mother's old publicity stills. I'd seen them all before. But now, I was drawn to them, as if they could give me some inspiration about where she might have gone. One of them was lying face down. I picked it up and saw that it wasn't my mother at all. It was a bland, lifeless studio shot of the young man who was now truly lifeless on my mother's bed. And it was inscribed. "To Glorious Glory, with all my love. Peter."

She'd been right about one thing. He was gorgeous. In the way that male models or soap opera stars can be called gorgeous. But the picture contained not a hint of the "warm and kind and gentle" person she had babbled about.

Curiosity is one of my main failings. Or virtues, depending on your point of view. I opened the back of the picture frame and slid the photo out. Just as I had hoped, there was a photographer's stamp on the back. Starburst Photos, with an address in the Chelsea photo district, not far from our apartment. Not bad for a beginner, I thought.

I slid the photo back into its frame. A plan was beginning to take shape in my head. The only way to prove my mother hadn't killed Peter was to find out more about his background, and who in his background might have had a reason to slash his throat. I could start with the photographer.

"Mitch!" I called out. "I think I'll go home. If that's okay."

He came out of the bedroom looking grim. "Harry'll want to talk to you later," he said. "I'll stick around for a while. At least as long as he'll let me."

He didn't need to tell me why. Early news about their prime suspect and what they were going to do about her.

There were several assorted persons in blue lurking about the corridor when I left. Even the lone woman among them eyed me sternly, but none of them said a word.

Down in the lobby, there were more cops and a small crowd of curious residents. One of them, a tiny woman with pink fuzzy hair and a huge black standard poodle on a leash, came right up to me and put her free hand comfortingly on my arm. "You're the daughter, aren't you?" she said. "What a shame. To happen in a nice building like this. Your mother must be absolutely out of her mind. With grief, I mean."

I shook her hand off and said, "Who are you?" Rude, maybe. But the state of my mother's mind was none of her bloodsucking business.

"Oh, just a neighbor, dear," she said. "Just a well-meaning neighbor. If there's anything I can do. . . ."

"Not a thing," I said. "Thanks."

Starburst Photos wasn't open for business but a catering crew and a couple of bartenders were busily setting up for a party. "You're way too early," one of the caterers chided me. "Nothing happens until ten."

"Where's Mr. Starburst?" I asked.

"If you mean Andre, he's upstairs having his hair done. I wouldn't disturb him if I were you." He bustled away to tend to a tray of cheese puffs.

I gaped around the huge loft. Photographic paraphernalia had been isolated at the far end under a raised platform partitioned off from the open space below. Upstairs, I gathered. I headed straight for it, mentally daring the officious caterer to stop me. He didn't. Upstairs was reached by an ornate spiral staircase that might have been rescued from some long-demolished Fifth Avenue mansion. I climbed it. And knocked at the carved mahogany door that surely had done previous duty in a parsonage.

"Not now, Brucie," came a peevish voice.

"It's not Brucie. It's an emergency!" I shouted.

"Brucie *is* an emergency. But come on in and make yourself interesting."

I opened the door and walked into someone's idea of an Arabian Nights fantasy. Heavy draperies, huge cushions, intricately woven rugs, peacock fans, a king-sized divan, and in the midst of it all, seated on a gilt throne, a skinny guy in a bathrobe was having his sparse black locks braided into a single long skinny pigtail. The hairdresser was a statuesque blonde my mother would have approved of enormously.

Andre was staring into a hand-mirror. "What do you think?" he asked. "I'm going as *The Last Emperor*."

I'd seen the movie, too. "You'd have to shave the front and have it start at the crown of your head."

"You're right, of course. But that's so permanent. And this is just for a silly costume party." He turned to the blonde. "That's fine, sweetie. Now why don't you go supervise downstairs for a while. We'll do the makeup later."

The blonde slithered down the spiral staircase and Andre regarded me thoughtfully. "You look so real," he said. "What on earth are you doing here?"

"Chasing a wild goose maybe." I was hesitant to blurt out my mission. "Have you ever photographed someone named Peter?"

"Peters abound, and they all want to be shot by Andre. Why?"

A little of the truth couldn't hurt. "He's been romancing my mother and I want it to stop. All I know is his first name. But she has a photo of him that says Starburst on the back."

"Oh, *that* Peter. What a sleaze! He orders photos by the gross. But no agency has ever seen him or them. He's not an actor. He's not a model. But he has been seen around town with quite a selection of, shall we say, matronly ladies. None of my business what he does with his pix. But he stiffed me for the last batch and that *is* my business. What do you want to know?"

"What's his last name? Where does he live? How old is he? Who are all these matronly ladies? And did you invite him to your party?"

"No to the party. I don't know the ladies. Somewhere between twenty-five and thirty. I'll have to check the address in my files. And he goes by the name of Partridge, but I think it's a phony. I'd also like you to look at his mug shot. Just to be sure we're talking about the same Peter. And who are you anyway?"

"Penny Crane." I took a small liberty with the I.D. No telling who might connect Penny Rhodes with Glory of the same name.

"Nice and plain. I like that. I'm really Andy Karp, but that sort of jars with the clientele." He rose languidly from his throne and pulled aside a heavy red and gold drapery revealing a small, exceedingly neat office area. A file drawer yielded a replica of the photo on my mother's mantel.

"That's him, all right," I confirmed.

"Is your mother rich?" Andre asked.

"Not rich. Just comfortable."

"I don't suppose our Peter would know the difference. Or care. As long as he can get something out of it."

"How about his address?"

He flipped the photo over. There was a form taped to the back that contained Peter Partridge's address on East Third Street, his phone number, and the notation in red ink that he was six months overdue on a bill of $216.50. I made a note and said thanks.

"Don't go yet," said Andre. "Forgive my asking, but you wouldn't happen to be the police, would you?"

"No."

"Because I don't think I'd like to have the police barging in. Not that I have anything to hide. But my clients are extremely sensitive. It would be bad for business."

He'd been very decent about the information, and I doubted that he would slash Peter's throat for $216.50. And I liked him.

"I'm not the police," I told him. "But they might come around. Peter's been murdered. In my mother's apartment. And my mother's missing. They think she killed him, and I'm trying to find out who else might have wanted him dead."

"Well, all I can say is congratulations to your mother if she really did off that slime. It'll be the sensation of my party tonight. Why don't you come and be a fly on the wall? You might learn more about Peter than you would poking about in the East Village. You'll have to wear a costume, though. No one admitted without."

"Maybe I will," I said. "Thanks."

The blonde returned to report that Brucie was having a fit over the crab blinis, and I left.

A cab took me to East Third Street where I walked up three flights to a black painted door secured with a hasp and padlock. Even as a teacher, I'd learned the usefulness of carrying a miniature tool kit to repair the results of school vandalism. The hasp came off easily and I slipped inside Peter Partridge's apartment. It smelled of cat, a very funky men's cologne, and dirty socks. The cat, a huge black monster, came yowling out of a closet and twined itself around my legs.

"Hungry, are you?" I said.

The cat continued yowling and twining until I started for the kitchen area, and then it was there before me. I filled its empty food bowl with some kibble I found on the windowsill, and got down to business.

I really didn't expect to find my mother here, but I looked anyway. There wasn't much territory to explore. It was a studio apartment with a sleeping alcove, one closet, and a tiny bathroom with the cat's litter box in the shower stall. The place was a mess: dirty clothes strewn everywhere, the bed unmade and the sheets grimy, take-out food cartons piled in the kitchen sink. But the closet and dresser bore evidence that Peter had been fastidious about his personal appearance.

The dresser also held a full-length photo of my mother, one that had been taken about fifteen years ago, in a skintight silver lamé gown cut down to her navel. I remembered that dress. Fifteen years ago it had embarrassed the hell out of me. Today I'd give anything to see her wearing it. The photo was inscribed, "To darling Peter, with all my love. Your own Glory."

She wasn't the only one who had contributed to Peter's gallery of conquests. There were about a half-dozen other photos on the dresser and more scattered around the room, all of them of fine-looking women who were probably, like my mother, a bit older than their pictures gave them credit for.

As Andre had said, "What a sleaze!" But whatever Peter had gained from his shoddy romances, he certainly hadn't been living the high life. His clothes were expensive and he had a pretty good stereo system, but that was it. Maybe my mother was the only one silly enough to believe he would marry her.

There was a fat little black book on the dresser and I pounced on it. Addresses, telephone numbers, most of them in Manhattan and most of them of women. My mother's was the newest entry in the R section. Starburst Photos was numero uno under the S's. I skimmed through the book, marveling at all the good addresses and the gullible women who went with them. But I wasn't about to start calling them up. Leave that to Harry Blaine. Toward the front of the book, something had caught my eye. I'd gone past it, and then paged back. It wasn't a name. It was an address. The same as my mother's but a different apartment number. The name attached to it was Audrey Allen.

My mother had said something at lunch about an old friend of hers living in the same building. Could this Audrey Allen be that old friend? It was a long shot. The building had at least a hundred apartments. Peter could have staked the whole place out as a prime hunting ground. But my mother could have panicked and gone to hide out with her old chum.

The cat had finished eating and was back, purring this time and rubbing against me. I reached down and scratched its head. It promptly rolled over and presented its belly for additional scratching.

"What am I going to do with you?" I asked. "I can't leave you here."

I found a cat carrier in the closet and left East Third Street after reattaching the padlock and hasp.

Uptown, downtown, East Side, West Side; I was spending more money on taxis in one day than I ever had in a week. The police were gone from the lobby when I reached my mother's building, but the doorman told me they were still upstairs. "But I made them take the body out by the service entrance," he added. "Can't have dead bodies disturbing the residents."

"Good thinking," I told him. No point in telling him that the police generally do what they want to do and that they'd probably chosen the less conspicuous way out. "Would you do me a favor? I'm going up to my mother's place now, but I don't want to take this cat up with me. Would you just keep it here until I leave?"

"No problem," he assured me.

"And there's no need to announce me. They're expecting me."

"Right, miss. And I'm sorry about your mother's trouble. Would you tell her that for me?"

"Absolutely. Oh, and by the way, when my boyfriend and I arrived earlier, did you announce us?"

"Well, no, I didn't. Your mother didn't answer, and I figured she was in the bathroom or something. And besides, you're family. But I knew she was up there, as well as Mr. Partridge. I let him in while she was out. She told me to do that. She wasn't gone long. I hope I didn't do wrong?"

"No. Nothing wrong. Thanks a lot."

Once in the elevator, I punched the button for Audrey Allen's floor. She was two floors above my mother, but in the same row so the layout of the apartment would probably be the same. If she was in, I'd question her about Peter. If she wasn't, maybe I'd see if I could pick the lock.

But I didn't have to. Audrey was in, and she was the same pink-haired woman who had asked me about my mother in the lobby. As she opened the door, the poodle started barking like crazy and leaping about in a frenzy.

"Down, Blackie!" she cried. "Damn dog's more trouble than he's worth. Come in, dear. Did your mother tell you where to find me? Does she want to see me now?"

"Not exactly," I said. "But can I talk to you anyway? You're an old friend of hers, aren't you?"

"Well, of course. And what are old friends for if not to help out when help is needed?" She led me into the living room, the same as my mother's but furnished to the hilt in antiques. I sat down on an Empire-style chaise lounge and Blackie tried to clamber into my lap. Maybe he smelled Peter's cat.

"That's enough!" Audrey scolded. "I really ought to take him to obedience school." She pulled the dog off me and hauled him away toward the kitchen. "I'll just give him some food and shut him up in here. Then you and I can have a nice little chat."

As she brushed against me, tussling with the dog, I caught a whiff of her perfume. I'd smelled it before. But what on earth had Audrey Allen been doing in my mother's closet?

I followed her to the kitchen and stuck my foot in the door just as she was closing it. She whirled on me, a long, thin, wicked-looking knife in her tiny hand. I shoved the door all the way open, knocking her arm away. She leaped backward and stumbled over the dog, who was doing his best to join in the fun. She landed on her tush but held on to the knife. The look on her face was pure malice. I felt pretty peculiar about mixing it up with a woman old enough to be my mother, but, hey, she clearly intended to inflict bodily harm on me. I kicked the knife out of her hand with one sturdy, sensible shoe, and then I sat on her. The dog licked my face.

"Where's my mother?" I demanded.

"Wouldn't you like to know," she sneered.

I bounced up and down on her stomach a few times.

"Get off me, you cow!" she snarled. She kept squirming and reaching for the knife, which had landed just out of her grasp. "Wasn't it bad enough she stole Sam away from me?" she screamed. "Did she have to take Peter, too?"

"Sam?" I gaped at her.

"Yes, Sam. Your father, you nitwit. We were all set to get married, and then *she* came along. I never forgave her for that. And then she dumped him when she was tired of him. But she got something out of it that I've never had."

"What's that?" I know, I know. I should have been asking better questions. But I was still trying to understand the answers she was flinging at me.

"You! A daughter. But she won't have one for long." She bucked like a bronco then, and I lost my seat on her stomach. If I hadn't been so stunned by what she'd been telling me, I would have tackled her instantly. But I didn't and she retrieved the knife and came at me again.

The shot came out of nowhere. Or rather through the kitchen door and right over my head. Audrey Allen collapsed in a spatter of blood from a wound in her shoulder. I whirled around and saw my mother standing there, still aiming the gun at her old friend.

"Mom!" I cried. "Where'd you come from?"

"Don't be stupid, Penelope," she said. "Get that knife away from her before she does any more damage. She's not dead, you know. I wouldn't want to kill her. Then she couldn't do time for murdering Peter. Not to mention all the sleeping pills she crammed down my throat. I don't know whether she was trying to kill me or just knock me out for a while. I've been in there vomiting ever since you got here. Now grab that knife."

I did as she told me. Audrey seemed unconscious, but she was definitely still breathing. Blackie was cowering and whimpering in the farthest corner of the room.

My mother was pale and disheveled and her eyes were red and slightly unfocused. I went to her and took the gun from her hand. "Hey!" I said. "This is mine. Where'd you get it?"

"If you're going to carry a gun, you shouldn't leave it in your bag when you need it. Adolph taught me that. Did I ever tell you about the cute little firing range in the basement of his house? I got pretty good with a .38. I almost used it on him once." She giggled. "I think I need to sit down now." She toddled away and arranged herself on the chaise in the living room.

With a wary eye on Audrey Allen, I picked up the kitchen phone and dialed my mother's number. Thank God, Mitch was still there. I gave him Audrey's apartment number and said, "You'd better get up here right away. Harry, too, if he's still there. Have I got a surprise for you."

When they arrived, Audrey was conscious and spitting venom. "Damn little twerp!" she screamed. "I wish I could do it again. And again. And you, too, Glory. I should have killed you years ago."

Harry was incredibly gentle with her. He calmed her down and told Mitch to call for an ambulance. He wrapped a couple of towels around her shoulder and carried her into the living

room. While we waited, he chatted with her and got the whole
story out of her. How she'd been out walking the dog and saw
my mother leave the building. A few minutes later, Peter had
arrived. That was when she decided to do it. She'd gone to my
mother's apartment with a knife from her own kitchen. She
rang the bell and Peter answered the door.

"Boy, was he surprised!" she said. "He didn't want to let me
in, but I just ran right past him. Then he ran after me, and I ran
into the bedroom. When he got there, I was ready for him. It
was so easy. He couldn't believe what was happening. I just
stood on the bed and grabbed him around the neck. He must
have thought I wanted to kiss him or something. He twisted
around, trying to get away, and that's when I did it. He fell back
onto the bed. And then I heard someone coming. I hid in the
closet."

My mother took up the tale. "She leaped out and pounced on
me after I talked to you, Mitch. And she dragged me up here at
knifepoint. I think she would have killed me, too, if I hadn't
gone with her. She held the knife on me all the way up the fire
stairs. When we got here, she ranted on for a while about how
she'd make it look as if I had killed Peter. And then she made
me take those pills. I didn't swallow all of them, though. Kept
some inside my cheeks, like a damned squirrel. But I still got
pretty groggy. I was coming out of it when I heard noises out
here. Turned out to be Penny." She smiled at me. "Lucky for
you I'm a light sleeper and a crack shot."

Later that night, while the three of us, Mitch, my mother, and
I were sitting around our dining table eating moo shu chicken
and shrimp with garlic sauce, and trying to avoid any mention
of Peter or Audrey, the doorbell rang. Blackie, who'd been
snoozing on the couch, set up a din. And the cat, who for the
moment was nameless, streaked off to the bedroom.

When Harry Blaine announced himself over the intercom,
my mother leaped from her chair and dashed after the cat. "I
look a fright!" she moaned. Harry would be disappointed, but
if she couldn't face him, she shouldn't have to. I set another
place at the table. When Mitch opened the door, Harry came in
carrying a stack of old LP records in both arms. He put them
on the table and sat down.

"Thanks for inviting me," he said. "I'm starving. I haven't eaten all day. Is your mother here?"

I hadn't invited him but Mitch wore a guilty smirk. "Lying down," I said. "She doesn't feel very well."

He looked pointedly at her half-empty plate and vacant chair. "Yes, well," he said. "I just wanted to tell her that we've got a signed confession and Audrey's going to be well taken care of. Your mother didn't do any permanent damage. I was wondering if she might sign a few record covers for me."

"Thank you. I'd be happy to." My mother was standing in the entrance to the living room. Her hair was sleeked back primly and her makeup was subdued, but she glowed from something that wasn't blusher. "It's very kind of you to come here to tell me that. I know you must be very busy."

Harry dropped his chopsticks and simply stared at her. My mother glided into her chair and smiled demurely at all of us. "Police work must be fascinating," she said. "I'd like to learn all about it."

It was on the tip of my tongue to tell her she could have found out everything she needed to know any time over the past three years from Mitch, but my dearly beloved, who can sometimes read my mind, kicked me under the table and I stuffed my mouth with a shrimp.

So now there will be two weddings but not together. My mother and Blackie have moved into Harry's bachelor digs in Queens while they have her apartment redecorated, and they're planning a honeymoon trip to Hawaii. "Why wait?" she said. "We're not getting any younger. Harry's so warm and kind and gentle, and he just loves to hear me sing."

Mitch and I will spend our honeymoon investigating drug use among the employees of a manufacturing plant near Philadelphia. It's our first big assignment and we're nervous and happy. But I sure hope I never have to come face-to-face with another pink-haired lady with a knife. At least, not without my mother along as backup.

Dorothy
Salisbury
Davis

TO FORGET
MARY ELLEN

THE TWO MEN SAT IN GIBBONS'S 1990 FORD TAURUS IN THE PARKING
lot of Freddie's Diner on the West Side of Manhattan. In
November it was already dark at five-thirty. Everyone on the
street, except the homeless, was bucking the wind, homeward
bound. The two men were unnoticed.

Joseph (Red) Gibbons was a retired New York detective. The
subject of unproven charges of corruption and misconduct,
he'd been given early retirement several years before. It was
widely suspected also that he abused his wife, but Mary Ellen
simply would not swear out a complaint against him. He was
an affable man most of the time, generous, with a glib tongue
and a ready handshake. He was also a bully, and it came out
when anyone of lower rank crossed him, or when he'd had a
few drinks, or, unpredictably, with his wife.

Billy Phillips was crouched down on the passenger side. The
round-shouldered Phillips had crouched so much of his life it

was his natural posture. On the move he was quick and simian; huddled in a chair or a car seat he had very nearly the inanimacy of a rag doll. In the neighborhood he was thought to be a kind man, he was very good to Marge, his wife, and he adored their ten-year-old son, William. There were rumors that he was connected with the Rooney Gang, but nobody suspected in what capacity. Some said it had to do with gambling. Phillips was a hit man, a paid killer. His wife took for granted that they lived on the horses and what she earned as a hairdresser in a neighborhood beauty salon. Billy was a good handicapper and every once in a while took off without notice for a few days at whatever track was in operation at that time of year.

Gibbons and Phillips had met only once before, when Gibbons was still a working detective. Phillips had made a rare slip-up: he had left evidence that would eventually incriminate him on the scene. Rooney had told him he might get lucky, Gibbons was on the case. By appointment he had gone to Gibbons's home, a loft in the West Thirties, and Mrs. Gibbons, Mary Ellen, had opened the loft door to him, not even curious about how he got into the building. He wouldn't have told her the truth anyway. He observed an ugly bruise on her cheek, but he recognized her as a battered woman more from the wary look in her eyes, the hang of her head, the sloping shoulders, especially the shoulders. The slope had particular meaning to him—it recalled his attempts to diminish himself, to become invisible if possible, in childhood, to slip under the blows aimed at him by a runaway father whenever he was coaxed home by the parish priest. Billy Phillips had never laid a hand on his own son, even in just punishment.

The night he had gone to Gibbons's home he was prepared to mortgage his life to get the incriminating evidence back in his own hands or destroyed. He represented himself to Gibbons as an intermediary, the messenger for a friend in trouble. He spoke as an outsider, even though he knew deep down that Gibbons did not believe for a minute he was there on behalf of anyone other than himself. No promises had been given. Both men realized, despite Phillips's sham, that they were prisoners to each other whether or not any word of commitment passed between them.

A few months after that Gibbons was retired. The evidence Phillips was concerned about never surfaced. The case, like his other homicides, remained open, but inactive. The police lacked both time and new evidence. His success was attributed in part at least to his never using the same weapon twice. After making a hit he took the weapon at once to Fitz Fitzgerald, a gun fence with an overseas outlet. When he needed a safe replacement Fitzgerald always came through for him.

Phillips had a beer now and then in McGowen's Pub on Eighth Avenue and he had seen Gibbons there a few times. They had made eye contact, but that was all. They'd not spoken again until the phone call from Gibbons that set up their meeting in the parking lot of Freddie's Diner.

Phillips appeared, as out of nowhere, got into the car and closed the car door almost soundlessly.

"Been waiting all this time to hear from me?" Gibbons asked him.

"I had a little package ready for you, but I didn't hear so I figured I'd better wait."

"Five years?"

"I thought maybe you'd forgot about it. Maybe you wanted to forget it."

"Cops and elephants don't forget. How big was the little package?"

Phillips shrugged. "I'm not a rich man."

"Maybe you're in the wrong business." Gibbons gave a snort of laughter.

Phillips didn't say anything. He felt like a mouse under the cat's paw.

"When the P.D. put me out to pasture, I went into the insurance business," the retired cop said. "I had a couple of good years in there before things dried up. I've got what my old lady calls a gift of the gab. It worked miracles when there was money around. The way things are now, half my clients can't pay their premiums. I can hardly pay my own . . ."

The more Gibbons talked about himself, the more uneasy Phillips felt. Why was he supposed to give a damn what Gibbons was doing? He was being set up for something and it was going to come like a kick in the groin. Was the old evidence still around? Was the case going to open again?

Gibbons sure as hell wasn't trying to sell him life insurance. But it had to have something to do with insurance. That made him even more nervous. Insurance companies had their own detectives. He pulled in tighter on himself, pushing back on the cushion, down on the seat as though he could disappear into the upholstery.

Gibbons continued, "Want to know what all this bullshit's about?"

"I want to know what size package you're thinking of, yeah."

The ex-cop chortled. "You've got it all wrong, my friend. It was you mentioned the package, not me. I've got a job for you, Phillips, something in your line."

He ought to have known, probably did. Only he didn't want to admit it. He didn't want the job, not for Gibbons. But he was afraid to say so. "You know how I make a buck these days? I handicap horses—all over the country. I guess you knew that, huh?"

"Twenty thousand," Gibbons said, ignoring Phillips's attempt to head him off. "Five when we shake hands, five when the job's done, and ten two years later. We can set the date."

Phillips bit his tongue. It was enough money to choke a horse. His instant calculations ran to where it would be safe to invest it, and how much it would grow to by the time William was old enough for college. It happened to him every time there was a possibility of real money. "What's the two year business?"

"Two years minimum. We're talking insurance. They don't pay till they can't get out of it. They want absolute proof whatever the claimant says happened did happen. We can handle that. We can see it happens the right way."

Phillips thought he had it now: proof that the deceased died by the rules set down in the policy fine print. Gibbons had got himself named beneficiary of some old Bridget or Norah he'd charmed with his Irish gab. Now he was ready to pull the plug on her. It had to look like a break-in or a street crime. High risk and tricky as hell. Twenty thousand wasn't all that much money.

But he said, "Tell me about it."

"I couldn't do that, Billy, without a commitment from you."

"I can't give you a commitment till I know what I'm getting into. Who? Where? How much time have I got?"

"I'll be working with you all the way."

Phillips was suddenly wary for another reason: Gibbons could be undercover, working for the cops again. He could've got religion. "I work alone," he said. "It's done my way or it ain't done by me."

"I buy that," Gibbons said, "but you might feel different in this case." The lights of a passing car flashed across his face. They caught the screwed-up eyes, the smug grin on his pudgy face.

"I do every case different," Phillips said, "but they all come out the same. See what I mean?"

"Whoever you take a contract on, they're dead. Is that what you're saying? What in hell would I be doing here if I didn't know that?"

"What's the job?"

"I want you to kill my wife."

Phillips wasn't prepared for that one, but he should've been, he thought: Gibbons the wife beater. He had an instant memory of the battered woman who opened the door to him that night five years ago. Gibbons would be working with him all the way. He believed him. And he hated him. Not that he'd loved any bastard he had ever done a job for. "I never did a woman," he growled.

"You know the sign in the window of the beauty shop where your wife works—UNISEX? Look at it that way."

The son of a bitch.

They met the next night two hours later in the same place. Freddie closed early. His main business came at noon from workers in nearby industry and warehouses. A few neighborhood stragglers hardly made it worthwhile to serve evening meals. By eight o'clock the only cars left in the lot would stay overnight. Freddie paid half his rent that way. Gibbons was one of his regulars, familiar to anyone who observed his comings and goings. No one did that night. Phillips considered himself invisible. He'd worked at it long enough, a master of every detail of misguidance. Even Gibbons didn't see him until he opened the car door and slipped in.

"I was thinking," Gibbons started, "you might want to come

up to my place and look over the setup. She's home most of the time except on card party nights, but I don't see what difference it makes whether she's home or not. Except on the big night, of course."

"The big night," Phillips repeated.

"Yeah." After a few seconds Gibbons said, "Ever have anyone hang on to you, Phillips? The more you shake them off the tighter they hang on. She's like that. When I can't stand it anymore I let her have it, and you know, the poor girl likes it? When I get over the rage, see, I'm sorry. Then she's all over me. Do this to me, do that. I go out of there hollering. If I didn't, I'd kill her."

"So why don't you?"

"Don't be a smart-ass," Gibbons said.

"You're still living in the same place?" Phillips asked.

"Same loft, same wife, same stinking elevator. You'll have to watch that."

Phillips had no intention of going near an elevator. Elevators were traps. If there weren't stairs . . . but he knew there were. He'd used them the one time he'd been there. He said nothing, however. He'd hear Gibbons out. He did things his way, but that wasn't to say it couldn't be changed to suit the circumstances.

"I got to tell you, we've been broken into twice. That's how I got the idea. I scared them off once. Next time I wasn't there. They beat up on Mary Ellen . . . Messed the place up. I figured it's a good idea for us to mess things up, too."

Us, Phillips noted.

"I could do it myself when I get there," Gibbons reconsidered. "No, better not. You never know how you'll feel when the time comes. We've been married thirty years, you know. If we'd had kids everything might have been different."

Yeah, you'd beat up on the kids, Phillips thought. He twisted in his seat. The family talk was making him nervous. "Let's stick to business, okay? Let's hear your game plan and I'll tell you if it'll work."

"It's so simple, it's scary. The first two floors in my building's industrial, see—in by eight A.M., out at five. I've got the fifth floor, right? I've been there fifteen years. But the owner's turning the third and fourth floor into apartments.

More bucks. All these classy apartments are ready. But they can't get occupancy certificates. The plumbing's fucked up. A few hundred bucks under the table, no problem. But it's not my business. The thing is, after quitting time there's nobody, but nobody, in the building."

There was never nobody, by Phillips's reckoning, but he said, "Okay, let's have the rest of it."

"A couple of nights a week I'm in the habit of staying out late. I don't stay over, but I stay plenty late. She knows where I am but I call her anyway, especially since the break-in. I got a downstairs key for you. You'll have to get rid of it good."

"I don't want your key," Phillips said.

"The night we settle on, you'll be in the hall outside the door when I phone. I'll let you know the time I'm going to call her and you'll wait a couple of minutes after you hear the phone ring. Then you'll ring the doorbell. Maybe knock and ring at the same time. The bell doesn't always work. I'll tell her to find out who it is, and when she calls out to you, you'll say it's Sergeant Nichols from the precinct. You brought a package 'round for me." Gibbons laughed. "That little package keeps turning up, don't it? Fact is, that's what happens once in a while. I'll tell her to open the door and it'll be that simple."

"Nothing is ever that simple," Phillips growled.

"But we can work 'round it?"

"Suppose I can't make it on target, or something gets in the way, like the real Sergeant Nichols?"

"There is no Sergeant Nichols. Then we start over another time. If you're not there she can't let you in, can she?"

"Have you got a revolver, Sergeant?"

"I've got my service .38. I was damn glad to break it out the night of the attempted robbery."

"What if your wife has it in her hand when she comes to the door?"

"She can't. I took it over to the office last week when things got uptight between her and me."

"Think she'd kill you if she got the chance?"

"Hell no. I was scared she might kill herself."

Stupid-head me, Phillips thought. Insurance companies didn't pay off on suicides. "I want that gun," he said.

"The hell you do. It's got my name all over it. I had to register it at the precinct when I retired."

"The weapon's no problem, but I want that one. I'll tell you why. This is how it's got to play to Homicide: No phone call. Let them figure out why she opens the door. You've told her time and again not to, right? So when she opens it, she comes on with your revolver—" Gibbons tried to interrupt. "Listen to what I'm saying. She comes on with the gun. The guy outside the door knocks it out of her hand. Maybe she gets shot in the scuffle. The cops can figure that out, too. That's how it's got to play to Homicide. In real life the shooter hangs up the phone before he leaves the premises. That way you know it came out like it was planned. Is there a witness on your end of the phone?"

"There won't be."

"You won't have to mess up the apartment. The shooter's got the piece. To him it's worth the kill."

"I want to think about it," Gibbons said. "That gun's like my right arm."

What bothered Phillips more than anything else about the job was his hatred of Gibbons. He didn't like working inside a building. He'd take fences over walls any day. And he didn't like it that the contract was on a woman. But every time he thought of Gibbons it was like something started crawling inside him. He could see his puffy face, his screwed-up eyes. And he knew that if ever he saw this man lay his hand on the wife he'd go berserk. It was like that when he saw anybody knocking a kid around. He'd almost got arrested once in a supermarket when he caught hold of a woman and pulled her away from where she was slapping the kid in its stroller. He didn't want to think too much about Mary Ellen. Where the hell was women's lib? She'd be better off dead, he told himself, than spoiling her life with Gibbons. But there was the twenty thousand dollars. The most he ever got for a hit was five grand.

The final meeting before the hit date occurred at Gibbons's loft. Mary Ellen played cards every other Wednesday night at the church hall. Gibbons would go over to McGowen's Pub for a few beers and then pick her up on his way home. When he told her he was staying home that night, that he didn't feel so great, she wanted to skip the card game. But when he blew up at her for it, she took off. He called after her that he'd pick her up as usual.

Phillips was watching from across the street. There wasn't much traffic, most of it the precinct cops taking in the whores from Eleventh Avenue and the crosstown Thirties: sweep night. There were night-lights on all the floors of Gibbons's building—pale, low-wattage bulbs you'd think would die any minute. And he couldn't see a homeless slob on the street, the cleanest street in town. Real treacherous. Gibbons's wife left the building at ten minutes to eight. He wasn't sure at first that it was her, the way she walked with her head up, her shoulders back, a tote bag swinging at her side. Good legs and noisy heels. It had to be her. The time was right and nobody else came out of the building. He could hear the clack of her heels far down the street.

That night he got into the vestibule the way everybody else did, by ringing Gibbons's bell and waiting to be buzzed in. He even took the elevator to the fifth floor. Never again. It climbed one floor after another as though it wouldn't make the next. Gibbons was waiting for him in the hallway. "Did you see her?"

"It must've been her. Nobody else came out of the building."

"I don't pick her up till ten, but I'd like to get you out of here as soon as we get things settled."

"Suits me."

"Want a drink?"

Phillips shook his head. "Let's get on with it." He sat down on a straight chair, having hooked it out with his foot from the round polished table. Mary Ellen kept a bare and tidy house. No plants, a couple of holy pictures. He thought about all the room there was in a loft. William, raised in a railroad flat, would go wild in a place like this. Phillips's nerves began to jump, the tension grabbed at the back of his neck when Gibbons returned.

"Fifty C-notes," Gibbons said, and took a packet of mixed old and new bills from a paper bag. "Want to count them?"

"You do it for me," Phillips said.

Gibbons put the already heavy bag down carefully on the table, removed the rubber band from the bills and slipped it onto his wrist. He counted the bills aloud, stacking them by tens on the table. "Satisfied?"

Phillips stood up and took his wallet from his slacks pocket. "Give me twenty of them." He stuffed them into the wallet and put it away. "Put the band back on the rest of them." He put the packet into his breast pocket.

They confirmed the date of the hit and the date and place of the final payoff. Phillips sat down again and they went through the setup one last time. Phillips looked around at the phone where it sat on a table between two easy chairs that faced the television set.

"What about the bedroom phone?"

"I told you, it's on a jack that's broke. I'm supposed to fix it but I won't."

Phillips got to his feet. A wall clock with one of those sunshine faces showed a quarter to nine. He motioned to the paper bag. "Let's have it."

"Take it."

"I don't want the bag. Hand me the gun."

"Goddamn it, take it yourself." The sweat glistened on Gibbons's forehead.

Seeing Gibbons sweat was balm to Phillips's nerves. "It's clean, right?" He reached into the bag and brought out the .38 police revolver. Beautiful. It looked as new as the day it came from the gunsmith. He flicked off the safety and rolled the cylinder. Every chamber was loaded. He reset the safety. "Thanks for the spares," he said. "Got any more?"

Gibbons sucked in his breath and let it out. "The rest of the box. It's on the closet shelf in the shoe box."

"Leave it there." Phillips put the gun in the pocket of his jacket, kneed his chair back into place, and went to the door. He looked back. Gibbons was still standing at the table, crumpling the bag, staring after him. He was shaking, Phillips realized. Gibbons was scared shitless. The stinking coward was scared of him. Phillips knew himself the man had good reason. "Let me out of here, will you?" he said.

Gibbons moved with a start. He tossed the bag on the table and strode to the door.

In the hall Phillips turned back. Gibbons stuck out his hand.

They had never shaken hands, and didn't then. Phillips made his hit face to face with his victim for the first time ever.

Nothing this night had gone the way Mary Ellen expected it to. She had left the house in a rage of her own and vented some of it clattering down the street. Like all her rages, it turned in on herself. She knew there was something wrong with her to take all the abuse she got from Red. It was sick to love him even more afterwards. At one time they'd taken counseling together from their parish priest. Red had insisted on it. The gist of what the priest had to say was, "Why don't you fight back, Mary Ellen?" "I wish to God she would," Red told the priest. But when she tried it with about as much punch as a kitten's paw, he'd twisted her arm behind her and said, "Don't you ever try that again."

She knew he was having an affair and she'd left the house convinced the woman would arrive at the loft as soon as she was safely out of the way. When Red blew up because she decided to stay home with him, she felt absolutely certain. She could taste the pain and pleasure of knowing them to be in bed together—in her bed. Her mind was on fire with the thought of actually seeing it. Give them enough time and then go back quietly. She tried to concentrate on the card game at first. Red would kill her. But she didn't really care. When an extra player showed up at the card game she gladly gave up her place. At twenty past eight she started back home, at half-past eight she left the elevator on the fourth floor and walked up the one flight of fire stairs. Before she even got near the loft door she heard the voices, Red's and another man's. She fled, ashamed and panicky. Red would kill her if he knew she'd come home, and he'd know why she did the minute she tried to lie about it. She got all the way back to the door of the parish hall and heard the scrape of chairs, the talk and laughter as the switch in bridge partners took place. She had no heart for the game and there wasn't a place for her anyway. There really wasn't a place for her anywhere. She felt ashamed, disappointed, crazy.

Whether suicide entered her mind she was never going to be able to say for sure, but she walked to the river, past the air force carrier *Intrepid* in its semipermanent dock, and through the scattered people out on a chilly weeknight. She walked out

on the long pier. Some way along it and close to the water's
edge, she found herself among materials set out for dock
repair: the barricade had been overturned, the lantern an askew
red eye. Backing out she sank her heel into a glob of tar. She
pulled her shoe out and tried to remove the gummy residue
with Kleenex, then with an emery board, finally with the nail
polish remover she had in her tote bag. She only made things
worse. The only place to deal with it was at home. She checked
her watch under the first high-density streetlight.

She avoided passing the church hall where Red would soon
be turning up to walk her home. If she hurried she could get to
the loft well ahead of him. She might not have time to clean the
shoe, but she could hide it away and not have to confess that
part of the night's silliness. And she'd pretend she hadn't heard
him say he would pick her up as usual. She took off her shoes
and ran the last part of the way home.

Homicide Detective John Moran and his partner Al Russo
took Mary Ellen and her lawyer back to the loft at seven in the
morning. She had been questioned throughout the night at
precinct headquarters. The lawyer, a smart young fellow
recommended by Moran himself, demanded that the police
charge her or release her. Moran was, to the extent his duty
allowed, on Mary Ellen's side. He had known Gibbons when
he was on the force; he knew him for a smiling Irishman with
a cruel streak in him, a lot of charm until it wasn't working.
Then he was a son of a bitch. He knew that Gibbons abused his
wife. A jury might come out on her side, too, but it would go
better for her if she confessed, let her lawyer spell out what a
bastard her husband was. And it would be better for Moran
himself if he could break the case now, before the brass moved
in.

He was dog-tired and well into overtime. His partner was
asleep on his feet and the suspect was a staggering zombie, but
Moran was determined on one more go-round with her. It
might be irregular to bring her back to the scene so soon, but
he got away with it. He wanted her to see the forensic crew still
at work, the scraping and the measuring, the chalked outline of
the figure who had lain there. She had been fingerprinted and
tested for powder burns. None showed up, but the tar and the

polish remover rendered the findings inconclusive. If she was guilty the whole tar and tar removal bit could have been calculated. The long pier had been checked out and at dawn a diving team was scheduled to search the river along the pilings for the gun. She readily admitted knowing there was a revolver in the house. It had been there for years. But she could not account for why it was missing now—unless her husband had taken it to his office. Or the man she'd heard him talking to had got it from him. The last time she had seen it was the night of the break-in when her husband scared off the burglars. The medical examiner had not yet offered any findings on the spent cartridge.

They went through the CRIME SCENE barricade in the first daylight. People on their way to work were routed away from the building and got no more out of the uniformed cops than that a police investigation was going on. But the rumors had it about right and a *Daily News* photographer was on hand. The minute he started shooting pictures the word went up, "That's her! That's the wife!"

Moran began what he hoped was the final grilling inside the entrance to the building. He wanted to know where the elevator was when she rang for it.

Mary Ellen swayed, a little dizzy when she looked up at the floor indicator. Her lawyer offered his arm. She threw it off. She was home and that was support enough for now. "It was on the fifth floor. That's what made me even surer she was up there."

"You took the elevator to the fourth floor yourself. Why not the fifth?"

"I didn't want them to hear it stop on our floor."

"But wouldn't they have heard it starting down for you? Or wasn't it right there waiting on the first floor, where you'd left it when you went out?"

"I've told you the truth. Are you trying to trap me?"

"I'm trying to help you," Moran said. "I don't know that there was a man up there at all unless you convince me there was."

"I heard him. That's all I can tell you."

"Were they arguing? Were they laughing? Come on, lady, you heard something. What was it?"

"Just voices. They were talking."

"Voices make words. That's how people communicate. Didn't you hear one word?"

She shook her head and swayed again.

The lawyer said, "Mrs. Gibbons needs to sit down, sir."

"So do the rest of us," Moran snapped. He pressed the button and the elevator door slid open noisily.

Mary Ellen did not allow herself to see that which she did not want to see. She was aware of men at work, the hallway filled with equipment, cigarette smoke, light that was blinding. She longed to be inside the loft with everything else shut out. She fought off the memory of that other return. Over the years she had rehearsed a like scene many times when Red was on the force. She clutched her lawyer's arm and looked only at the ceiling while they edged their way around the floor tape. Moran allowed her to use the bathroom, given the all-clear by the crew.

There were only three rooms to the loft, the bedroom, the kitchen, and the very large living room. The round table with its four chairs had been dusted for prints. It was available to them. Moran seated the group the way he wanted them, allowing Mrs. Gibbons to keep her back to the area under investigation. If he wanted to make her look there, he could. At the moment he wanted her cooperation, not her collapse. He resumed his questioning; Russo activated a small tape recorder.

"Suppose, just for a minute, Mrs. Gibbons, you had not heard those voices, what would you have done?"

"I'd've let myself in real quiet. If there wasn't a light on in the big room—that's what we call this room, the big room—if there wasn't a light on here, I'd have sneaked through and turned on the light switch to the bedroom just as I opened the door."

"How would you have felt if there was no one there?"

"Don't answer that," the lawyer intervened.

"You'd have been disappointed, right?" Moran amended.

"I was disappointed when I heard those voices. Oh, yes. I wanted her to be there with him, if that's what you want me to say."

"All I want you to say is the truth." Moran drew a deep, raspy breath. He wanted a cigarette, but he'd smoked his last one before leaving headquarters. "Let me tell it the way I see it, Mrs. Gibbons. You were absolutely sure you'd catch them here last night if you came back early. In your bed! In *your* bed. So when you got the chance early in the evening, you took the revolver from the closet shelf, from a shoe box, right? And tucked it into that bag of yours. Lots of room. No problem." He paused. She was shaking her head. "So what's wrong with it?"

"I'd've been scared Red would catch me taking it."

"Was he home *all* the time? Didn't step out for cigarettes, a breath of air? Didn't get a telephone call that kept him on the line—a call from his other woman, let's say, so he'd be glad to see you disappear in the bedroom?"

"You're wrong, wrong, wrong. That just didn't happen." She put her head down on her arms on the table.

Moran tucked his hand under her chin and forced her head up. His face close to her, he said, "Let's go back to the question. If you didn't hear those voices, what would you have done?"

"I told you I'd have sneaked in."

Moran interrupted. "And if you'd found them in bed, naked as baboons, making love so hot you could smell it?"

Her whole forlorn expression changed. She smiled, her dead eyes caught fire. "Yes!" she cried encouragingly. "Yes!"

Christ, Moran thought, she's enjoying this.

When the medical examiner agreed that the fatal bullet had probably come from the box of cartridges found on the shelf of Gibbons's closet, pressure mounted within and outside the police department for the arrest of Mary Ellen Gibbons. The insurance representatives kept to the background, but the company made it plain they wanted to see a case developed along the lines of murder for profit, the direction toward which the district attorney's office was already inclined. While Gibbons had written the policy and paid its premiums by pouring virtually all his commissions into it, Mary Ellen was co-signatory. Indeed their investments and bank accounts were in both names. The only noticeable irregularity in the Gibbonses' finances was that in the past eighteen months he had, on several occasions, failed to deposit their monthly dividend check from mutual funds. This, however, coincided with his extramarital affair with a woman who testified to "his generous care of her."

As for physical evidence, the weapon itself had not been found. Given the tides, the muck, and the undertow of the Hudson River, this was not surprising. The grappling for it went on. None of the fingerprints brought up in the Gibbons home indicated a visitor that night. There were simply no witnesses to confirm that part of Mary Ellen's story. Testimony to her erratic behavior was ample. Her distracted behavior at the card party was readily testified to, as was the hour at which she cut out of the game. A young couple came forward who had seen her bumbling around the pier repair site. They were afraid she might fall or jump into the river and turned back themselves, not to be involved. They had intended to report her to the first cop they encountered, but by the time they came on one they decided that their imagination had exaggerated her strange behavior.

Mary Ellen never wavered in her account of that night's activities. She admitted that although she had known of her husband's affair for a year, and had found out where the woman lived, she had not until that night tried to confront them. Detective Moran tried to believe, along with almost everyone on the case, that she had contrived the story to cover the murder of her husband. But he could not reconcile her responses under questioning with murder for profit. He was superseded in the case, not taken off it, but dropped down a couple of notches in authority. The Police Benevolent Association was adding pressure: one of their own had been murdered.

Her arrest, Moran knew, was imminent. Without quite realizing how it happened, he found himself back where he had started, on Mary Ellen's side. As he said to Al Russo, who had answered the complaint with him that night, "You saw that place—all the comforts of a zoo. That money wouldn't mean much to her if she was to get it."

"Wait till the lawyer's bills come in. She'll need it then."

Moran thought about what Russo said. It was out of sync. And that was what he felt about the whole case. The money angle would make sense if Mary Ellen was the victim, her husband the one to profit from her death. No one would pay those premiums without expecting to collect. That's what made it crazy: he paid the premiums. He had to believe she was going to die first. And here she was, about to be charged with his murder, frozen into a story she hadn't moved a shadow's length away from.

On Saturday morning Moran went over the prints again. It was the third day after the homicide. Most of the recent prints had been identified, including those of Mary Ellen's sister— whom she was staying with now—and a plumber. Moran studied Gibbons's prints on the table. Those marked FRESH were in one place where, he figured out, Gibbons would have been facing the door. He got out the crime scene photos of the table and chairs. He was a few seconds identifying the one item on the table.

It was a crumpled paper bag. His association was instantaneous. Now. Not originally. The bag had gone to the lab. It would take time to bring up prints on the rough paper. Moran tore through the transcripts of Mary Ellen's statements—when questioned she did not remember the paper bag at all. Her husband might have gone out after she left the house, but not before it. Moran turned to the autopsy report: there had been no food intake after that night's early dinner. Gibbons did not smoke. The inventory of personal effects showed his wallet to have contained ninety-eight dollars. It was still in his pocket when he was shot. Eighty cents in change had spilled out on the floor. Moran turned everything around and made himself assume Mary Ellen to be telling the truth. The paper bag fit the payoff tradition. Someone had come to the loft with it, or for it? The man whose voice Mary Ellen claimed to have heard was real. He had been there. So what went wrong between him and Gibbons? If they'd been quarreling she'd have known that much at least from the pitch of their voices.

Moran went back to the monthly dividend checks Gibbons had failed to deposit. They totaled $5,100. But something else showed up: Mary Ellen was not as ignorant of their finances as he had supposed. On several occasions she had requested a bank printout of their accounts. So she would have been aware that Gibbons was siphoning off the occasional dividend check. She *could* have been aware. Was it one more example of her masochism to have known and been silent?

Yet another possibility occurred to the detective. Suppose a killer hired by Gibbons had gone to her and told her he was being paid $5,000, say, to kill her. Say he asked her to make it ten and he would turn the gun on Gibbons. Would she finally, finally, have taken the offense against her husband and said, "Go ahead. Kill the bastard!"?

Phillips had run down the four flights of stairs that night knowing he should have gone back into the apartment and taken the paper bag. But too much blood had spattered and there was too little time. When Gibbons failed to pick her up at ten she'd come home on her own. Poor sick woman, he had done her a good turn and he hoped she'd appreciate it some time. Now he had to forget Mary Ellen and make new plans for himself.

On the street he stood a moment sucking in the air to clear his head of the reek of gunpowder. His hearing was coming back. A noisy argument was building mid-block. The cops would be close at hand when Mary Ellen wanted them. He went the other way and set himself an ambling gait with little simian spurts now and then. If anyone noticed him at all in the twenty blocks uptown and the two long blocks west, he'd be taken for a harmless drunk. In fact, he picked up an empty wine bottle, discarded it, and kept the brown bag it was wrapped in. He worked the revolver into the bag without taking it from his pocket.

It wasn't ten o'clock yet when he reached Mickey's Place, the hangout of the Rooneys. Rooney was out of town, Phillips was glad to hear. Fitz Fitzgerald was the one he wanted to see, without Rooney putting his nose in. Fitz was shooting pool. He had three more balls to clear the table. Phillips went into the back room, called the "conference room," and waited for him. He tried to remember the names of the former gang members whose initials were carved in the table. Fitzgerald came in flushed with a win. He looked scrubbed and, as usual, wore a white shirt and striped tie. He looked like a bank teller, and his daytime job wasn't far from that mark: he worked in a check-cashing shop. He looked no more like a gun fence than Phillips looked like a killer. The first thing he asked was if the gun was hot.

"Plenty. You don't get it unless you got a place for it outside the U.S.A. And I don't mean Ireland."

"You know I ain't political, Billy. Let's have a look at it and you can tell me how much you want."

"Half what you can get for it, and I'm willing to wait for mine." He slipped the gun from the bag.

Fitzgerald's face went white. He knew a police special when he saw one. He began to back off.

"It's okay with me if you put it on ice for a while," Phillips cajoled. "I'm going out to the West Coast tracks in the morning. Just put it on ice and I'll check with you at the end of the week."

Fitzgerald moistened his lips. "Rooney won't like it, Billy. He keeps saying, 'Some of my best friends—'"

Phillips cut in, "Does he have to find out? It's you and me doing business here."

"He finds out most things, don't he?"

"Yeah, when some fink tells him."

"I ain't no fink and you know it, Billy."

"What in hell would I be doing here if I didn't know that?" The words had a familiar ring: it was what Gibbons had said talking him into the job.

Marge Phillips was about to leave the house on Saturday morning when the phone rang. She hoped her perm customer wasn't canceling.

"Is Billy back yet?"

"He's not, but he's due in around noon."

"It's Fitz Fitzgerald, Marge. I got to deliver a package to Billy and it's got to be this morning, Rooney's orders. Could I bring it around to you on my way to the shop?"

"Ah, Fitz, I won't be here, but William's home. I'll have him watch out the window for you. It'll give him something to do and keep him out of mischief till his father gets here."

Fitzgerald hesitated. "The kid wouldn't open it, would he?"

"Not if you tell him he mustn't. He's very good that way."

Moran was in the squad room unwrapping his lunch when the report came through of a ten-year-old boy dead on arrival at Roosevelt Hospital. He'd been shot while playing with a .38 revolver. Moran stuck the sandwich in his pocket on his way to the desk. "I want to roll on this one, Sergeant. I'm looking for a .38. Maybe I'll get lucky."

Judith
Kelman

THE
ABSENT
PRESENT

"TALK FASTER, MELISSA. SHE'LL BE HERE ANY MINUTE."

Melissa Gordon perused the committee list and scrawled Sarah Richards's name next to "Refreshments." Sarah ran Eating Is Alimentary, a successful catering operation in Greenwich, Connecticut. Dindy Draper, heir to the Draper dried pasta fortune and veteran organizer of dozens of elegant charity balls, would capably manage the decorations. Penelope Treat, who arranged corporate meetings in her capacity as publicity VP for Viscount Press, had agreed to find and book the hall. Joyce Ferman, executive editor at *Fine Living*, had signed on to oversee the souvenir yearbook. In addition to coordinating the overall arrangements, Melissa would take charge of programs, invitations, and the special class awards. It was going to be the finest twentieth reunion in Parcher School history.

"I think we've about covered everything," Melissa said.

"Then what do we do with dreary Rhonda Drear when she shows up?" said Penelope.

"I honestly don't see why you had to invite her to the planning meeting, Melissa. The problem with you is you're too damned nice," Dindy said.

"She called and asked to come. How could I say no?"

"Try 'no.'" Dindy said. "It's easy. You press the tip of your tongue to the roof of your mouth and—"

The buzzer sounded, announcing that a Ms. Drear was on the way up to Melissa's Park Avenue penthouse. A tense hush gripped the assemblage followed by a burst of giggles.

"Remember, this is 'Help me, Rhonda,' we're talking about. Whatever we give her to do, she's guaranteed to screw it up," Penelope said.

"Be fair. Maybe she's changed," Melissa said.

"Sure, Melissa, and maybe the pope has become a Baptist."

"Come on, everyone. We have to think of something fast," Dindy urged.

"No problem, ladies," Joyce intoned. "I just thought of the perfect job for our Ms. Drear."

Rhonda drew a greedy breath and viewed herself in the polished brass elevator door. For months she'd been anticipating this meeting, this moment. As her spiritual advisor, Madame Zarushka, had predicted, her twentieth high school reunion would mark the turning point in her lackluster life. Her crucial energy sectors would fall in fresh alignment. Rhonda could envision the consequences. Love, luck, and material rewards would suddenly pour her way like a mighty river diverted by a giant karmic dam. She had waited thirty-eight years for her time to come.

And it was coming on June Eleventh.

With Madame Zarushka's enthusiastic support, Rhonda had prepared for her renaissance. Strict diet and tortuous daily sessions with a personal trainer had lopped off her excess inches and pounds. Countless hours and dollars spent with a personal shopper had replaced her dowdy wardrobe with elegant, figure-flattering classics. After the nose and chin job, a makeup artist had taught her eye-fooling techniques to enhance her chintzy cheekbones and plump her anemic upper lip. At the Bernie Bernini Salon, her hair had been shorn, shaped and highlighted at outlandish, yet worthwhile, expense. A weekend seminar in Creative Positivity had squared her posture and enabled her to release her long constipated charm.

She looked and felt, in a word, terrific.

The transformation and her frequent sessions with Madame Zarushka had virtually exhausted the proceeds of her mother's whole life policy. But Rhonda was not in the least concerned. After her triumph at the class reunion, she would find a wonderful, high-paying job. It would be the start of the successful career that had long eluded her. Madame Zarushka had read her future resumé in the stars, and it ran two pages.

As Rhonda saw it, she was well past due for some good fortune. Destiny's dark shadow had dogged her from early childhood.

She had been born two weeks late. The overcooking had doomed her to a difficult birth and consequent problems with spelling, fractions, and the frequent, disquieting sensation of a toilet flushing deep inside her head. Then, when Rhonda was six, her father had left their rent-controlled apartment for a pack of cigarettes and never returned. Rhonda didn't remember the man, much less his brand, but she presumed both must have been extraordinary.

Rhonda's mother had worked hard to provide her with every possible advantage. Rhonda had attended Parcher School and private college with the aid of partial scholarships and the loans she was still attempting to repay. Through her mother's diligence and dedication, Rhonda had enjoyed the opportunity to disgrace herself in Manhattan's finest dance, drama, and elocution classes.

It was Mother Drear's dearest wish that her sole offspring would marry young and well. Mother had wanted Rhonda to have several accomplished children of her own, many devoted friends, and a fulfilling vocation. But the fates had conspired to thwart the dream.

Rhonda would have been well liked, but there was always a jealous or perverse peer to turn the others against her. She was a sickly child, prone to gastric upsets and respiratory infections. In middle school, an ill-timed case of chicken pox had kept her from being tapped for the honors track and doomed her to second-rate courses and teachers.

In high school, one of those inferior teachers had been her true undoing.

Miss Caroline Crawshaw.

The name alone was enough to ignite Rhonda's rage.

Ninth- and tenth-grade English had been a torment under that woman's tutelage. Nothing Rhonda produced was good enough. Everything had to be reworked and rewritten. Her best stories and papers came back bloodied with niggling criticisms. When Rhonda balked at correcting what she knew to be excellent work, Miss Crawshaw had penalized her with unthinkably low grades.

Those C's and D's had ruined an otherwise exemplary record. Those grades had kept Rhonda out of the honor society and off the list of distinguished scholars marked by an asterisk on the Parcher School graduation program. Those grades had caused her rejections from Columbia and Cornell, left her with nowhere to go but the all-female Mount Hillard, where it was impossible to find a date, much less a husband.

Too late, Rhonda had realized that it was probably what that miserable spinster had intended all along. If Miss Crawshaw had to live her solitary dried prune existence, she was determined to inflict the same fate on innocent students like Rhonda.

The elevator arrived. Drawing the sort of deep, calming breath she'd learned in Creative Positivity, Rhonda stepped in and requested the penthouse. The uniformed operator nodded and smiled. The old Rhonda would have thought he found her ridiculous; the new, improved model accepted the attention as a compliment.

On the cushioned ascent, she expelled the heinous Miss Crawshaw from her mind. She was at the threshold of a monumental moment. This reunion was going to change her life.

Melissa's apartment was stunning, and so was Melissa. They all were. Rhonda's eye caught the Hermes scarf at Joyce Ferman's neck, the Chanel suit on Dindy Draper, and the doorknob solitaire flashing on Sarah Richards's finger. Ten carats minimum, she estimated. Probably as flawless as Sarah had always been. Penelope Treat was her standard elegant self in crimson silk with crocodile accessories.

I fit in, Rhonda assured herself in the upbeat silent self-talk she'd learned in Positivity class. I am every bit as attractive and appealing and accepted as any one of them. Maybe more so. At closer range, she noticed the crow's feet on Joyce Ferman and the scatter of gray strands in Melissa's bangs. Sarah Richards's legs were mapped with blue veins, and given a certain tilt of her head, it appeared that Penelope was sprouting a second chin.

The rest of Rhonda's awkwardness evaporated as Melissa led her into the dining room and motioned her toward a tapestried chair at the antique Chippendale table. But as she sat, she noticed that the demitasse cups were drained, the pastry tray reduced to leavings and crumbs.

"Am I late, Melissa? You said two-thirty."

"Sorry. If I did, I meant two. Coffee?"

Rhonda accepted a cup and the apology. This was going to be wonderful. She would not allow thirty foolish minutes to spoil it. She smiled and waited out a long, gurgling flush behind her ear.

"How've you been, Rhonda? You look different," Sarah said.

"Do I?"

"You look wonderful," Melissa said. "Tell us what you've been up to."

Rhonda flapped away the awkward question. "The usual, you know. Let's talk about the reunion, why don't we? I can't tell you how much I'm looking forward to it."

Dindy's eyes narrowed. "You certainly do look different. I'd hardly recognize you."

"Well, it has been an age," Rhonda chuckled. She wanted to tell Dindy Draper that she hadn't changed a bit. Same gaunt, dissipated look. Same nasty sneer. Probably still spreading her spindly legs for anything in pants. Dindy was one of those envious snits who'd always been against her, Rhonda knew. But she was determined not to let old furies stand in her way. She thought of the way Madame Zarushka had taught her to deal with anger.

"Release it. Let it go. Think of the black crows flying away,

Rhonda dear. Let only the beautiful doves return to roost in your soul."

Joyce Ferman was smiling at her, flashing those perfect teeth. "We were hoping you'd agree to take on a very important job, Rhonda."

"Of course. Anything."

Joyce's smirk passed like a candle flame from woman to woman. "We want you to be in charge of the class gift."

Dindy Draper bit her lip to keep from snickering. Sarah Richards averted her gaze and stared at her engagement ring. A cloud of concern crossed Melissa Gordon's expression as she went to the kitchen to replenish the pastry tray. Penelope Treat was the only one controlled enough to risk a word.

"Perfect job for you, Rhonda. Simply perfect."

Rhonda's heart fluttered like a trapped bird. Were they making fun of her?

"But what sort of gift can we give? The school shut down a year ago."

Penelope didn't flinch. "Exactly why you're the one we want in charge. Since we can't give the usual furniture or equipment or new classroom, we need someone whose mind works in a whole different way. Someone with your sort of creativity."

Rhonda fought her rising panic. "But how do you give something to a school that doesn't exist anymore?"

Joyce held herself in stiff control. "Who says a class gift has to be for the school? It can be something for the class. Right, ladies?"

"Right," the others chorused. "Leave it to you, Rhonda. You'll think of something."

Absorbing their trust and compliments, Rhonda pushed aside her terror and focused on another of Madame Zarushka's visualizations.

"Let the thoughts flow like ocean tides, my dear. Out with the bad. In with the fresh and pure."

"What's the budget for this gift?" Rhonda said.

A pulse worked in Joyce's jaw. "We're trying to keep costs down, Rhonda. It's not the expense that counts, it's the symbolism."

"Symbolism. Absolutely," said Sarah.

Out with the bad. In with the fresh and pure.

"You don't have to come up with something right away," Joyce said.

"Definitely not. Take your time. You can report back to us in a couple of months," said Penelope.

"Or you can even surprise us at the reunion," Dindy chimed in. "Wouldn't that be fun, everyone?"

Out with the bad . . .

The incoming tides carried a rush of inspiration. Warmed by the flash of brilliance, Rhonda flushed and laughed aloud.

Melissa had returned with the pastry tray. "Everything all right, Rhonda?"

"Better than all right. I just thought of the perfect class gift."

"What?" Penelope said.

"Actually, I'd rather do as Dindy said and keep it a secret." Her laugh was heartier this time. The others exchanged dubious looks, but Rhonda was not bothered in the least. She knew her idea was perfect. It was going to ensure her triumphal moment and all the stellar events to follow.

"Wait until the reunion, my fellow Parcherites," she said with a rakish heft of her brow. "My class gift is going to be the best surprise of all."

Dindy Draper was the last to arrive. Melissa had set a gracious luncheon on the sideboard: poached salmon, grilled chicken salad, French bread, Viennese pastries, and a compote of seasonal berries.

Breezing through the dining room, Dindy heaped her plate and hurried to the table.

"What's with you, Dindy? Your pants on fire?" Joyce said.

"Not at all. I just wanted to eat before you-know-who shows up and kills my appetite."

"Good point," said Sarah popping a mammoth strawberry into her mouth.

Melissa shook her head. "You people are really terrible. Give Rhonda a chance. She was perfectly fine at the last meeting: pleasant, agreeable. I saw a dramatic difference from the clumsy eighteen-year-old misfit she used to be."

"Right. Now she's a clumsy thirty-eight-year-old misfit. Admit it, Melissa. It would certainly be more pleasant and agreeable taking care of the last minute details if dreary Drear weren't around," said Joyce.

Melissa passed crème fraîche for the berries. "Well, it so happens she's not coming."

"Praise the lord and pass the ammunition," Penelope said.

Sarah poured herself another touch of Dom Perignon and tipped the bottle over Penelope's stemmed crystal flute.

"To what do we owe this wonderful good fortune?" said Joyce.

"I don't know exactly. Rhonda called this morning. She said she was all tied up," Melissa said.

"So much for the class gift," Dindy said with a snicker. "I guess she's too embarrassed to show up and admit she couldn't think of anything."

"Leave it to Rhonda to take that outrageous assignment seriously in the first place," said Joyce.

"So happens you're both wrong," Melissa said. "Rhonda told me to tell you it's all set. She's taken care of the class gift, and she can't wait for us all to see it."

The musty room echoed with the woman's desperate cries. Six hours, and the voice was finally starting to dim like a spent battery. "This is crazy," she wailed. "Simply insane."

"I am terribly disappointed in you. Terribly," Rhonda said. She stood with her arms crossed and her jaw jutting forward like a hood ornament. "I certainly expected far more from a person of your abilities."

Rhonda giggled in giddy self-appreciation. She had Crabby Caroline Crawshaw's voice and mannerisms nailed to perfection. Normally, she had no particular skill for mimicry. But twenty years of active loathing and simmering recollections had locked this particular likeness firmly in her mind.

A toilet flushed deep in the center of her forehead. Seat of the third eye, Madame Zarushka called it. Window to the soul. Rhonda imagined the flush drawing her wretched old teacher down the drain with a churning rush, carrying her off to join the rest of the sewage.

"Please, Rhonda. Enough. You must let me go now. I'm an old woman. My heart."

"Heart? You? Now there's a good one."

Miss Crawshaw's gray eyes were pooled with anguish, and her face had erupted in dusky blotches. Hours of screaming struggle had whipped her hair into albino cotton candy. And the tail of her blouse hung from her skirt like a dog's tongue. Quite the new look for Miss Prissy Perfect whose stiff form and stern visage had always been a study in hard right angles.

With enormous satisfaction, Rhonda noticed how the woman had shriveled in her own skin. In high school, she'd loomed large as a redwood. Tough and knotty. Impervious to fears or feelings. Now, her spotted flesh hung on the wasted frame like spattered rags.

"If you let me go, I promise I won't say a thing to anyone, Rhonda. I'm not interested in punishment. All I want is to be left in peace."

"And you will be," Rhonda said with great sincerity. "No way I'm hanging around this creepy, empty place. I only stopped by to see how you're coming along. Or would 'going' be more accurate?"

Fear glinted in the old woman's expression. "My cats. They'll starve without me."

Rhonda shook a finger. "Now, now, Miss Crawshaw. We're prevaricating, aren't we? I didn't see any cats when I came to your place to pick up the garbage."

"They were sleeping in the kitchen."

"That's what you are, you know. Garbage. Sack of stinking, rotten trash. Do you have any idea what you did to me, *Miss* Crawshaw? Do you ever lie awake nights and think about the lives you ruined?"

The dull eyes blinked slowly, like a frog's.

"Don't play innocent with me, you old hag. You know exactly what you did. It was all deliberate, every bit of it. All you wanted was to humiliate me, put me down, make nothing out of me."

"That's not so, Rhonda. You must believe me."

"Wrong. That's two points off for gross inaccuracy, Miss Crawshaw. I don't have to believe you or do any other damned thing you say. Shame, shame. There goes your A."

"I don't understand this. What is it you want from me?"

"Asking questions out of turn," Rhonda said clacking her tongue. "What am I going to do with you?"

A tremor wracked the woman's frail frame. "Is there something you can cover me with? I'm so cold."

"No wonder. You've got ice water running in those varicose veins of yours. Remember the ninth-grade essay contest? Remember how you held my paper up like it was a dead spider and said, 'Rhonda Drear. You come right up here and take this back. I don't want to see it again until it's something you can be proud of.'"

The old woman nodded dully. "I encouraged all my students to do their best work. That was all I wanted for any of you."

"You call that encouragement? You tell me my work is an ass-wipe, and I'm supposed to be inspired? Well, *now* I am inspired. I'm inspired to go out for a nice dinner. Then, I'll go home, luxuriate awhile in a bubble bath, and enjoy a delicious night's sleep full of the sweetest imaginable dreams. See you tomorrow, dearie. Don't let the bed bugs bite. Or the rats."

"Please, Rhonda. At least, let me use the bathroom before you go."

Rhonda planted her hands on her hips and frowned. "I'm afraid that's quite impossible. You know it's strictly against the rules to leave the room in the middle of a lesson."

She paused with a hand on the door. "There's a bucket under your desk, Miss Crawshaw. And don't forget: neatness counts."

Melissa Gordon returned from the bedroom toting a red sequined gown on a padded hanger.

"It's stunning, Melissa. Red's definitely your color," Penelope said.

"You don't think it's too flashy?"

"If you've got it, flash it," Dindy said. "Speaking of which, what's the flash on the awards? Why all the secrecy?"

Melissa picked an imaginary speck of lint off the Galanos she'd purchased for tomorrow night's festivities. "No reason. I just thought it'd be more fun for you to hear them at the dinner."

"Nonsense," Penelope said. "Since when did you know any one of us to have a lick of patience?"

"Come on, Melissa. Give," Joyce agreed.

Draping the gown over the arm of the couch, Melissa drew

a breath. "All right, but you have to promise, no arguments."

"Like hell we do," Sarah said.

Avoiding the ring of curious eyes trained on her like sniper rifles, Melissa extracted a folder from her Louis XIV sideboard, cleared her throat, and read from a printed sheet inside.

"The honorees at the Parcher School Class of '73 reunion are as follows: King and Queen will be Mark and Penelope Treat."

Penelope met the resultant scatter of applause with an aristocratic nod. "Thank you, thank you. You're too kind, really."

"We know that, Penelope. So don't push your luck," Dindy said.

"Most Accomplished: Joyce Ferman. Least Changed: Sarah Richards. Most Prolific: Marcy Byer."

"Is it true she has ten children?" Penelope gushed.

"Ten children, ten novels. And two more of each on the way," Melissa said. "Most Famous: Linda LaVigne."

"Did you see her in *Rattler*?" Dindy sniffed. "The woman was positively putrid."

"Maybe so, but Linda's lack of talent is known to millions and millions worldwide," Melissa said, closing the folder. "And that's about it."

Joyce's eyes narrowed. "Wait a darned minute, Melissa. What about 'Most Changed'?"

Melissa flapped a hand. "Did I leave that out? It's Rhonda Drear."

The rumble of dissension built to about a six on the Richter scale.

"No way," Dindy said.

"I agree. Rhonda's the class dork. Why should she come away with an award?" Penelope said. "Poor Dindy here isn't getting anything. Of course, you'd win hands down if there was a bitchiest category, dear."

"Why thanks, Penelope. That means a lot, coming from an expert on the subject like yourself," Dindy said.

"They're right, Melissa. Rhonda may have improved, but that doesn't make her any star player in my book," Sarah said.

Melissa held her tone level. "I knew that would be your reaction, but I've given this a lot of thought. The truth is,

Rhonda was branded as an outcast from day one. Once we picked her to be the fall guy, the poor girl didn't have a chance. Everyone was always teasing her, excluding her. With all that, how could you expect her to be anything but awkward and inappropriate?"

There was a guilty silence.

Melissa allowed it to settle and went on. "Remember how Roger Ruskin glued her skirt to the chair in Biology? Remember Cody Keller asking her if she'd like to go to the junior prom, and when she said yes, suggesting she find herself a date? Remember that time you called her and recorded her trashing everybody on the phone, Dindy?"

"And then you played the tape over the loudspeaker after morning announcements?" Sarah said and winced.

Melissa nodded. "Rhonda deserves a medal for just surviving all our cruelty. Despite us, she's managed to become a stylish, attractive woman. And courageous. After all we did to her, who'd expect her to come to the reunion?"

The women traded looks of contrition.

"And not only is she coming, she's gone out of her way to offer her help."

Joyce raised a sheepish hand. "I move that we unanimously approve the choice of Rhonda Drear as the 'Most Changed' member of the Parcher School Class of '73."

There was a rush of relief followed by affirming hoots and whistles. Melissa beamed. "I can't wait to see her face when she hears."

"The reunion is going to be absolutely perfect," Penelope said.

Melissa's smile faded. "I dearly hope so. But there's still one critical piece missing."

This time the ring of eyes was expectant.

"I still haven't been able to get hold of our number one honoree, the class choice for best teacher," Melissa said.

"Well, keep trying, Melissa. Work on it," Sarah said.

"We'll all work on it," Joyce said. "Caroline Crawshaw has to be available. That woman was my inspiration."

Sarah nodded. "Mine, too. In a way, she made me what I am."

"She touched all of us at the Parcher School," Dindy said

with unaccustomed solemnity. "She left her mark on so many students. More than she ever imagined."

The room was hot and musty. Rhonda recoiled from the stench of urine and fear. The camcorder she'd purchased that morning at Forty-seventh Street Photo was nowhere near as light as they'd made it look in the box. Damned thing was boring a hole in her shoulder and poking her hard in the eye.

"Pick up your head, Miss Crawshaw," she snapped. "Look into the camera, for Chrissakes."

There was a wisp of wordless voice. Something between a squeaky hinge and a hissing radiator.

Rhonda settled the camcorder gently on the floor. Fourteen hundred dollars, not counting the tapes and batteries, so she was damned well going to take care of the dumb machine.

And she was going to take care of Miss Crawshaw as well. The odor intensified as she approached the bound bag of bones. Holding her breath, Rhonda grabbed a fistful of the coarse, frenzied hair and pulled until the old woman was sitting more or less erect. Her eyes stuttered, and she made a feeble sound.

"Listen to me, Miss Crawshaw. I don't buy this weak act for one minute, you hear? This is the final exam. You pass, or you have to take the course over. You read me?"

The lips worked, and Rhonda caught the silent plea.

"All right, you old biddy. You want water, I'll give you water. Anything to get this over with."

The fountain in the hall ran warm and rusty. Perfect. Searching for a container, Rhonda spotted an old milk carton in a hill of debris at the end of the hall. Judging it suitably repugnant, she filled it and returned to class.

Miss Crawshaw drank in greedy gulps. Draining the carton, she eyed Rhonda with bloody distaste. Somewhat revived, she tested her parched voice.

"All right. I'm ready now. Let's get on with it."

"You remember your lines, Caroline baby?"

"Yes."

"You forget your lines, it'll cost you a letter grade. You understand me?"

"Yes, Rhonda. I'm afraid I understand you perfectly."

Hefting the camcorder to her shoulder, Rhonda stepped back

and set the focus. She checked the settings, captured the old bag in the center of the lens, and flipped the ON switch.

"Action . . . camera. Go for it, Caroline, you old crow. And remember, this could be the performance of your life."

Melissa's husband fastened the string of diamonds at her neck and smiled at his wife's image in the vanity mirror.

"Magnificent. All that's missing is the smile."

"I'm just so worried about Miss Crawshaw. Where can she possibly be?"

He ticked off the possibilities as if he were summing up a knotty case for the jury. "On vacation, having a face-lift, off with a secret lover, at fantasy camp. Who knows?"

"Sorry, Tim. I can't make light of this. The woman is eighty-three. In all her eighty-three years, she's been the sort you could set your watch by. And now, she seems to have vanished in thin air. Her doorman hasn't seen her in days. Her neighbor checked the apartment and found the woman's cats alone and hungry. Even her sister hasn't the vaguest notion where she might have gone."

He frowned. "We checked the hospitals and police reports and every Jane Doe cadaver over thirty in the city's morgues. There's nothing you can do at this point but try to forget it and enjoy the reunion. You'll give her the award in absentia. The photographer will tape it so Miss Crawshaw can watch the replay as soon as she turns up."

Melissa ran a comb through her hair and dabbed the puddled tears in her eyes. "Do you really think she will, Tim?"

"Caroline Crawshaw's a strong woman, honey. Old in years, maybe, but I'd say she's got plenty of life left in her. My bet is she'll show up any time now with a terrific new story to tell."

His prediction spurred a tiny smile. "I thought you never bet unless it's a sure thing, Timothy Gordon."

"It is, darling. I can feel it in my bones."

Cocktails were at six, dinner at seven-thirty. At six-fifteen the first in a steady line of limousines and luxury sedans stopped in front of the Essex House on Central Park South.

Melissa and Tim stood at the door to greet the guests. Inside, a trio of musicians played songs selected to spur memories of their Parcher years. Photographs and displays of memorabilia furthered the sentimental mood. Old friendships were remembered and reaffirmed. There was the exchange of fond embraces and overwrought compliments.

"Barbara Zeimans. I swear, you haven't changed a bit," Dindy gushed.

"You mean I looked thirty-eight in high school?"

Between greetings, Melissa scanned the proceedings with a critical eye. The room was magnificent, the accents and appointments flawless and elegant. Having sampled the food, she knew the dinner would be superb. Ditto the selection of wines, champagnes, and cognacs. Everyone looked resplendent in their formal attire and appeared to be having a wonderful time.

If only their treasured teacher were not missing.

Melissa tried to cling to her husband's reassurances. He was the skeptical legal eagle. If he truly believed Miss Crawshaw was alive and well and simply off on some mysterious trip, maybe it was so.

It had to be so.

Melissa had left desperate messages everywhere: at the woman's apartment house, at the shops she frequented in her neighborhood, with the ladies in her bridge group, at the orphanage and the literacy program where she was a prized volunteer. She'd even left word with the several infirm elderly people Miss Crawshaw visited regularly bearing gifts of hot meals and companionship. If anyone heard from the woman, they were to urge her to come to the Essex House this evening.

Melissa sighed. No matter how perfect everything appeared, the reunion would not be the same without their favorite teacher.

"Great dress, Melissa. Great party, too."

Melissa turned to the sight of Rhonda Drear in a stunning Valentino knockoff. With her upswept hair and the high color in her cheeks, Rhonda came as close as she conceivably could to being beautiful.

"Welcome, Rhonda. You look fabulous."

"Thanks. You, too. But why the long face?"

Tears brimmed in Melissa's eyes. She swiped them away.

"It's nothing. Forget it. You go on in and have a wonderful time."

Rhonda stood firm. "Not until you tell me what's wrong."

Bursting with anguish, Melissa took Rhonda by the arm and led her down the hall toward the ladies room. Once the door had closed behind them, she allowed the stifled sobs to escape.

"It's so awful. I can't stop thinking something terrible must have happened to her. An accident maybe. She might have been mugged and left for dead."

Rhonda's eyes were huge. "Who? What are you talking about?"

Melissa sniffed and struggled to collect herself. "Everyone's pretending it's nothing, that it'll all be fine. But I can't pretend. As long as Miss Crawshaw is missing, I can't enjoy the reunion or anything else."

"Miss Crawshaw?"

"Caroline Crawshaw. Don't you remember her, Rhonda? She was everyone's favorite teacher. We all loved her so."

"You're looking for Miss Crawshaw?"

The woman seemed to be in shock, Melissa thought. Her expression was clouded, and her head was bobbling like a toy on springs. "I understand, Rhonda. It is a terrible blow to all of us. We wanted Miss Crawshaw here so we could give her our favorite teacher award. I've been trying to reach her for days, but she's gone. Vanished without a trace."

Rhonda paled and sat heavily on a stool at the mirror. "Vanished."

Melissa could see Rhonda's distress. She tried to blunt it with reassurances. "Tim's sure there's some simple explanation, that she'll turn up. So let's hope he's right, why don't we. Maybe a miracle will happen and Miss Crawshaw will show up in time to accept her award tonight."

But Melissa's intentions missed their mark. Rhonda's cheeks puffed, and her hand flew to her mouth. She raced into a stall. Melissa stood numbly, listening as poor Rhonda got sick to her stomach.

She emerged moments later, pale and shaken. Melissa felt a hard tug of empathy.

"Sit, Rhonda. I know you're upset, and so is everyone. But I have some wonderful news for you as well. Guess who else is getting an award tonight? And it's the most exciting award of all."

Long after Melissa powdered her nose and returned to her hostessing duties, Rhonda sat in the ladies room, staring at the rug. Again and again, she imagined the magical moment in gruesome detail. She conjured the sound of her name resonating over the speaker system, the hot surge of pleasure as she approached the podium, accompanied by the sound of her classmates' heartfelt approval and applause.

She felt the weight of the videocassette in her Judith Leiber purse. The large-screen television and tape VCR she'd rented were waiting on a cart in the banquet manager's office. It was all arranged. She'd replayed the scene dozens of times since that first planning meeting so many months ago. But this was not the way it was supposed to happen.

After she played the tape of Miss Crawshaw confessing her personal and professional misdeeds, her classmates were supposed to erupt in rapturous cheers. In a frenzy of appreciation, they were to crowd around her, spewing thanks and admiration.

She'd been positive that was to be the special, pivotal event Madame Zarushka had predicted.

A toilet flushed. Rhonda couldn't tell if it was in her head or beyond the marble wall. She groped through the dizzy haze enveloping her for a viable idea. There had to be a way out.

Desperate, she found a pay phone and dialed Madame Zarushka. No one was home. A service answered at the offices of Creative Positivity. No, she was told. There wasn't anyone on call. No, the program directors had made no provisions for emergencies.

Her sole remaining quarter glinted up at her from beneath the damning videocassette. All she had with her was the change, three dollar bills, and her lowly green American Express Card. Somehow, that would have to be enough.

Suddenly, her future loomed with startling clarity. Madame Zarushka had predicted a cataclysmic change, and it would be so. She would have to flee her inherited rent-controlled apartment. All her things, including the new wardrobe, would have to be left behind. She couldn't dare to try to claim her remaining savings at the bank. They would be searching for her everywhere.

Somehow, she'd have to vanish without a trace, become a nameless, faceless nothing. That at least should be simple for someone with her extensive experience.

Slipping the quarter in the phone slot, she dialed nine-one-one to report a kidnapping and relate the location of the victim. Slipping out the hotel's back door, she headed for the subway and oblivion.

It wasn't all bad, Rhonda thought, using the skills she'd mastered in Creative Positivity. As Madame Zarushka often said, nothing was all bad. One person's calamity was another's good fortune. Or as Rhonda's mother had liked to put it, no matter how thin you slice the ham, there are always two sides.

Plodding down the subway steps, Rhonda clung fast to her last remaining positive thought. With any luck, the Parcher School Class of '73 would have the gift they most dearly wanted.

Lucy Freeman

THE GREAT TABOO

AFTER HIS FINAL MORNING PATIENT LEFT, DR. WILLIAM AMES PICKED up the phone to ask his service for messages. The sweet-voiced woman announced, as though it were a regular occurrence, "Lieutenant Jack Lonegan of the Nineteenth Precinct called. He asked if you would contact him as soon as you were free." She gave the number.

Dr. Ames smiled as he dialed. The year before he had helped Lonegan, then only a detective first-class, to solve the murder of Jonathan Thomas, one of his patients. Had another patient been murdered? Ridiculous. No psychoanalyst in the world would come up against such odds—the murder of two patients within a year.

He said to the policeman who answered, "Lieutenant Lonegan, please. Dr. William Ames returning his call." Within a few seconds he heard Lonegan's deep, friendly voice, "How *are* you, Doc? It's been a long time. I thought we were going to get together now and then for a Scotch."

"I was waiting for you to call. You're the busy one, judging by crime statistics. So you're a lieutenant now. Congratulations!"

"Yeah. Thanks to you. If you hadn't caught Jonathan's murderer, no promotion for me. I owe you one for that, Doc."

"You don't owe me anything, Jack. I was happy to help."

There was a long pause at the other end of the wire, then Lonegan said, "Doc, I need your help again. There was a murder last night in my precinct and a patient of yours is involved."

I wasn't able to help Helene Garth in time—her husband carried out his threat, Dr. Ames thought. He said grimly, "Tell me the details, Jack. When did he do it?"

"When did he do what, Doc?" Puzzled voice.

"When did Albert Garth kill his wife?"

"You on junk, Doc?" Jokingly.

"You know me better than that. Once in a while too many Scotches. But a drug addict I'm not."

"Garth didn't murder anyone," Lonegan said. "You got the name right but not the gender of the corpse. The body we found in the dead of night lying in that small park belongs to a man. Albert Garth, that well-known stockbroker, was the one killed. His home address was in his pocket. He had one hundred and fifty dollars in his wallet, which shows the killer didn't want money so it must have been someone he knew. Stabbed three times in the chest. No sign of the weapon."

"Have you talked to his wife?" Dr. Ames wondered whether his patient was involved.

"Mrs. Garth said her husband never came home last night. It was most unusual for him to stay out late," Lonegan added. "Said they hadn't been getting along."

"She was telling the truth, Jack," Dr. Ames said. "I was trying to help her decide to divorce him. He brutalized her. Black eyes, punches in the breast. A mean man." Then he asked, "How did you know my connection to Mrs. Garth?"

"Easy. She told me you were her shrink," Lonegan said. "I protected you, Doc. I didn't tell her you knew me."

Dr. Ames chuckled. "Thanks. It's been quite a while since anyone protected me."

"And I'm asking you now to help me once again, Doc." A plea in that irresistible voice.

"You mean as I did in Jonathan's case?"

"That's just what I mean."

"Who are the suspects?"

The lieutenant's laugh was ironic. "Don't needle me, Doc. You know them better than I do. That gorgeous Mrs. Garth must have told you lots about her life that she didn't spill to me in two hours of questioning this morning in her palatial living room."

"Was he stabbed in the chest at the park, or someplace else and then driven there?"

"My guess is he was dead on arrival, then dumped on the ground. I'll tell you the suspects. First, Helene Garth, his second wife. Then his first wife, Marietta Garth. His daughter Amy, by the first wife. Helene Garth's mother, Mrs. Annette Benson, who hated him. And her son, Helene's brother, Evan Benson. Plus maybe an enemy or two in the financial world who wanted revenge for lousy tips in the market."

Then Lonegan added, "One more. I forgot Helene's close friend, the actor Noel Marvin. He was recently in a show with her where she did that great dance number. He played the likeable, comic character . . . Likeable, comic characters commit murders regularly," he added bitterly, "but his alibi holds up about as well as the rest."

"How did you check alibis so quickly?" Dr. Ames was impressed.

"The two detectives working under me are whizzes. They've been checking since eight this morning. They learned that the daughter, Amy, did not spend the night in her room at her college in Poughkeepsie, as she said she did. That the first wife said she walked by herself for hours in Washington Square but no one saw her. That Noel Marvin walked all the way from Broadway to his apartment in Greenwich Village but no one saw him either. That Helene Garth was in her apartment waiting for her husband to come home and went to sleep at midnight. That her brother, a fairly well known artist, spent the evening painting in his apartment. And that his and Helene's mother, Mrs. Benson, watched television alone in her apartment."

"Looks like you've got work on your hands, Jack." Dr. Ames was sympathetic.

He heard Lonegan sigh, then came the request: "I've got to depend on you for the psychological approach once again, Doc. Any one of them could have killed Garth. They all had a motive. Please help me out."

"Jack, I like and respect you. But I don't have the time to be a psychoanalyst *and* a detective."

"Not even if it involves the life of your pretty patient? There's no proof, Doc, that she didn't murder him. She's just as much a suspect as anyone else. And I think she has the strongest motive of all. He beat her up regularly, she said. And then there's the money. At his death she gets a cool million."

"Money isn't everything," Dr. Ames said lamely. The beatings, Helene had told him, were brutal, an even stronger motive than money, he thought.

"In the case of murder, money often figures big, Doc. I ask with all my heart, will you give a hand? Strictly speaking, a 'head'?"

In spite of that silent inner voice which cautioned him against it, Dr. Ames felt an urge for adventure, rebellion against sitting in a chair hour after hour, day after day, year after year, listening to patients. Though his job was to help the individual better protect himself by understanding his self-destructive impulses, why should he not occasionally help bring someone who had committed murder to justice, thus protecting society?

He sighed again, then said, "Before I make a decision I'd have to talk to Mrs. Garth, because she's a patient and I need her approval. She's supposed to show up at two P.M. I'll ask if she has any objections."

"Can I call you around four and see what she says?" Hunger in his voice.

"Of course. Good talking to you, Jack."

After he hung up, Dr. Ames wondered why, during the six months she had been on the couch, Helene Garth had not mentioned her involvement with Noel Marvin. Perhaps Lonegan was jumping to the wrong conclusion, perhaps it was not an affair but a friendship. Or perhaps she did not as yet trust her analyst enough to confess what she believed might detract from a favorable image of herself. A husband who beat her might be acceptable but not an adulterous relationship.

Promptly at two, Helene Garth walked in the door of Dr. Ames's office. She had a soft, seductive voice and the slim shape necessary for a Broadway star. Curly blond hair streamed below her shoulders, shy blue eyes stared at him as though she were a schoolgirl, he, a stern principal.

He led the way into the room with the green leather couch, the room in which, as one poetic patient put it, "The hidden secrets of the mind whirl off the four corners out into Central Park below to get carried away by the wind." He asked, "Mrs. Garth, today will you please sit in the chair? We must talk. I'm so sorry to hear of your husband's death."

She sat down, looked at him helplessly, tears in her eyes as she said, "It was a nightmare. I'm trying to pull myself together."

"Do you want to tell me what happened?" If she could talk about her feelings, rather than deny them, she would be better able to handle them.

"I feel I've talked my head off. The police questioned me for hours this morning. They're trying to find clues to the murderer." She said slowly, "I went to the bedroom about nine last evening, undressed, and watched television, waiting for Al to come home from a dinner meeting. When he didn't arrive by midnight, I turned off the television and fell asleep. When I woke at eight he still wasn't in bed. As I've told you, he sometimes stays out all night with other women. The police arrived about nine and I answered all their questions."

"Did your husband ever mention a fight with anyone? Do you know of possible enemies he might have on Wall Street?"

She smiled in spite of her grief, said, "You sound just like the detective. No, Al didn't mention fighting with anyone. Except his first wife."

Dr. Ames suddenly thought that perhaps in spite of her denial and look of innocence, Helene's fury might have risen to the point of murder. Spurred on by some shred of self-preservation, either in panic or deliberately, possibly she had killed the man who so often beat her, had somehow driven him to the park or had an accomplice who carried him.

He asked, "Who do you think might have killed your husband?"

"I don't know . . . Maybe his first wife, Marietta, who loathed him. And, I hate to say this, but my mother also detested him after seeing me with black eyes and bruises on my face and body. She has begged me to leave him. My older brother, Evan, who is divorced and lives alone, also knew of Al's cruelty to me."

Thinking of her failure to mention the actor with whom she was involved, Dr. Ames asked, "Why didn't you tell me you are friends with Noel Marvin?"

She blushed. "I thought your opinion of me would be even lower if you knew I was having an affair with another man while still married to Al. I was afraid you would dismiss me as a patient. Maybe the real reason I wanted to go into analysis was that I needed the courage to leave Al and marry Noel." Then, sadly, "Why couldn't I just break away after all those beatings?"

"Does Mr. Marvin know about your inheritance?"

"I tell him everything."

Not like you hold back on your analyst, he thought, then said, "Mr. Marvin might have killed your husband and left him in the park, knowing you would inherit a large sum of money and might marry him."

"Jesus, no!" She gasped, said, "Noel couldn't kill a fly. He's too sensitive. Stab a man to death? Never."

"How do you feel about him now that you are free of your husband's cruelties?"

Tears again filled her eyes. "I don't know, Dr. Ames. I'm confused."

As well she might be, he thought. She would have to understand more of the reasons why she had chosen a barbaric man as husband, then fled into the arms of a stranger before she could be happy with a man. He said, "By the way, Lieutenant Lonegan, the detective in charge of the case, has asked me to help him by interviewing everyone who is a suspect, in the hope of turning up what he calls a psychological clue. I wanted to ask how you felt about this before I made the decision."

Without hesitation she replied, "I think you should do all you can to help him. I want Al's murderer found. Or,"— hesitating a moment—"do I?" Then, with conviction, "You must believe me, I didn't kill Al. I wanted to leave him, God knows. But I couldn't kill anyone. I kept hoping Al would change. Part of me will always love him for marrying me, for letting me be in his life for a while. I know I'm far from a mature person, and this must have angered him deeply."

Her latest dream might furnish a clue as to the murderer or whoever she suspected, Dr. Ames thought. In a dream we cannot deceive ourselves about what we truly feel, as we do in wide-awake life.

He asked, "Did you have a dream last night?"

"As a matter of fact I had a terrifying dream. My brother Evan and I were running along a beach on a warm, sunny day. Suddenly Evan said, 'Look, Helene, look!' A black, slimy object was rolling in on the tide, pushed higher and higher up on the beach with every wave. It was obscene, a dead octopus with some of its tentacles cut off. A blackened, crippled monster. I screamed in fear. Suddenly dark clouds blotted out the sun. Evan said, 'Let's bury it so nobody can see its horrible shape.' He dug a deep hole in the sand. We pushed the octopus-monster into it, then covered it up."

"Did you and Evan often go to the beach when you were children?"

"We had a summer home in Westhampton and Evan and I spent all our days on the sand." Added, "There are no octopuses in Westhampton. Only crabs."

"What does the octopus in your dream remind you of?"

"All those slimy tentacles, clutching at you, choking you to death, like Al tried to do." Her hand went involuntarily to her neck.

"He tried to choke you many times. Like an octopus."

"You mean an animal can stand for a person in a dream?"

"That's a common displacement from the unconscious part of the mind. The language of the dream is the language of the child and the savage. Your dream seems to contain the wish that you and Evan could get rid of your husband's body so no one would find it."

"I love Evan," she mused. "He understands my agony and

tries to protect me. He keeps telling me to get a divorce, like he did."

Would he kill for her? Dr. Ames wondered.

"How would you feel if I interviewed your brother? And your mother? And Noel Marvin? Lieutenant Lonegan asked me to do this."

"Please see anyone you wish." Then she confessed, "I have even been afraid that whoever killed Al might now come after me."

"Why?" He felt puzzled.

"Well, if it was his first wife, Marietta, she might resent my inheriting most of his money. Money that would have been hers."

"To whom do you leave it in your will?"

"I don't have a will. I never thought about Al dying. I guess I'd leave half to my mother and half to my brother."

"Aren't you afraid someone you love might prove to be the killer?"

She was silent. He then asked, "Shall I make a guess as to who it might be?"

She laughed nervously. "How could you know, at this point? You probably think my mother paid some crook to kill Al and free me. Protect me from further physical harm."

"It could be," he said.

"Mother?" She sounded stunned. "I was joking. How could you suspect her?"

"Because of the powerful maternal instinct to protect one's child."

She looked at him dubiously, said, "I can't imagine my mother as a murderer. She can't even raise her voice in an argument. I'd love to know what you think of her."

Love my mother, love me, he thought. He did not tell her he mentioned her mother because of the dream about the octopus. Hiding the monster could have represented her wish to protect her mother from being discovered by the police. All children at times will hate the parent, for no parent is perfect enough to warrant a child's complete love.

"When is the funeral?" he asked.

"There isn't any. Al didn't want services or burial. He instructed his lawyer that he be cremated."

The fifty-minute hour was up. Dr. Ames said, "Thank you for your honest answers. I'm sorry I had to ask some hurtful questions."

"Thank you for wanting to help me both professionally and personally." She smiled wanly at him.

After she left, he was not sure, in spite of her approval, that he wanted to get involved in finding the killer. He would have to decide in one hour, when Lonegan, a detective who never stopped pursuit once he made up his mind, had said he would call.

Promptly at four, just after the patient who followed Helene had left, Dr. Ames told his service he would take the four o'clock call.

"Hi, Doc. Right on time," said the deep voice. "Did Mrs. Garth object to your helping me?"

"No, she didn't."

"Will you?"

Dr. Ames said slowly, "I really shouldn't."

"I have an idea, Doc. If I can set up all the interviews for one day, will you do it? That's all I ask—one lousy day. You figure out what it costs to cancel all your patients for that day and I'll make sure you're reimbursed."

Dr. Ames enjoyed his first laugh of the day. "You're determined to get my opinion, aren't you?"

"I think you're great, Doc. I learn a lot from the way you think. But, most important, I think you can help solve this case."

"And if I fail?"

"At least we both tried. Trying is better than not trying, when you know you should."

That did it. Dr. Ames relented. "Okay, Jack. I'll cancel all appointments for a week from today. I'll spend morning to midnight interviewing anyone you want. Don't worry about paying me. Consider it my contribution to New York's finest."

"I'll see you get some reward."

"Forget it. Just arrange the interviews."

"I'll talk to all the suspects and set the time for you to visit." Then Lonegan added, "All except Mrs. Garth. You've already interviewed her, I trust." Sudden sharpness in Lonegan's tone.

"Yes. She says she didn't do it. Could never do it. I believe her."

"That's your privilege, Doc. But I have to think of everyone as a possible murderer. Nothing personal, you understand."

"Of course not. Not more than you'd consider it personal if I turned up evidence against someone else."

The detective ignored the jibe, said, "I'll phone you ahead of time and give you the names, addresses, and hours of the interviews.

"I think you had a hunch we'd be working together again, Doc." Lonegan sounded amused.

"Maybe. But I didn't think it would hit so near home twice in a row." Dr. Ames winced.

"Just lucky, I guess . . . I mean me," Lonegan added hastily. Then, "Good luck, Doc. Hope you come up with a winner. I mean a loser, as far as we're concerned."

"Thought you'd decided it was Mrs. Garth." Sarcastically.

"No proof. But I'm digging away on that lady's alibi. Sure she didn't tell you anything I should know?"

"Not a thing, Jack. Only a dream. Are you interested in her dream the night of the murder?"

"Doc, the day we convict someone on a dream we're really in trouble."

"You can say that again, partner. Such stuff as dreams are made of would hang every one of us on the spot."

And yet, the analyst thought, as he started on his way home, there was something in Helene Garth's dream if he could decipher it further, that might point to the killer. That fragment of truth always at the core of a dream. An elusive fragment. Not enough, as yet, to make any sense.

The next day at noon, between patients, Dr. Ames called Lonegan who, his service reported, had phoned at eleven. "Got a pen handy, Doc?" Lonegan asked.

"Fire away, Jack."

"Here's the lineup for Wednesday. Mrs. Garth's mother, Annette Benson at ten in her apartment, Two Sutton Place. Then you walk a few blocks north to 381 East 63rd Street to talk to Evan Benson, her son, Mrs. Garth's brother. At two P.M. you show up at Two Fifth Avenue to interview Mrs. Marietta Garth, the murdered man's first wife. Her daughter Amy is coming down from Poughkeepsie in the morning and I asked her to be at your office at four P.M. Figured you'd want to talk to her when she wasn't with her mother. The last appointment is at six P.M. with Noel Marvin, the actor, who will also come to your office after he finishes his matinee."

Dr. Ames said wryly, "Looks like a busy day. I'll call you, Jack, at precinct headquarters after I've seen the last suspect. Will you wait there for my call?"

"I won't move until I hear from you, Doc. Once again, thanks beyond words. Good luck."

"I'll need it," Dr. Ames muttered, then thought, That's a strange thing for a psychoanalyst to say, we are taught not to believe in "luck" but to help the patient understand the importance of the direct messages from his unconscious.

The Sutton Place apartment in which Helene Garth's mother lived was spacious and sun-filled. From the corner of Mrs. Benson's living room, where he sat on a flowered chintz couch, Dr. Ames could see the East River and an occasional ship passing on its way out to sea or upstream to Long Island Sound. Trees covered the dead end of 57th Street, the small neighborhood park where Albert Garth's body had been discovered.

Mrs. Benson resembled an older version of her daughter, her once-fragile features set in hardness, her once-slim body burdened with additional weight. She greeted him with a friendly look, said, hand outstretched, "When the detective telephoned and asked me to see you, I was happy to do so. I wanted to thank you for helping Helene as a patient. I can see changes in her already."

Then she asked, "Would you like coffee? I always drink three cups a morning."

"If you've made it, fine. Black, please."

She bustled off to the kitchen and he looked around the room. There were photographs of Helene as a solemn baby, as a waiflike girl in ballet costume, as the striptease dancer in her recent musical *Leading Lady*. He studied the photograph of a young man with blond hair and an esthetic face vaguely resembling Helene's, undoubtedly her brother Evan.

Mrs. Benson swiftly returned with two china cups on a silver tray. As they sat down on a white couch she said, "I don't know why you'd want to know about my uninteresting life. I was born in Racine, Wisconsin, came to New York at twenty-one, worked as secretary in a large public relations firm. My boss was a young man just starting his career as an executive. We fell in love, married, had two lovely children. When my husband died seven years ago, he was fairly rich so none of us had to worry about our next meal."

Dr. Ames asked, "Did your husband ever punish the children physically? By striking them?"

She tightened her lips as though thinking, then said, "Once or twice he may have lost his temper at Helene. Evan was always a quiet little boy, but his sister would occasionally talk back to her father and he slapped her around a few times."

Like her husband had later done unto her in even angrier passion, Dr. Ames thought. Once abused as a child, the victim unconsciously seeks further abuse, feeling it is better to be struck in fury than ignored, at least there is the "touch" of another person—a hostile touch is better than none at all.

"How did you feel when he slapped your daughter?" Dr. Ames asked.

"I wanted to stop him, but he was a powerful man. When he lost his temper you didn't dare oppose him. But he soon would cuddle and kiss her to make up for his meanness."

And the inconsistency of first the violence, then the show of caring, would confuse a small child, who would wonder, How can my father both hate and love me? It was no accident Helene had married a man just like her father.

"Did your husband ever strike you, Mrs. Benson?"

She looked embarrassed. "Once. When I dared speak up for Helene. She had come home an hour late from a high school dance."

"How did you feel about Albert Garth's treatment of your daughter?"

"I thought he was a nasty beast in spite of his handsome looks and his money. I saw Helene's bruises when she would come here, crying. I wanted her to leave him. But she insisted she had to stay married at least two years to give it a try."

"Do you think Garth's money was one reason she stayed?"

"Helene is not a poor girl. Her father left her a substantial trust fund. And she earns money when she appears on Broadway. I think it was more than the money."

"Such as?"

"Why, love of course, Dr. Ames." As though he, a prominent psychoanalyst, should surely know this.

"Do you really think it was love that Helene felt for her husband? A man who beat her up?"

"What would *you* call it?" A perplexed tone.

"A kind of adolescent love, not a mature love, which includes respect and understanding. She should have waited until she knew more about him before she married him. Where were her protective psychic antennae?"

Mrs. Benson laughed nervously. "You're way over my head. You doctors of the mind are too complicated. I'm just a simple mother."

Dr. Ames believed Mrs. Benson was not the slayer of her hated son-in-law, even though she might verbally protest his assaults on her daughter. He could predict her indignant "Of course I didn't kill Al!" were he even to suggest she might have murdered him. He would spare both her and himself the indignity of such a moment.

He stood up. "Thank you for the coffee, Mrs. Benson, and your cooperation."

"Is that all, Dr. Ames?" She sounded disappointed.

"You've been very kind to give me this much time. I thank you for the pleasure of meeting you. I'm only sorry it was a murder that brought us together."

Evan Benson, who lived a few blocks north of his mother at 381 East 63rd Street, resembled the photograph on his mother's desk, except he was far taller than Dr. Ames expected, standing about six feet. He seemed a gentle man, similar to the quiet little boy his mother had described.

"Come in, Dr. Ames." He led the way into his large apartment. The windows looked westward at the towering buildings of midtown Manhattan. As he turned to look around the room, twice the size of the average city apartment, Dr. Ames suddenly felt he was standing in the midst of a blaze of fire. The walls were lined with paintings that portrayed billowing flames of red, orange, and yellow, leaping from the depths of black caverns. Devils with pitchforks raked the naked bodies of men and women into the fires as dead-white angels stared in helpless agony from the corners of the paintings.

If these paintings came out of the soul of Evan Benson, it was indeed a tortured soul, Dr. Ames thought, for if ever he had seen it, this was murder on canvas.

"Yes, they're all mine." Evan answered the unspoken query. Then said in a quiet voice, "They bring out quite violent reactions in most beholders. I think that's why I paint them."

Dr. Ames made a mental note: This is a man who, while appearing gentle, says he likes to bring out violence in others. Then he said of the paintings, "They're very original."

"I sell quite a few, believe it or not. And for high prices."

"I believe it," Dr. Ames said. "I admire not only your concepts but the brilliant colors."

"Want a drink before lunch?" Evan asked. "The maid, who also doubles as housekeeper, is making us shrimp salad and coffee."

"I don't drink this early in the day, but I will relish the shrimp salad and coffee," Dr. Ames replied, and thought, Mother, daughter and son share a warmth and charm that is disarming but they also share a vulnerability to life's hardships.

Evan poured himself a Scotch. "So you're my sister's shrink." He spoke with admiration, not scorn. "Shrinks look more like actors every day."

"I take it that's a compliment." Dr. Ames smiled as he sat down on a black velvet couch.

Evan lowered himself into a green contour chair facing Dr. Ames, and said slowly, "I suppose Helene tells you everything as part of her therapy."

Dr. Ames, detecting a slight note of fear in Evan's voice, asked, "What do you mean by 'everything'?"

Evan looked startled, explained, "I only meant like—well, what a bum I am, earning my living by painting, which she doesn't consider work."

"Your sister doesn't think you're a bum, far from it." Reassuringly. "She speaks of you as a very gifted, successful artist and says you are her only protector. She loves you very much."

"That's good to hear." The boyish eyes, blue like his sister's, showed gratitude. Then they suddenly widened in alarm. "Or maybe not so good to hear. Maybe you think that to protect her I murdered the madman she married."

"I have no idea, nor do the police, who killed Albert Garth. That's the reason I'm asking a few people some questions. The detective in charge, a friend of mine, thought I might find a clue by talking to all of you. It may well be none of you is guilty, that an outsider committed the murder as Garth walked in the small park. Or it could be someone who had a grudge against Mr. Garth because he gave him the wrong financial advice. Or even a mistress he kept secret."

"Do you ask patients to express their murderous feelings?" Evan asked admiringly.

"Psychoanalysts often deal with murder," Dr. Ames said. "The murderous wishes that lie in all our minds." Then he asked, "Do you have any idea who might have stabbed Mr. Garth?"

"I really don't, Dr. Ames." Then Evan added, in serious voice, "I want you to realize, though, I am not only capable of murder, but I have committed it five times."

"Oh?" Dr. Ames said, surprised.

"In Vietnam I murdered—or at least I consider it murder— five human beings. On orders, of course, to kill the enemy so we could stay alive. It was murder, nonetheless. Murder without batting an eye."

Dr. Ames now understood why Benson painted the scenes of hell. He exploded on canvas where it would hurt no one, all his feelings of fear and rage over the horror that had been Vietnam. An artist, forced to kill, would try to combat his grief and guilt by painting away the terror.

"The detective said you were painting the night of the murder." Dr. Ames's tone was questioning.

The answer was swift, emphatic. "I didn't leave this room." Then he smiled. "I think it's time for shrimp salad and coffee. Mother told me she was seeing you earlier this morning and I gather you will visit the first Mrs. Garth this afternoon so you'll need nourishment."

As Dr. Ames speared his last luscious shrimp, he said, "Thank you very much, Mr. Benson, for your hospitality. You have been extremely thoughtful." Then he asked, "How long were you married?"

"It lasted almost two years," he said, "then I lost all interest in her, and she, in me. We sought a mutually desired divorce. There were no children. She has since remarried and has a son. I am awaiting the woman of my dreams, I guess. Maybe I also need to be psychoanalyzed."

"If you decide you wish to be, I can recommend several fine analysts."

"What about yourself?" Evan asked.

"An analyst cannot have two patients from the same family," Dr. Ames explained.

As he opened the door to leave the sumptuous apartment, he said, "If you want the name of another psychoanalyst, please call me."

The look on Evan's face was now one of agony, as though he did not know how to apologize for his unhappiness at living alone, despite the magnificent paintings he had produced. Dr. Ames felt as near tears as he had been at times in his own analysis.

The taxi raced south along Franklin D. Roosevelt Drive, then westward on Fourteenth Street and down to Two Fifth Avenue. Albert Garth's first wife lived in an apartment on the tenth floor.

No man could have picked two wives more opposite in appearance, Dr. Ames thought, staring at the woman who opened the door. She was tall and willowy, clad in a black silk pants suit. Curly jet-black hair was drawn high on her head. Her facial features, while pleasant, seemed rather sharp.

Her look was one of mild annoyance. She wasted no time, said, "Come in, Dr. Ames. I warn you I'm seeing you only because the detective who called threatened that I'd be tossed in jail, or other such refined words to that effect, if I refused. I am outraged beyond belief to think I am a suspect in Albert's murder. It's ridiculous to think I'd kill a man who has been giving me generous alimony, while under his stinking will I don't get one red cent. Though I guess I should be grateful the alimony continues even if he's dead."

Dr. Ames wondered why she had to defend herself so

strongly. As she talked she preceded him into a room over-looking the arch of Washington Square, a half-halo encircling the statue of the father of the United States. The room was decorated in black and white, its only color the red, blue, and yellow of a large abstract a la Mondrian.

He felt that if it were winter she would not even have been gracious enough to ask him to take off his coat. He was glad Evan had provided shrimp salad and coffee. He was accustomed to hostility from patients; he welcomed it as a sign they were losing the fear of expressing inner hatred, not really hurled at him but at the parent of childhood—a previously denied hatred that in subtle, oblique ways had been destructive. But this hostility in a somewhat social setting was as unpleasant for a psychoanalyst as it would be for anyone else.

Marietta Garth looked about forty-five and, judging by her anger at him, a man who had done nothing to hurt her, he could well imagine the fury aroused by a man who *had* hurt her. He pictured violent scenes between her and the late Albert Garth. Unlike his second wife, this woman could have fought back with a vengeance.

She did not ask him to sit down, but he did so anyway. She sat stiffly upright on a chair facing him, glaring as he lit a cigarette, as though defying him to get information from her.

"Mrs. Garth, I am not here to accuse you of anything," he assured her. "Nor to question you at length. That is Lieutenant Lonegan's province. I am here to ask your help in trying to find out who could have killed your ex-husband."

"I could have! Cheerfully!" A vindictive tone. "But I didn't. Nor did my daughter. Amy wasn't even in New York at the time. How stupid can a detective be? Imagine ordering her to miss classes and come to the city to be interviewed as a possible murderer."

"Perhaps Amy wants to help find her father's killer. She might recall something that was a clue."

"Well, I don't want to help. I'm glad he's dead. You can't imagine what an insufferable, egocentric, selfish human being Albert was. You psychoanalysts all think punishment comes from within. That a man suffers enough from his own psychotic behavior. But I don't believe it. Monsters like Albert F. Garth—'F' for fucking, or rather *non*-fucking, as far as I was concerned—deserve the same beating they give others. I'm not a bit sorry he was knifed to death. You can't imagine the torture of lying next to a man night after night, year after year, wanting him desperately to touch you, to say one loving word, only to have him turn his back to you, rigid with hate. It makes you feel despicable. As though you were not a woman. And you hate him because he can't be a man."

A different look suddenly flashed in her eyes, a look of curiosity rather than anger. She asked, obviously referring to Helene Garth, "Do you think she did it?"

"No one has been accused," Dr. Ames said.

"What do you expect from me? A confession?"

"Only if you murdered him."

"I've told you and that stupid detective that I most assuredly did not," she said haughtily. "As a taxpayer I am paying that inept man to find out who did. I'm not going to do his dirty work."

"But you might help if you know anything about Mr. Garth's past that might lead to the murderer."

"If I knew who he—or she—was, I'd pin a medal on them." Defiantly, "I don't care if the killer goes scot-free."

He wondered what more he could get from her except further verbal vitriol. He asked a last question. "Do you want to tell me about your childhood, Mrs. Garth?"

"The hell I do!"

He was amused at her childish defiance, at how much she *was* telling him in choice of words and tone of voice. Suddenly she asked, as curiosity got the better of her hostility, "Do *you* have any idea who killed Albert?"

"I don't," he admitted.

Her tone softened. "Please don't think I'm a complete shrew, Dr. Ames. It's just that for so many years I put up with such aggravation, not to mention terror, that I haven't energy left for one ounce of sympathy over his death. Or care who killed him."

He told her, as he had told Helene, "You chose this man as a husband. Nobody forced you to marry him. He must have met some of your unconscious needs."

Her glare returned. "I don't believe all that conscious and unconscious crap."

"That's your privilege, Mrs. Garth." He thought, And that's why your life, lady, is so unhappy, and why you chose a pathological man like Garth. His second wife has just enough of the instinct of self-preservation to seek help, but you are more self-destructive, so you will live out the rest of your life in furious complaint.

"Where are you meeting my Amy?" she snapped.

"At my office. I'm on my way there now."

"It's a waste of time. For both of you."

He ignored her remark. "Thank you for seeing me against your will."

"I want you to know you're the first psychoanalyst to step inside this apartment," she said.

He was hard put to know whether she said it with pride or regret, as he waited for the elevator.

Dr. Ames felt strange walking into his office at three-forty-five in the afternoon; usually he was in it five or six days a week from eight in the morning until early evening. He now had the leisure of fifteen minutes before Amy Garth was scheduled to see him. He called his service to find out if there had been messages.

"Please phone Lieutenant Lonegan right away," begged the familiar voice. "His number is—"

"Never mind, I know it by heart," Dr. Ames said sarcastically.

He dialed and heard Lonegan's "Hello," said, "I'm reporting in. Three down. Two to go."

"Glad you reached me, Doc, before you saw Amy Garth." There was concern in Lonegan's voice. "The doorman called this morning and confessed he saw Amy and her father arguing violently in front of his apartment at about seven-thirty the night he was killed. He was scared at first to tell me this, then decided he'd better tell the truth."

"Exactly what did he say?"

"He heard Garth scream at her, 'I'll see you in hell first.' She had a 'mad look' on her face, he said."

"Is Amy Garth on drugs?"

"I don't know. I thought that's one thing you might find out."

At that moment the office doorbell rang and Dr. Ames said, "I think she just arrived. I'll call you right after I've seen the last person, Noel Marvin."

"I'll be waiting right at this desk, Doc. Oh, try to find out where Amy spent the night, will you?"

"Okay." He hung up, walked out to his reception room. Amy was a pale edition of her mother, though she lacked the angry look and, he guessed, the biting words. He felt sorry for any daughter of Marietta and Albert Garth.

"Please come in, Miss Garth." He led the way into his office. "I'm sorry to interrupt your work at college, but Lieutenant Lonegan thought it important I see you."

She wore high white boots, a navy blue miniskirt and white sweater tight against her small breasts. Her brown hair swung low to the middle of her back.

"Oh, wow!" She walked to the window, looked down at Central Park, a blanket of tall green trees. She turned to him with a faint smile, added, "Far out!"

"Please sit here, Miss Garth." He patted the brown tweed chair.

"First time I've been in a shrink's office," she said confidentially.

He doubted she could have murdered her father; patricide was an act rare in young women unless they were psychotic. But she might know something about his death or sense a guilt in someone else. Even though a sadistic father inspired murderous hatred in a daughter, she would be apt to conceal it from herself to keep what she thought of as his love.

"You must be very upset over your father's death," he said sympathetically. She would be the one person whose feelings ran deep. Hated or loved, or both, she was his only child, and while he could abandon a wife or two, he was not likely to desert a daughter.

"What kind of man was your father to you?" he asked.

Tears welled up as she spoke. "He was never easy to live with. He had a ferocious temper. Mother and he fought like cats and dogs. My father and I had our fights, too, but he never really hurt me."

"Can you think of anyone, Miss Garth, who might feel angry enough at your father to want to kill him?"

She turned in the chair, looked out the window as though stalling for time. Then she whirled around to face him again. "Not my mother," she said. "I know you interviewed her today. She probably told you how much she hated my father. But my mother couldn't kill anyone. She wouldn't know what to do with a knife." She added swiftly, "I read in the papers that my father was stabbed several times with a knife."

"They haven't found the weapon. They think the killer took it with him. Probably tossed it in the nearby East River."

"I hope they find his murderer." The cry of the bereaved child. "I'll never see him again! Never!"

She broke down and sobbed as though she had lost her whole world. And for the first time that day Dr. Ames was glad Lonegan had asked him to interview the suspects. If nothing else, he at least offered this pathetic young lady the chance to release some of her grief for a father who was suddenly and savagely murdered.

She quieted down after he handed her several tissues. She apologized, with a nervous laugh. "I owe you a box of Kleenex." Then, with sudden eagerness, "I wish I could answer your question as to who I think killed my father. But I really don't know."

"If you had to make a guess, who would it be?"

Silence, then she said, "I'm no help at all. I can't think of anyone."

Dr. Ames said, "Frankly, I have no idea either." Then ventured, "Could it be Helene Garth?" thinking she was Lonegan's choice.

"I don't believe she would ever kill anybody." Thoughtfulness in her voice. Then, with great reluctance, "The only one who might have a reason is that young actor, Noel Marvin, Helene's friend. My father told me he knew—" She stopped, blushed, then went on. "Daddy had never used that word before, but he said Helene was 'fucking' Noel Marvin. Noel seemed like a man who might kill if my father taunted him. Noel's very nervous and can be kind of explosive. Have you met him?"

"Not yet," Dr. Ames said.

"Helene introduced me to him one evening. He's a strange guy."

"By the way," Dr. Ames tried to sound casual, "the doorman at your father's building told detectives he heard you and your father arguing violently at nine–thirty outside the night he was murdered. Detectives also checked your alibi and learned you did not sleep in your dormitory that night as you said you did."

She looked distressed, then explained, "The whole thing is so sad that I didn't want to tell anyone. I caught the ten-twenty P.M. train to Poughkeepsie after our argument on the street. My mother had told my father I was living with a man in his college apartment, though officially I have a room at the dorm. Johnny, who is in his last year, and I plan to marry in the fall. Daddy sent for me to find out if this was true. He threatened to cut off my allowance and take me out of college if I didn't stop seeing Johnny at once. I told him I couldn't do this, that we were very much in love and intended to marry."

"That explains what the doorman overheard. Your father saying he'd see you 'in hell first.' "

"My father is—was—a very selfish, stubborn man. He meant what he said. He would have taken me out of college, rather than let me marry Johnny. Even so, I wish he hadn't died."

"You've been very helpful, Miss Garth, and I thank you for traveling all the way from Poughkeepsie," Dr. Ames said. "I hope we meet someday under more pleasant circumstances."

"I do, too, Dr. Ames." She stood up, put out her hand in gratitude.

As the door closed behind the white boots and blue miniskirt, Dr. Ames thought, She is a very appealing young lady and, according to her, I am about to meet the man she thinks may have killed her father.

He awaited the last suspect of the day, curious to find out what kind of man Helene had chosen as successor to her difficult husband. He wondered if by any chance Amy had intuitively identified her father's murderer, if out of the mouths of babes again came truth. Or, was she lying and had she killed her father, who not only deserted her but threatened to separate her from a young man she desperately loved. This had to reawaken all the fury and heartbreak she felt when her father abandoned her and her mother for another woman. Many

murders were committed because the one who has been
deserted preferred to take the life of someone he loved rather
than give him up to somebody else.

Promptly at seven P.M. the buzzer sounded and Noel Marvin
walked in. The six-foot slim man had the actor's usual
handsome face. His hair was blond, his eyes, flashing brown.
He tried to repress his desire to leave as soon as possible.

He slid into the patient's chair, faced Dr. Ames, lit a
cigarette, and said, "You don't have to believe me, but I did not
kill Albert Garth. I wanted to. He was such a shit to Helene.
But I didn't think it was up to me to rid the world of him.
Because he was so sick and self-destructive, I thought she
would soon leave him. Don't you think I was right?"

Dr. Ames replied, "Either that or he would have killed her
one night in a drunken rage." Then he asked, "Did you ever
see her after one of his assaults?"

"She turned up one night with both eyes blackened and her
arms bruised when she was appearing with me in a Broadway
play." The actor clenched his fists.

"What was your reaction?"

"I was furious at him. I wanted Helene to leave him at once.
But I didn't want to kill him. I don't think I could kill anyone."

"By the way, I saw you in *Leading Lady*, thought you were
excellent," Dr. Ames said. "You played the part with great
humor and warmth."

"Thank you." Noel let out a huge puff of smoke. "That's
salve to a wounded ego."

"One of the critics described you as quietly dramatic."

"I should hope so!" he exclaimed. "I'd hate to see an actor
who wasn't."

"When did you and Helene meet?"

"During the casting of *Leading Lady*. We became 'good
friends,' as they say. I don't have to beat about the bush with
you. We've had great sex. She told me she wanted to leave
Garth, an aging Prince Charming with enough money to buy
her a million silver slippers. I went to their home twice for
supper at his insistence. Once I met his daughter Amy, a pretty,
pathetic little thing."

Suddenly Noel said, as though divulging a deep, dark secret,

"I hope it's okay to tell you this. One night I ran into Albert at the home of a mutual friend who turned out to be one of Albert's Wall Street clients. Albert had just made a killing for him in the market. This friend was giving a party to celebrate. I was shocked to find it an all-male affair."

"Who was this mutual friend?"

"I'd rather not say. I don't think he ever saw much of Albert other than as his broker." Noel added hastily, "I'm not gay. And until then, I didn't know Albert was. He evidently could swing both ways."

This introduced an important element into the murder, Dr. Ames thought. From what Helene and, most recently, Marietta, had told him of Garth's sexual behavior, it was no surprise to him to learn Garth was bisexual and occasionally sought homosexuals. Such men needed the reassurance of a second penis to express their sexual desire. To touch or see the penisless creature—woman—threw them into such sexual panic that an erection was impossible. Only if a psychoanalyst understood such a man's fear could he try to help the patient give up the fixation acquired in childhood in which he felt attracted to the same sex.

"Do you know for a fact that Al Garth was homosexual?" Dr. Ames asked.

"Not for a fact," Noel said. "There were no signs of it that night. Several of the men were openly kissing and hugging each other tightly. But he didn't join in."

"What was he doing there?"

"Celebrating his great kill on the market for our homosexual host, I guess."

Noel Marvin had helped perhaps more than he intended, Dr. Ames thought. Helene had mentioned nothing of her husband's possible homosexual proclivities nor had she shown awareness of any homosexual tendency in him. But then, like many women, she was what Dr. Ames thought of as "emotionally illiterate," unaware of her own hidden sexual feelings and those of others.

Dr. Ames thought that Garth also might have been the sort of man who, horrified at the idea of sexual contact with another man, vicariously enjoyed in fantasy the thought of sex between two males. Or, just as some girls will flirt with men yet retreat from any act of sex, Garth might have enjoyed taunting younger men trapped in homosexual urges. Perhaps under intense need, pushed by liquor to the edge of what he thought obscene desire, Garth even gave in at times to his homosexual passion.

Without knowing the man except through the words of others, Dr. Ames guessed that as a boy Garth had been so repressed sexually he never dared touch what he believed to be the "mutilated" bodies of a girl—girls without penises—and when he did so as a man, the relationship did not last.

Noel looked at his watch; it was Wednesday and he had to hurry back for the evening performance.

Dr. Ames said, "I thank you, Mr. Marvin, for taking the time to come here. I think you have helped out in a way that is very important. I'll let you know what happens."

Noel stood up, looked for a moment out the window at the fading sun over the park, said in awe, "What a place to be psychoanalyzed in! Relaxes you on the spot."

They both laughed. Dr. Ames felt greatly relieved that his interviews with possible killers had ended. He had seen the last suspect but failed to unearth the iota of a clue showing that any one of those nearest and dearest to Garth, both in love and in hate, was the killer.

Before calling Lonegan, Dr. Ames sat quietly at his desk, going over the day's interviews. All at once he put two and two together, analytically speaking. He recalled suddenly the way Helene's brother had talked of murdering five men in Vietnam—"I had to kill to stay alive." He also mentioned he needed to be psychoanalyzed, intimating he had serious problems, and, as Dr. Ames had left, Evan Benson had the look of agony on his handsome face, as though he did not know what to do to save his tortured soul.

For some reason, Dr. Ames recalled the famous Schreber case, which Freud had titled "Psycho-analytic Notes Upon an Autobiographical Account of a Case of Paranoia (Dementia Paranoides)." In it Freud formulated his theory that paranoia was a defense against homosexual desire. If a man felt homosexual yearnings that caused panic, he became paranoiac, imagining the other man hated him.

As Freud put it: "It is a remarkable fact that the familiar principal forms of paranoia can all be represented as contradictions of the single proposition: '*I* (a man) *love him* (a man),' and indeed that they exhaust all the possible ways in which such contradictions could be formulated.

"The proposition 'I (a man) love him' is contradicted by: I do not love him—I hate him.' . . . Consequently the proposition 'I hate him' becomes transformed by *projection* into another one: '*He hates* (persecutes) *me*, which will justify me in hating him.' And thus the unconscious feeling, which is in fact the motive force, makes its appearance as though it were the consequences of an external perception: 'I do not *love* him, I *hate* him, because HE PERSECUTES ME.' "

Dr. Ames promptly telephoned Lonegan at police headquarters awaiting his words. The latter asked anxiously, "Find anything, Doc?"

"I think so," he said. "I'll need your help. Can you arrange to meet me at the home of Evan Benson? It's right near you at—"

"I know it by heart," Lonegan interrupted. "It's at 381 East 63rd."

"It's just a gamble," Dr. Ames warned.

"What else is my life but a gamble?" A snort of laughter.

"Remember, it's only a hunch, Jack."

"I love hunches. Sometimes they're the best leaders. Shall I bring sandwiches for all of us?"

"Let's eat later. We can have a few drinks first."

"Whatever you say, Doc. Meet you in the lobby of Benson's apartment house in twenty minutes."

As soon as he hung up Dr. Ames called Evan to make sure he would be home. He asked if he could drop in for a few minutes, saying he wanted to see him again.

Evan said with a laugh, "You want me to be psychoanalyzed so soon?"

"That's one thing we could discuss," Dr. Ames said.

"I'll have drinks on the coffee table," Evan said.

Lonegan was waiting in the lobby when Dr. Ames arrived and they ascended to the eighteenth floor. Evan looked surprised when Lonegan also walked in. Dr. Ames introduced them, Evan passed the Scotch around, then they sat on separate chairs, chattered aimlessly for a few minutes as Lonegan admired the paintings.

Finally Dr. Ames said to Evan in a low voice, "Tell us what happened with Albert Garth. Why did you kill him?"

Evan sighed, took a long swallow of Scotch. "You found out, did you?" he finally said. "You're a fine psychoanalyst, Dr. Ames, probing the depths of a man as always. Yes, I killed the son of a bitch. He didn't deserve to live, the way he beat up my sister all the time. That was one strong reason. But there was a second, even stronger one."

He fell into silence until Dr. Ames requested, "Tell us about it."

Evan swallowed another portion of Scotch, went on, "He called me that night about nine. I had dined a few times with my sister and him at their penthouse and thought him an obnoxious man interested only in himself. He asked if he could come here at once, said he had just heard high praise of my paintings by Emily Genauer and thought it about time he owned a Benson. He wanted to see which painting he liked best and would buy it on the spot."

Evan fell silent again. "And then?" Dr. Ames asked.

"When he walked in he suddenly grabbed me, kissed me lightly on the lips, said, 'I felt like doing this ever since we first met, Evan.' I was furious—and scared. After he picked out a painting he offered to pay $25,000 for it. I accepted gratefully. It was a large painting; he said he would pick it up during the week.

"Suddenly he walked over, started to fondle my penis, wanted to kiss me again. I protested. He wouldn't listen. He said, 'You tempt me, you're such a handsome, quiet man. You look like your sister, you even move like her. I want you.' He started to pull down my trousers.

"I was furious. I thought, so that's what the $25,000 is for. Not for my painting, but my body. Something exploded inside. I never had sex with a man before and didn't intend to experience it now. I saw the silver letter-opener gleaming on my desk. I grabbed it, plunged it into his chest three times. He didn't even defend himself, just fell to the floor, dead, as though he expected me to kill him for what he demanded.

"I waited until I knew the area would be deserted, about two

A.M. We have no doorman that late so I could walk out, holding up Albert as though he were drunk. My car was parked in front of the building, no one was in sight as I pushed Albert in. We drove the few blocks to 57th Street, I know well that small park in which I often sat and looked at the boats moving up and down the river. I dragged Albert out of the car, carried him into the park, lay him on the grass and fled."

Dr. Ames said sympathetically. "To allow your penis to be touched by a man was taboo enough but a man married to your sister was the great taboo."

He thought, Albert knew his wife would not stay with him much longer, her desertion would also cause him to regress sexually so that, with enough alcohol to free inhibitions, he could give in to his homosexual urges. He unconsciously chose someone near and dear to her and as nearly like her as possible. The physical beatings he had to inflict on a woman were also indicative of his sexual problem, Dr. Ames believed.

He now understood Helene's dream the night of the murder. It represented a deep wish. The crippled, slimy octopus-monster washed up on the beach symbolized her murdered husband as he lay bloody and dead on the white carpet (the sand). Her associations to the dream, as she talked of cutting herself with the shell, told of a need to punish herself for daring to wish her cruel husband would die. Though she had not murdered him, she felt as guilty as if she had.

In her dream she and Evan had stood alone on a deserted beach, as they so often had as children, and as they now stood, two against the world. Evan had unconsciously carried out her wish as well as his own to get rid of a man who wanted to sexually mar him.

Dr. Ames hoped an understanding judge would be lenient with Evan, take into account the young man's terror at a sexual assault and love of a sister who the victim had so often hurt physically.

It was nearly ten o'clock when the two men sat themselves in an empty booth in the rear of a bar on Third Avenue, near the Nineteenth Precinct headquarters where they had taken Evan. He would soon be released as he produced money for bail.

"I'm buying, Doc," Lonegan announced. "What'll it be?"

"A final Scotch before dinner," Dr. Ames said.

"Two Scotches and water, doll," Lonegan called to a passing waitress.

"What kind of sentence do you think Evan will get?" Dr. Ames asked.

"Depends on the judge. Whether he thinks, at least in the case of Albert Garth, that the attempted rape of a man by a man is as criminal as a man trying to rape a woman."

"Do you have faith in the judiciary, Jack?" Dr. Ames asked.

"My faith in the judiciary can be measured by the amount of Scotch in this watered drink." Lonegan nodded at the glass the waitress set in front of him.

"Tell me, Doc," he then asked, "why were you so sure Mrs. Garth was innocent?"

"After years of treating men and women on the couch you can generally sense when they speak the truth."

"Tell me something else, Doc. Why does a beautiful dame like that marry a guy like Garth?"

"She thought she was in love."

"Wasn't she?"

"She was caught in the fantasy of love."

"What's a fantasy?" Apologetically, "I don't know beans about your profession," added in a mutter, "though you know plenty about mine."

"A fantasy is a distorted idea carried with you since childhood. A child sleeping in the same room with his mother and father sees them in the sexual act and has the fantasy his father is murdering his mother. He is too young to know about genital sex, but he feels anger. He interprets the act of sex as one of violence."

"You mean Mrs. Garth's idea of love wasn't love at all?"

"Right. It was like masochism. Childhood sensuality. And hatred." He added, "She was too upset to think straight. When we get upset, our unconscious thinking often takes over our logical thinking. If you'll pardon the jargon, Helene Garth was controlled by unconscious guilt. Her brother sensed this and part of him, when he killed Albert, was acting in behalf of his sister. Just as he murdered in Vietnam for his country."

"Did she egg him on to kill her husband?"

"Good question." Dr. Ames smiled at Lonegan approvingly.

"Perhaps she consciously did, as well as unconsciously. She may have built up her brother's hatred of her husband by telling him of the beatings. Or at times he saw her damaged face and reached his own conclusions. He became both her protector and her imagined forbidden lover. They seem to have been very close all their lives."

He went on, "There are many reasons for the murder, Jack. Evan may well have been repelled by what to him was an obscene temptation. Too terrorized to reason, or to flee, his frenzy erupted in the violence he had learned to act out on enemies in Vietnam. Added to his slaughter of five unknown victims on the battlefield was now the slaughter of a known victim. A man who had threatened him sexually and regularly was vicious to his sister."

Lonegan looked at Dr. Ames in mixed envy and admiration, then said, "Sometimes I wish I'd set out to be a shrink."

Dr. Ames smiled. "It's not too late if you feel the urge."

"There's as much chance of that, Doc, as you turning in your diploma for a shield."

"No way!" Dr. Ames laughed. "I'll enjoy my sleuthing vicariously through you. You're the super-sleuth."

"And you're the super-shrink, Doc."

They sipped away in silence.

Warren
Murphy

LOOKING FOR
MISTER GREEN

I'M NOT GENERALLY AFRAID OF WOMEN BUT I WAS PREPARED TO MAKE
an exception in the case of K. O. Khatchaturian.

I first met her while I was sitting in the back of a quiet New
York City courtroom and she came galumphing in through a
side door, six hundred pounds of sinew and gristle, this wild
expression on her face, looking like a Lane Bryant contract
killer who'd just sniffed out the world's last anorexic.

My seat was in the back row on the aisle and I slumped
down, hoping this apparition would go away and not try to
shoot up the courtroom, but instead she stomped directly in my
direction.

When it looked like she was definitely, irrevocably coming
toward me, I started to slide along the hard bench, prepared to
slide all the way to Hoboken if I had to, but instead she
lumbered into the row in front of mine, then leaned forward
over the back of the bench, staring down at me.

"Are you Devlin Tracy?" she demanded.

"Depends."

"Depends on what?"

"On whether or not you're planning to hurt me."

"Very funny."

"Not to me. Who are you anyway?"

"My name is K. O. Khatchaturian."

She glared at me, waiting for me to make a joke about her name. I'd just as soon start telling bald jokes to George Foreman. So I didn't say anything, but I did reach behind me under my jacket and press the button that started my hidden tape recorder. If this Visigoth was going to work me over, I was going to have a record of it for the ACLU.

"They told me at the district attorney's office that you were nosing around on the Lauren Carlson case. Were you?" Her tone was nasty, hectoring, and among the things I do not like before lunch is being the hectoree.

"What business is it of yours, kind lady?"

K. O. Khatchaturian looked like her name. She was big, real big. Maybe not as big as me, but the last woman I met who was as big as me was a Jell-O wrestler at a Mensa convention. Anyway, I always thought big people were supposed to be jolly and fun-loving, but this woman exuded anger like a swamp does water vapor. Her fingers were gripping so hard into the back of the bench that her knuckles were white. Her fingernails were all bitten down as if she lived on a diet of fang. She was blond, and don't get me wrong, even if she was big, she had good features and, in the unlikely event that she'd ever smiled, she might have even been pleasant-looking. But I wasn't waiting for a smile, not from this one. I like women who remind me of expensive French target pistols. K. O. Khatchaturian reminded me of a World War II surplus bazooka.

Now she looked unhappy at being called a lady.

"I've been retained by WIT—Women In Trouble—to work on the Lauren Carlson defense," she said coldly.

WIT. I should have known.

"You a lawyer?"

"No," she said. "A private detective."

"What's the neighborhood coming to?"

WIT is this strident gang of harridans who are out to prove

that all men are rapists and that capitalism made them do it. They show up spreading chaos, confusion, and communism wherever they go. But what, I wondered, did they have to do with the Lauren Carlson case, which seemed like your common garden-variety wife-kills-husband celebration?

The husband—that was Leonard Carlson, age 47—had his car jacked up in the service station he ran and was working on something underneath it when his sweet Lauren came along and shoved the car off the jack. The wheel landed on his head.

Then Lauren went out a back door, walked home and brewed herself tea, and probably would have gotten away with the whole thing if one of the neighbors hadn't been passing by the garage and seen her slam her weight against the car and knock it off the jack onto poor Leonard's dome.

Now how was WIT going to figure out that this was somehow Leonard Carlson's fault?

I kept watching K. O. Khatchaturian, knowing the dismal truth that she was going to tell me all about it eventually.

Her jaw started working, but before she had a chance to hurt anybody with it, the bailiff came in and called the courtroom to order.

"Listen, Tracy, I—"

"Shhh. The judge is coming."

"Here come de judge." Nasty again. "I suppose you're impressed by that."

"I'm impressed by anybody who can send me to jail," I said.

"I don't like traditionalists."

"And I don't like you, so sit down and shut up."

I stood up when the judge walked in and sat down when he sat down. I didn't really have any business in court, but I just wanted to see for myself what Lauren Carlson looked like.

Khatchaturian finally lowered herself onto the seat in front of me, blocking out the sunlight for the whole western hemisphere, and listened while the bailiff and the court clerk went through the usual court routine.

This was a small criminal court, over on the East Side of Manhattan, and it didn't attract much attention. There were only a handful of civilians in the courtroom and none of them looked shabby enough to be a reporter. I guessed that all that would change as soon as WIT started banging its drums for

Lauren Carlson. They could give Al Sharpton lessons in press manipulation.

The bailiff called the first case, the people versus a gentleman named Tyrone Walker.

A short man in a lawyer's pinstripe suit stood up in the first row.

"Sorry, Your Honor. Mister Green isn't in court."

The judge nodded. "Postponed a week," he said in a bored voice.

The bailiff called another case. He liked to read them off as *The People* versus so-and-so or *The People* versus somebody else and I always wondered why *The People* weren't ever versus anybody they ought to be versus. Carl Sagan, for instance. I was versus Carl Sagan. The only astronomer who ever made a living by shouting the sky is falling, the sky is falling. Where are all *The People* when I need them to save me and Spaceship Earth from Carl Sagan?

Another pinstripe stood up, another announcement to the court.

"Sorry, Your Honor, Mister Green isn't in court."

"Postponed a week," the judge said again.

K.O. Khatchaturian turned around and growled at me. "Where the hell is this Mister Green? Who is he, the public defender or something?"

"No."

"Well, he ought to be in here so we can get this show on the road."

"Mister Green isn't even a person," I said. "It's just a code phrase for money. If Mister Green isn't in court, it means that the lawyer hasn't been paid yet by his client."

"And the judge postpones the case just for that?"

She sounded incredulous.

"Yes."

She shook her head like a hamster's and I wished her eyeballs would fall out. "That's just like this corrupt system," she said. "It runs on money. Justice for sale to the highest bidder. A disgrace."

Sometimes I don't know why I bother, but I tried anyway. "It makes things work better," I explained.

"I'd expect you to be an apologist for them." She pronounced "them" as if it were underlined.

"Look, Sluggo," I said, "a defendant comes in here and he gets a lawyer at the last minute and the lawyer pleads or a trial date is set or whatever it is they do and then the lawyer doesn't get paid and he drops out of the case and the whole thing gets delayed while Tyrone gets himself a new lawyer and it drags on forever. But if the lawyer's been paid, he's going to stay with the case until it's over and Tyrone gets sent away. It's efficient that way. That's why Mister Green is important."

"Naturally you take their side. A lackey for the system."

"Try imperialist running dog. I haven't heard that one in a while either."

"All right. Running dog."

I closed my eyes, although I was a little reluctant to do that around this vampire. "I don't know why you're on my case, lady, but I didn't invite you here. Why don't you go back to your training camp or something?"

"'Cause I've got to talk to you first. It's not any more pleasure for me than it is for you."

"The best I'll give you is a scoreless tie."

Mercifully, we were interrupted when the bailiff called out "The People versus Lauren Carlson," and Khatchaturian spun away from me. Lauren Carlson was a tall pretty blonde who looked plainly out of place in the blue prison holding uniform. A female guard held her elbow and led her into the courtroom. She was handcuffed and clasped her hands together in front of her like a choir singer.

Another pinstripe got up in the front row and walked past the swinging gate of the bar to stand at the prisoner's side. Another man, obviously one of the prosecutors because his suit looked cheap, hustled into the court from a side room.

"All right, what do we have here?" the judge said.

"Fred Koehler for the state, Your Honor. This is a bail application by the prisoner. She has tentatively been charged with homicide in the death of her husband. We are preparing to go before the Grand Jury tomorrow for a first-degree murder indictment and the state opposes any bail being set on Mrs. Carlson."

The judge looked to the other lawyer.

"Judge, we have evidence that shows clearly that this was an act of self-defense. Mrs. Carlson, under any circumstances, poses no threat to society and is not a threat to flee the jurisdiction. I have been retained by Women In Trouble to represent Mrs. Carlson. As you know, this is a prestigious organization and we request that Mrs. Carlson be freed into our custody without bond."

"That's unheard of, Your Honor," the prosecutor snapped. "We don't know anything about any new evidence. What we do know is that this woman pushed a car onto her husband's head and killed him and we have an eyewitness who will testify to that murder. She might very well flee the jurisdiction, faced with that evidence."

"The officers of WIT will guarantee Mrs. Carlson's appearance, Judge," Pinstripe responded.

And so on like that. Yabba dabba doo. It's what lawyers do and I guess it advances the cause of justice, but they're so damned loud about it. I personally haven't liked a judge since Roy Bean.

Anyway, during all of this, I was watching Lauren Carlson. Her head was down and she seemed to be staring at her hands in an image of penitence.

And then, surreptitiously, she polished the fingernails of her right hand on her blue dress and looked up at the judge.

I could almost see him calculating. On the one hand, he had to live with the District Attorney's office and didn't want to tick them off too much. On the other hand, if WIT was getting involved in the Lauren Carlson case, it was going to be headlines and sure to be on the eleven o'clock news. What was more important, good will from prosecutors or good publicity from feminists?

Score one for the feminists.

"On the representations made here by defense counsel, I will set bail for Mrs. Carlson at a nominal five thousand dollars," he said.

"Thank you, Your Honor," Pinstripe said. He turned to the young D.A. "We'll post it this afternoon," he said, then walked through the swinging gate as if he wanted to be out of the courtroom before the judge changed his mind.

As the guard was leading Lauren away, Khatchaturian turned to me triumphantly.

"Good. Now we can get going on this defense."

"Good luck with it," I said. I got up and walked toward the hallway. Lauren Carlson's acquittal might be on Khatchaturian's agenda but it wasn't on mine. I've always thought that you can learn the most about people by watching them when they don't think they're being watched, and Lauren Carlson buffing her fingernails at her murder arraignment told me all I needed to know. The woman was guilty as dirty underwear, and now, despite all my usual rules for life, namely lie low, stay out of sight, and do as little as possible, I was stuck with the job of proving it. I fingered the little piece of paper in my pocket that had gotten me into this mess in the first place even as I heard K. O. stomping after me into the hallway.

She shoved a business card into my hand and I shoved it into my pocket unread.

"It would be useful," she said, "if you would convince your insurance company to free up the insurance payment on the late Mister Carlson."

"It would be useful if you would take your head out of your nether regions. The woman killed her husband. We should give her money for murdering him? And Garrison Fidelity is not *my* insurance company. They're just a client. I'm only a P.I."

I knew K. O. was trying to restrain her temper because I could see little beads of acid sweat breaking out on her forehead. No doubt she would rather have kicked me in the groin, slapped me across the face with a brick, and left me for dead. She struggled to keep her voice calm.

"It doesn't have to be today. Look, Tracy, we are told that the insurance company listens to your recommendations. Now we're going to get this no-billed by the Grand Jury tomorrow. I guess what we'd like is for you to tell Garrison Fidelity to pay right up then, instead of waiting six months the way these bastards always do. Mrs. Carlson can use the money and your insurance company can use the good will."

"You're so sure you're going to get this dropped by the Grand Jury?"

"No doubt about it," she said smugly.

"Risky. If the Grand Jury no-bills it this time and then new evidence comes up, Lauren can go before another Grand Jury and face indictment all over again."

"We'll take that chance. So how about it? Tell Garrison Fidelity to release that money immediately. It'd be a nice gesture."

"So is this." I stuck my thumb to my nose and waggled my fingers at her. "That gesture's an old favorite of mine."

"Look, Tracy, WIT is involved in this now. By tonight, the press is going to be all over this case. It would look good for you and your company to be on the right side. To say that Mrs. Carlson was not the villain but a victim in this case and you don't want to victimize her any further by delaying payment of what is rightfully hers."

"If the company asks me, I'm more likely to say don't pay a cent until you have to, because this woman's guilty."

"Come on, Tracy, it's only fifty thousand dollars."

"Have a nice day."

Only fifty thousand dollars.

That's what K. O. had said and, in a curious way, she was right. Fifty thousand dollars wasn't enough. Wives didn't go dropping motor vehicles on their husband's skulls just to collect fifty thousand dollars. Murder only starts to make sense when you get into six figures. It's the Mister Green factor. Find the money and you find the motive.

Of course, money's not the only reason for murder. I think that in the sixteenth century, somebody killed for love. You could look it up.

I was back in my office on West 26th Street, my nerves all ajangle from my brush with death in the person of K. O. Khatchaturian. Sarge and Chico, my two partners in the private detective business, were out of town. Sarge because he is my father and therefore obligated to go with my mother to some kind of goddam mah-jongg festival in Fort Lauderdale, and Chico because her interminable sister was having another one of her interminable plumbing operations out in the boondocks of western Ohio. She has one a week, it seems, and all in all she makes a hell of an argument for genetic engineering that could create a woman with PVC tubing.

So I was alone and in an awful state. Taped to my back was

a voice recorder with the glass-grinding tones of K. O. Khatchaturian stored on a tape. I would just have to throw that away as soon as possible so I never ran the risk of hearing her again. And in my pocket, I had her business card which I now fished out and dropped into the wastebasket, again without looking at.

On my desk, I smoothed out the last small piece of lined paper from my pocket. It had been delivered in yesterday's mail, addressed to "Devlin Tracy, Private Detective." I guess whoever wrote it got my name out of the paper when we got a little ink a week before because we'd solved something that had to do with gurus and murder and insurance fraud.

I had opened the letter and found a small clipping, only a few paragraphs, about the death of Leonard Carlson and the arrest of his wife. When I shook the envelope, a crisp hundred dollar bill fell out. This is a sure way of getting my attention.

Then I opened the note. It was printed in large block letters in a not-too-experienced hand.

DEAR MISTER TRACY.
HERE IS $100 DOLLARS. IT IS ALL I GOT.
YOU USE IT TO SEE THAT JUSTISS IS DON. MISTER CARLSON WAS A NICE MAN.

It wasn't signed and there was no return address. I looked at the hundred dollar bill. It had had some writing in one of the corners, but it looked to have been erased. I held the bill up to the light and I thought I could see the name "Jimmy" and a few words—"Have some fun"?

I tried rubbing a pencil on it, like the detectives do in the movies all the time, to try to get an impression, but all I got was a hundred dollar bill that dirtied your hands whenever you touched it.

So. So now I was stuck with a hundred bucks from somebody who wanted me to do something but I didn't know what. That was yesterday morning. And then, yesterday afternoon, I found out from Garrison Fidelity Insurance that they held a fifty thousand dollar policy on Leonard Carlson's life with his wife as beneficiary. A nice coincidence. They didn't really ask me to look into the case, but since I was going to anyway, I already had been paid once and I figured I could get paid again from the insurance company.

That was not a bad deal, and let's face it, nobody's really knocking our door off the hinges with work, so I made ready to provide that one hundred dollars worth of justice.

My first stop had been the D.A.'s office to find out what I could about Lauren Carlson—nothing—and one of the big-mouths there must have told that feminist barracuda about me, which accounted for me being cornered in that courtroom.

What an awful day. Now I faced the big decision of whether I should calm my nerves with a drink or calm my nerves with two drinks. I might as well tell you, I drinks a bit. And I smoke, too. I also wear deodorant and smelly K-Mart aftershave in public places, especially in California, 'cause I like to watch the allergics drop like flies around me. Let them sue. Some Frenchman described my *P&L* when he wrote his will: "I have nothing, I owe much, the rest I leave to the poor." Sue away, *mes amis*.

Before I even had the chance to make my big decision about one drink or two, the telephone rang.

"Hello, Groucho," I said.

Groucho is what I call Walter Marks. He is a vice president of the Garrison Fidelity Insurance Company, where I used to work as an investigator before slipping into this private detective swamp with Sarge and Chico. Now I don't work for him anymore. He's just another client.

In truth, most of the time he's our *only* client but he doesn't know that and what one doesn't know doesn't hurt, do one?

"Don't call me Groucho," came his answering snarl.

"How about Gummo? Did you know there was another Marx brother named Gummo? And there was a Marx sister named Bimbo? Of course, she never made it into the act. Well, at least not the vaudeville act. She spent a lot of time *doing* the act, but—"

"Trace, shut up."

"I'm all ears."

I had decided. I would have *three* drinks to calm my nerves. After K. O. and Groucho, both in the same day, I deserved at least that much.

"What is going on with Lauren Carlson?" he demanded. Did

I say that Groucho is little? That's why he never asks for anything; he always demands and that is why I always ignore him. Until little people learn to act right, they should either be resolutely ignored or crushed underfoot like bugs. Starting with Carl Sagan and moving right on to Paul Simon. I hate him, too. *And* his stupid music.

"It's really an interesting case. I'm so glad you assigned me to look into it."

"Stop trying to con me and just tell me what is going on?"

"Okay. I went down to the D.A.'s office. They've got a witness who saw her kill her husband. Then I went to the arraignment. I damned near lost my life doing this for you, Groucho, because WIT was there and they had this big Amazon bonecrusher and I barely escaped—"

"WIT? Women In Trouble?"

"Yes. And they conned the judge into letting Lauren out 'cause they're going to tell the Grand Jury tomorrow it was self-defense even if it is pretty hard to figure out what you're defending yourself against when you drop an automobile on your husband's cantaloupe. And then this Valkyrie wanted me to ask you to be ready to release the insurance money immediately. Did you ever hear anything so stupid?"

"I'm thinking of doing just that," Marks said.

"She got to you, didn't she? Well, you don't have to be afraid of her, Walter. I know she's bigger than you, but just kick her in the shins. Those big ones can't stand being kicked in the shins and—"

"Who are you talking about, Trace?"

"K. O. Khatchaturian."

"Never heard of the person."

"She's a private detective for WIT. Definitely a low-class woman."

"Be that as it may, I never heard of her. I was visited by some other detective with WIT. A lady named Kohones. Do you know her?"

Kohones? Surely he jesteth.

Not a chance.

"This Kohones said that they've dredged up evidence that shows Lauren Carlson is innocent and that WIT is planning a big media do about it. We could come off looking good if we'll speed the policy payment to her."

"Want to buy a bridge?"

"What?"

"You've been sold a bill of goods, Gummo. This Kohones must be some hustler. How the hell can you reasonably think about paying off an insurance policy to a probable murderer? You're going to look like an idiot. A bigger idiot than usual. Every nut who has one of your policies is going to wind up bumping off the spouse and sending you the bill."

"Well, I don't think it would be quite that bad, Trace," he huffed.

"Have it your own way, but I'm sending you a written memo opposing what you're doing."

"In writing? You? Why?"

"So that when they fire your dumb ass, I still have the company contract. I don't want to be a party to this insanity."

"You're making a mountain out of a molehill," he said.

"They'll be burying you in a molehill. It'll just be big enough."

"Good-bye," Groucho snarled. The phone clicked dead in my ear.

Let's face it. Some people just can't deal with constructive criticism.

I reached for the bottle of vodka that I keep in the bottom drawer of the desk all three of us share and it was gone. That meant Chico had hidden it on me before going off to her plumbing convention. She's always on me about my drinking.

Now, let's see, if I were an insidious but beautiful Eurasian, where would I hide a bottle of booze from an alcoholic degenerate?

Naturally she would put it somewhere I would never look, so I walked to the file cabinet and found it in the back of the bottom drawer.

Sorry, Tojo, you lose again.

Actually, even if she is always complicating my life by hiding my liquor and trying to get me to wear clean shirts and stuff, having Chico around had its benefits. For instance, one of the good things is that the drinking glass in the bathroom is now always clean. When it was just Sarge and me in this place, the damned thing looked like a terrarium for growing moss and lichen.

So I brought the clean glass back to my desk and was ready to pour my very first drink of the day when the office door swung open.

I expected something else awful to happen to me, but instead there was a pretty woman standing there. She was smiling as she looked at me and the bottle of vodka in my hand.

"My malaria," I said and coughed. "It kicks up this time of the year and vodka and quinine water is the only remedy."

"Where's the quinine water?" she asked.

I snapped my fingers. "No wonder I'm not getting any better."

"I'll tell you what. I know a place nearby that gives good quinine and I'll spring for lunch. Interested?"

"My mother doesn't let me go to lunch with strangers. Quick, tell me everything about yourself. Even the sordid stuff."

"I'm Whimsey Kohones. You met my partner today, Khatchaturian?"

"I said sordid, not nauseating. She's not coming to lunch with us, is she?"

"No."

"All right. You're her partner?"

"Yes. She said she gave you our business card."

"I threw it away 'cause I thought the ink was poisoned. Anyway, I already have the 900-number for Dial-a-Snarl."

"She's very intense, isn't she?"

"No. Death is intense. She's just hateful. You're sure she's not joining us?"

"Positive."

"Okay. Let's go." I put the vodka back in the desk. "There's something you ought to understand, though."

"What's that?"

"I'm not easy."

So it turns out that Whimsey Kohones and K. O. Khatchaturian are partners in a private detective agency in California. They do a lot of work for WIT and that's how they got into the Lauren Carlson thing.

"What exactly *is* this Lauren Carlson thing?" I was into my second vodka and feeling expansive, especially since Kohones didn't hold me to watering it down with tonic. Not that she would have noticed anything anyway. She had this big platter of food in front of her, enough greens to straighten out the legs of Captain Bligh's entire crew, and she was digging in with both hands. Why is it that all the pretty women I run into really like to eat? Does it have something to do with enjoying life? Maybe that makes you pretty. Maybe that explains why K. O. Khatchaturian was probably in a car wash someplace eating bug-squash scraped from windshields.

She finally finished chewing and answered my question.

"Lauren's been battered," she said.

"Her husband's got a wheel rim where his forehead used to be. He's not in such good shape either."

She shook her head. "No. We've found a witness, an expert witness. I'm going to see him today and I think he'll testify that Leonard Carlson systematically beat his wife for years. We're talking broken bones, Devlin—"

"Call me Trace."

"Okay, Trace, we're talking broken bones, not black and blue marks. And yeah, she pushed the car on him because she was afraid he was going to beat her again, and that's why she's going to get off on self-defense."

"He wasn't beating her then. He was beating on the car's oil pan."

"It doesn't matter. The case law is pretty well settled. A pattern of beating creates a climate in which a woman fears for her life. She's allowed to take whatever opportunity she can to save herself from the next attack."

"Even if I agreed with you, which I don't, why are you talking to me? What do I have to do with it?" I asked.

"I was talking to your boss, Walter Marks, about getting Lauren's insurance money released quickly. He said that you were the only one who could recommend such action. So I asked K. O. to keep an eye out for you."

"Sorry for you, but Groucho . . . Walter . . . lied. He just didn't want to give you an answer so he laid it off on me. I don't make any decisions for Garrison Fidelity. I'm only another hired hand."

She looked saddened but nodded understandingly. "Oh well."

"And you two are working on her defense, but you seem to be spending a lot of time worrying about Lauren's insurance money. Why is that?"

She shrugged. "'Cause we want to get paid. WIT is a good client. High visibility. But they don't come up with the money without a fight. We've learned our lesson. Nowadays, one of us works on the case; the other one works on getting us paid."

"Mister Green," I said smugly. "Your partner gave me all this sanctimony and now it turns out that her world revolves around Mister Green, too."

"Who's Mister Green?"

"Ask K. O."

When she found out that I couldn't help her get paid, Kohones wanted to ditch me, but I convinced her that since we were both interested in truth and justice, we could probably do more by working with each other. And let the chips fall where they may.

"Suit yourself," she said and let me follow her to Flower East Hospital where we got ourselves ushered into the office of Dr. Robert Muller, acting director of emergency services.

He was tall and laconic, a Californian both by appearance—tanned—and manner—laid back almost to the point of coma.

He waved us to seats then asked us about the weather. Then he asked us if we wanted coffee. Then he asked us how we liked New York City. My ears were falling asleep.

Finally, he got around to saying, "About Lauren Carlson," and I got around to turning on the tape recorder under my jacket.

He hoisted a thin sheaf of papers from his desk. "In the last year, she came into the emergency room here six times for treatment. I was working days on the floor then, and as chance would have it, I treated her all six times."

"And?" Kohones said.

"I don't have any doubt that her injuries were the result of being beaten."

He looked down at the blue sheeted reports. "One-thirty P.M., April 3rd, multiple bruises and abrasions of the chest and shoulders. One-fifteen P.M., June 16th, multiple contusions and chipped bone in the left wrist; one-forty-five P.M., September 3rd, contusions of the upper back thighs." He looked up. "I remember that one clearly. It looked like she had been whipped, but when I asked her about it, she said she had fallen downstairs and scraped herself on the nylon rug." He started reading again. "One-twenty-two, December 28th, hematomas of the face . . . that was a black eye. One-oh-nine, January 18th, bruised ribs, no fracture. And one-fifty-six P.M., March 1st, hematomas of both upper arms, bruises around the neck."

"Accident prone," I said. "She falls a lot."

"That's what she wanted us to believe and that's what she always said. But not so. The injuries weren't consistent with falling. They were consistent with being used as a punching bag."

Doctor Muller looked at both of us, all sincerity and public spirit. "I've got a couple of X-rays in here, too, from her visits and I stand ready to testify if necessary."

Very noble, very California. Upright defender of women and other endangered species.

I bent over to look at the medical reports but that was just for show. I can never make any sense out of technical stuff but just my looking at it seems to impress people.

"Ever meet Mister Carlson? I mean before his wife turned him into garage kill?" I asked.

He shook his head.

"Isn't that a little unusual? I mean, don't the batterers sometimes bring the batt*ed* into the emergency room?"

"Sometimes they do. It inhibits the victim from talking. But as I say, Mrs. Carlson never talked anyway. Always, a fall, a stumble, an accident, dropped something on herself. Carlson didn't have to come in. I guess he knew she would never say anything." He essayed a small smile. "The loyal wife. An old-fashioned virtue," he said.

"A freaking imbecile," Kohones said.

He realized he had been politically incorrect and he quickly said, "Of course."

I grunted.

"So, there you have it, open and shut," Kohones told me out on the street where she was trying to get a cab.

"Maybe yes, maybe no, I don't know yet."

"You're hopeless," she said.

"My most endearing quality."

"Do what you want. Between the good doctor there and some other stuff, I think we've got enough to get Lauren off tomorrow. If we do, will you push through her insurance check so we can get paid?"

"You have my word. Pull it off and I will do my best to make Mister Green appear."

"I get it. Mister Green is money."

"I love a quick study," I said.

I went to see the woman who had watched Lauren Carlson dump the car on her husband. Her apartment building was past the Lower East Side, into the Lowest East Side, one of those areas of Manhattan that politicians are always promising to rebuild to bring about the renaissance of the inner city. In other words, a slum that was never going to be anything more than a slum until they get rid of the people who make slums. The woman wasn't home, or at least she didn't answer the doorbell. Maybe she thought I was K. O. Khatchaturian come to call.

Outside, I looked across the street and saw people working at a ramshackle cinderblock building with a faded sign overhead that read CARLSON'S GARAGE. I was surprised since I would have thought it'd be shut down.

I went across the street and soon wound up talking to a man named Guido Romeo, who said he was the garage's assistant manager. He treated me like a process server until I told him what I was doing and then he became downright brotherly.

He left the running of the gas station in the hands of two teenagers and took me into the back room to talk. Now this place was just your regular run-of-the-ghetto gas station but the back office looked like a transplant from a Loire Valley chateau.

The walls were paneled and there was a large rosewood desk. There were built-in bookshelves, filled, as far as I could tell, with books on the stock market. Piles of *Wall Street Journal*s were stacked neatly against one wall, and there was a television set, a fax machine, and a console telephone with three outgoing lines.

I pretended not to notice anything out of the ordinary, and when Guido motioned me to a chair alongside the desk, I turned on my tape recorder. I don't know why. I can never make head nor tail out of the tapes later. They're always just a lot of people complaining about things, but it's a habit and one of the few I have that isn't totally self-destructive.

"So tell me about Leonard."

"He was the salt of the earth," Guido said. "Everybody who worked for him, you know what we called him? Lovely Len. Is that what you want to know?"

"Yeah. Stuff like that."

"Okay. He wasn't just a good guy. He was the best. I worked here for him for twenty years. Six days a week for twenty years we had lunch in this room. Every day. We'd eat pastrami from across the street and play gin rummy. He sat where you're sitting. He couldn't play gin rummy at all. We paid only a quarter of a cent a point and I clipped him every day. And every day, he'd write it down in the scorebook." Guido pulled an inch-thick ledger from a corner of the desk and opened it to row after row of dates and amounts. "And every Saturday he'd total what he owed me and pay up. Five, ten bucks a week, but he always paid. He was that honest kind of guy."

Then he stopped talking. I waited for a moment.

"Whyn't you asked me questions? Maybe that's easier," he said.

"Did Leonard ever talk about beating his wife?"

"Huh?"

"Beating his wife, Lauren. Leonard ever talk about that?"

"Len never beat his wife. He was nuts about his wife and then the slut goes and does what she did."

"Why'd you call her a slut?"

"Because she was. She was always tipping around on him. I seen her myself one night in a restaurant uptown with some guy. I think that's why Len never went home for lunch. Afraid he'd find her in the rack with somebody. I think that happened to him once when they was first married."

"You know the guy she was with?"

"Nahhh. Just another guy."

"Well, running around on her husband . . . that might be reason for him to beat up on her," I said.

"Never. Len told me about that. He said he was going to have to see a doctor 'cause she was always falling down. He would go home at night and she'd have bandages on because she fell down."

"She fell down a lot."

"Exactly. That's why he was going to their doctor about it. I don't understand stuff like that, but Leonard said it was like she never used to be clumsy and now she was and maybe she just wasn't having accidents but in the back of her mind she wanted to have accidents. He said it was something like that guy Fraud says, something like that."

"I never heard of Fraud."

"He was like a big shrink, you know, and he said people sometimes do things because they've got needs. You know, people have needs."

"You think Lauren had a need to fall down?"

He shook his head. "You're pretty dumb for a detective, you know."

"Everybody tells me that. But what I'm stuck with is this. Lauren kills her husband but she's got medical witnesses who'll swear that she was always in the hospital because her husband beat her up. I can't make a case for anything else, not even murder for money, because all Leonard had was a stinking fifty thousand dollar insurance policy. That's not enough for murder."

Guido fixed me with a surprised look. "Insurance? Leonard didn't need insurance. He had five million dollars."

"Gasoline prices aren't *that* high."

"Look around, Tracy. All those papers. They're all stock market stuff. Leonard spent most of the day in here working on his investments. You know, some guys play golf. Leonard played the stock market. He'd been doing it all his life and he made a whole lot of money doing it. He showed me his brokerage statement once. Five million and change he had."

"If he had all that money, what the hell was he doing living on this block? This isn't exactly Palm Beach. His wife must have raised hell about that."

Guido shook his head. "She didn't even know about the

money . . . not until . . ." He thought for a moment, then leaned forward and planted his thick forearms on the desk between us.

"Last year, it was. My seven-year-old kid got hit by a car. Bad accident. He needed a lot of reconstructive surgery on his leg and, like a jerk, I had forgot to pay my Blue Cross. I was trying to get the money by taking a mortgage on my house in Staten Island, but the damned bank was screwing around and taking forever. Leonard came in the next day with a check made out to me for fifty thousand. He told me there was more where that came from if I needed it. Well, I used it for the operation and a month later I got the mortgage check. I remember it was a Saturday, April 1st, April Fools' Day, you know, I thought it was kind of a joke. So I came into the city and went down to Leonard's house to sign over the fifty thousand but Leonard wasn't home so I gave it to Lauren. Her eyes lit up like a Christmas tree when she saw it and I told her that Leonard had lent me the money. I'm sure that she never knew he had that kind of money until I opened my big mouth. The Monday after that when I came in to work, I asked Leonard about it and he just sloughed it off. 'All good things come to an end,' he said, something like that. And we didn't talk about it anymore."

He stopped talking and there didn't seem to be much more to get out of Guido, so I stood up and thanked him and he said, "You find out the truth, okay?"

I nodded. "By the way, how's your boy? What's his name—Jimmy?"

"Timmy," he said. "He's coming along fine. He's gonna be all right. He loved Leonard, too. On his birthday when he got home from the hospital, Leonard gave him three hundred dollar bills inside a card. Timmy really loved him."

I walked down the block to the Carlson's address. It was a typical run-down row house apartment building, not the kind of place where you'd expect to find a multimillionaire.

On a hunch, I went into the foyer and rang the Carlson's doorbell but there was no answer. If Lauren had already made bail, she was probably out being fitted for widow's weeds. Or maybe getting a manicure.

I roused one of the neighbors, some grisly busybody, and got her talking and finally got out of her the name of Leonard Carlson's family doctor.

"He's in the neighborhood. That's why we like him. Everybody likes a doctor in the neighborhood. That's why we all go to him. 'Cause he's in the neighborhood."

So I went to talk to him for a few minutes and he told me what I thought he would and then I went back to the office to play back the tapes of the day. And also to have a drink. I was thinking maybe I had earned it.

I hadn't realized until I listened to it again on tape, how annoying and nasal Doctor Muller's voice was.

"At one-thirty P.M., April 3rd, multiple bruises . . ."

And Guido Romeo: "She didn't even know about the money . . . not until . . ."

I listened to them a long time. Usually, my partner Chico does this brain end of the business with the tapes, but if she's always going to be out of town fooling around with her sister, I figured I'd have to start doing more of that for myself.

I did do it for a while and it got me so tired I took a nap on the couch. When I woke up it was dark and I dug out of the wastebasket the business card that Khatchaturian had given me earlier in the day. There was a Manhattan phone number penciled on it and I dialed and K. O.'s savage voice came barking across the line at me.

"Khatchaturian speaking."

"Good evening, sir or madam. May I speak with Miss Kohones, please?"

The phone clanked down. A moment later, Whimsey Kohones picked it up.

"This is Trace. What first? The bad news or the really bad news?"

"Surprise me," she said.

"Okay, the bad news first. I found Mister Green."

She wanted to hear all about it in person so we met in a coffee shop near her borrowed apartment. I hadn't counted on her bringing Joe Palooka along, but since she had I decided I was going to make this quick before K. O. got peevish and started to chew on my ankle.

"So what have you got for us?" K. O. wanted to know even before they sat down at the small table.

I ignored her and turned toward Kohones.

"Leonard Carlson was worth five million dollars. He made his money in the market. Lauren killed him for the dough."

"Lauren killed him because she was a battered wife fearing for her life and trying to preserve one little shred of human dignity," K. O. stated angrily.

I ignored her some more. Kohones, at least, was quiet and listening so I talked to her.

"Lauren didn't know about the money until last April 1st. That was a Saturday. On Monday, April 3rd, she made her first trip to Doc Hollywood in the emergency room."

"Carlson beat her," K. O. said.

I kept looking at Kohones. "She beat herself. A half-dozen times. She always went to the hospital between one and two o'clock so she could claim that her husband came home for lunch and smacked her around. But Carlson never went home for lunch."

"I don't believe it," K. O. said. "This sounds like some kind of whitewash, trying to crucify a woman who has committed no crime at all."

I told Kohones, "Carlson was a numbers nut. The guy who works at his garage has a record book. They played gin rummy every day at lunch. The dates are all in there. Carlson *never* went home for lunch. And of course, she didn't kill Leonard for the few bucks of insurance. It was for the five million in stocks."

Kohones finally spoke. "That's all pretty thin," she said.

"Yeah, but it's a start. Lauren was sleeping around on her husband and he knew about it. That might be why she didn't just try for a divorce to get her hooks into his money. Carlson loved her and—"

"Yeah, he loved her," K. O. snarled. "That's why he beat her."

"Love won't be why I beat you if you don't shut up," I said.

"Carlson legitimately worried about his wife. There's a family doctor. Carlson went to see him to try to get the doctor to figure out why Lauren was falling so much. The doctor confirms that. He said that when he asked Lauren about it, she just got defensive and denied that she had ever fallen. I figure that was just her way of getting the doctor to butt out."

I signaled the waitress for another cup of coffee.

"Still thin," Kohones said.

"Sure it is. But it's enough for the cops to work on. They'll dig up the boyfriend and he'll talk and the doctor will talk and Guido will talk and it's murder. Five million dollars. That was the missing Mister Green."

Kohones was smiling, which almost counteracted K. O.'s sputtering.

"Anyway, that's the bad news and the really bad news is I don't think you two are going to get your fee. My company's not going to pay it and I don't think Lauren can get her hands on any of Leonard's dough once she's indicted. If you're smart, you'll get WIT to back off from her right away. Maybe that way, they'll pay you some money just in gratitude for saving their butts. If you want, I'll give you the names I've got. You can give them to the D.A. Maybe it'll make you look good." I looked at K. O. "Well, at least half of you."

"What about you?" Kohones asked. "You found this all out. Don't you want to look good?"

"No," I said. "If I get famous, next thing you know, the phone'll be ringing off the hook and everybody'll be wanting to hire me and I can't put up with that. And besides"—I fished the crisp hundred dollar bill from my jacket and laid it on the table—"I've already been paid."

I went back to the office to sleep on the couch. I do that a lot when Chico's out of town.

Before I did though, I wrote a note at the desk to little Timmy Romeo.

Dear Timmy,
Justice is done for Mister Carlson. And he told
you to have fun with this money so spend it on
something neat.

I signed it with my name and then I put the note and the fresh hundred dollar bill in an envelope, sealed it, and addressed it. It would go out in the morning's mail.

Then I slept like a baby. I always did when JUSTISS WAS DON.

Justin
Scott

THE
COMMISSIONER'S
MOLL

THE NEW POLICE COMMISSIONER, FORMER CHIEF OF DETECTIVES JOE
Grove, figured the night was too cold for a full-bore riot, but he
stopped by Tompkins Square anyway to let his cops know he
was thinking about them. The previous commissioner had
sucked up to the politicians, but in Joe Grove—a huge man as
black as asphalt and tough as Bed-Stuy—they had a cop's cop
bossing the job. A good thing, that night, because the mayor
arrived to take charge in a tuxedo and suddenly every Dwight
Gooden in the neighborhood was pitching bricks at the TV
cameras.

The Commissioner dispatched the Tactical Patrol Force to
escort His Honor safely home to Gracie Mansion. "Try and
keep the damned fool there," he ordered his aide, but the
damage was done. A mob charged out of the park, led by a
bare-chested weightlifter swinging a motorcycle chain at the
shortest cop in the line.

Officer Kathy Dee two-handed her baton into the mutt's knee, just like they'd taught her at the Academy. He slammed her to the pavement with his momentum, but he went down, too, screaming, while she was already tucked and rolling back to her feet.

Commissioner Grove was impressed. It took brains and balls to stick to training when instinct screamed to waste shots at the head.

Up close, she impressed him again: a demure little Irish blonde encased in riot helmet and plastic shield like a brand-new doll in a box. Kathy Dee was round and clean and smooth and her hair glowed like a sunny day. Mature men would confide over a couple of cold ones that they would like such a wholesome girl for a daughter; were that not possible, they'd admit after a few more, they'd be glad to have her as someone else's daughter.

The Commissioner ordered her transferred, forthwith, to One Police Plaza to brighten his days as his driver.

Kathy Dee protested that she was bucking to make detective and there was no legitimate way she'd earn her gold shield driving the Commissioner's limo. The Commissioner knew she had a point: she would make no friends down in the squads, not with the coven of middle-aged Irish who ran headquarters cranking out gossip about the big, black commissioner and his little blond driver.

For him, the downside could be howls of sexism, racism, and bossism. The Irish would hate his guts, as might the women. But male blacks, Hispanics, Chinese, maybe even the Italians, would probably cheer, Score one for the ethnics. Screw 'em all, he decided. Bossism was a damned good way to remind everybody who was boss. He glowered menacingly and heaved up his enormous frame behind his desk, a sight known to curl the toenails of top brass.

The young lady stood firm. She had dreamed of becoming a police officer since she was eight years old, she explained, when the teacher said her legs were too short to be a ballerina. Now she dreamed of being a detective and was busting hump for her master's at John Jay, nights.

"Your old man on the Job?" the Commissioner growled.

No. Her father worked for the city, in the Water Department.

She was the first cop in her family. The Commissioner, who usually left speculation to the irresponsible, found himself wondering what made people want to be good.

"Got a boyfriend?"

Kathy had been shifting her weight foot to foot, like a runner waiting for the light to change. She stopped; her smile got bigger and brighter and totally unreadable. "No time for one."

Joe Grove had the distinct impression that was all she'd spill on that subject. Fair enough, cops with no secrets made excellent firemen.

"What do you want to be a detective for? Ten people a day are killing each other for drugs and money. Back when I started out, murder was rare enough to be interesting. Today we got dogfights—one mutt shoots another. Sociopaths with automatic weapons and not one ounce of human emotion. Gets so you catch a normal murderer with a normal human motive, you want to let the poor bastard go."

"You're a detective."

Joe Grove shook his head. "Behind this desk, I'm the Job's defender, cheerleader, and head executioner. I ain't got no time to play detective."

"But you wanted to be a detective, like I do, right? And they say you were the best homicide investigator on the Job."

Joe laughed. "Well, damn, don't you have the silver tongue. Better I teach you how to be the first female police commissioner."

Kathy thought he was laughing at her and went red in the face. "I request to be sent back to patrol force. I'll work my way up on my own. I don't *want* your help."

"You're gonna be my driver, Irish, and that's final. Now there are two qualifications for an officer who's privileged to chauffeur the PC. One, she forgets everything she sees and hears; two, she keeps her trap shut."

"I have a photographic memory and my high school yearbook called me 'Kathy the Mouth.'"

"Jesus F-ing Christ. What am I going to do with you?"

"Teach me to be a detective," she said. "That way you won't lose your touch stuck behind this big desk and I'll become a good detective."

"It's more than knocking citizens down with a nightstick. What makes you think you've got the stuff?"

"Straight A's in Police Science."

"What I'm saying is it's no longer a career I'd recommend to a bright young woman."

"I'd like to find out for myself, please."

"Don't you get it?" Joe started to shout, saw the disappointment cloud her face, and remembered two thousand years ago when he thought the Job was a gift from God. "Okay," he sighed. "You find a case worth solving—worthwhile *and* interesting—and I'll partner with you. Show you the ropes."

"You'd be my partner?"

"Only if you find me a murderer I can respect. Don't waste my time chasing mutts. Find me a human being—till then, you drive when my regular driver's off, run errands and make yourself useful. That's my final offer."

He thrust out a hand big and black as a wrecking ball. Kathy hesitated a split second—aware that the Commissioner would not have extended this invitation to an ugly woman. But she was also aware that, despite his reputation as the mentor from hell, every one of Joe Grove's protégés had made Detective Lieutenant by the time they were thirty.

"You can start by enrolling in a Spanish course. Pretty soon that and Chinese is all they'll talk in this town. And I think I'd like you better in plainclothes . . . Not too plain."

Soon the dark-hearted Celts who ran Headquarters were slathering in their sleep. Bad enough that the Commissioner had Kathy Dee as some sort of roaming personal assistant, slipping a link in the chain of command: God knew what she reported to him in private. Far worse, as Joe had guessed, were their suspicions of pleasure behind closed doors. When she carried the morning's Unusual Occurrence reports into his office, and shut the door behind her, there wasn't an Irish cop in the building who believed things were kosher.

"Found a good one," she said, handing Joe the stack. The commissioner read them, unhappily. Six months into his administration, police morale had improved, with a cop's cop at the helm, but nothing else had changed in the city. New York still had a nightly murder rate that rivaled a nation at war: three kids slaughtered by a fourth with a MAC-10; four bodega owners in three separate boroughs shot by robbers; two drug dealers burned alive by competitors—

"Didn't we get this yesterday?"

"This is today."

—another cash machine killing; old lady dragged to death; livery cab driver found face down on his back near Riverside Drive—

"Funny typo here, 'Face down on his back.' "

"That's how they found him. Little Rick Garcia."

"You're shitting me. His head was on backwards?"

"The M.E. confirmed it. I just phoned him. And get this—Little Rick's cab was parked at the car service he drove for."

The Commissioner grinned. "Damn. You *know* what I like."

Kathy Dee folded her pretty little hands on her modestly crossed knees. "I *know* what you like."

Deputy Inspector Foley, the Commissioner's official aide, disengaged his ear from the door and slapped his forehead. Foley's clerk whispered into the telephone, "They're doing it, again," and a bureau chief waiting in the reception room crossed himself. Commissioners were granted certain leeway, but for decent failings like drinking whiskey at breakfast. This girl was half his age and blond, Jesus was she blond. The good news was she was only part Irish. Her personnel file, diddled out of Fat Nellie by a computer hacker who knew the codes, revealed a German grandmother on one side and a Swede on the other, which explained a lot.

Inside the Commissioner's office, Kathy Dee explained that Little Rick had priors for assault and armed robbery, cab driving being a sideline. He ran with a crew called the Bolivar Boys, which hung out in the back room of the Bolivar Car Service on Amsterdam Avenue, twenty blocks and one precinct south of where he had been found face down on his back.

"Wonder why they didn't just shoot him?" mused the PC. He glanced at the Amsterdam Avenue address—83rd Street in the relatively sane Two-Oh—and gave Kathy the nod. "Okay, Irish. He's yours. There's a pizza joint up there called Caesar's. Bring us a couple slices of white for lunch."

She charged out the door like a kid heading to the movies. Joe gazed thoughtfully at the imprint she'd sizzled on his retina, then picked up the telephone to unwind by terrorizing his Brooklyn borough commander.

Kathy Dee swung by the morgue, wondering if the medical examiner had unearthed some additional cause of Little Rick's death. The M.E., fearing from her original call that the Commissioner might take a special interest in this case, had reviewed the postmortem himself. He rolled the body out on a gurney and whisked back the sheet.

Kathy's stomach jumped. Little Rick looked as though he had lost a saber duel. When she looked more closely, she realized the gaping wounds were only autopsy incisions, sewn loosely shut with big loops.

"As you can see, no bullet holes, no punctures, no tire tracks."

The body had lain on the sidewalk about an hour, the M.E. estimated. There was swelling where his neck had snapped.

"I thought his head turned around."

"I left it like this when I was done. You want I put it back?"

"That's okay."

The killer hadn't hit him, hadn't bludgeoned him, kicked him with karate feet, or employed mechanical aids. Beckoning an assistant, the M.E. demonstrated how Little Rick's killer had gripped his head with both hands and turned it "like a twist-off bottle cap."

"Strong hands."

"Believe it. Look at the build on this guy."

Little Rick had a heavily muscled torso laced with old knife and razor scars. Healed gunshot wounds pocked his bulging chest and arms like raindrops on a pond. No wonder the Commissioner asked why they didn't shoot him. In Manhattan, guys like this died in a hail of automatic weapon fire, not of a broken neck. Kathy Dee asked if it could have been an accident.

The medical examiner started to snicker, reconsidered his visitor's connections, and answered politely that no, it could not have been an accident that killed Little Rick. He did not fall off a skateboard or trip on empty crack vials. A person tall and strong, and very likely fueled by enough angry adrenalin to double his strength, had performed terminal chiropractry on what had been an exceptionally thick neck planted on a powerful and—judging by the wounds Little Rick had survived previously—savvy street fighter.

The Bolivar Car Service—"We Go Where Yellow Don't Dare"—shared its stretch of Amsterdam Avenue with seven beer bars (bridge and tunnel kid joints that Kathy Dee recalled from her college days), Caesar's Pizzeria, a maternity shop into which a trio of graying West Side mothers were wheeling strollers, stores that specialized in lamps, in stuffed bears, in toys, in items for and about cats, a glazier, an Armenian luggage repairer, a hardware store, and a terrific dress shop that cops could not afford to patronize even if they had the long slinky body to wear the fashions in the window.

Elderly Lincolns and Cadillacs with tinted plastic peeling from their windows crowded the avenue, double-parked in front of Bolivar. On the sidewalk, girls in tight pants and women who had brought babies down from the tenements above the storefronts were flirting with the drivers. "Señorita," leered a guy sitting on a double-parked Sedan de Ville. "No parking." He had an arm in a sling and a bandage on his brow and he pursed his lips and made an offensive sound, like a wet kiss.

Kathy Dee flashed her tin and addressed him in Spanish. The guy in the sling looked genuinely puzzled. She repeated herself in English, advising him to update his vehicle inspection sticker, which had expired.

"Hey, no problem, you take my space." Shielding the sticker with his good hand, he slid into his car and drove off. Kathy entered the narrow storefront. A dispatcher behind a plywood counter worked a telephone and a CB. Behind him, partially curtained, was a large room. A half-dozen drivers, bandaged like the guy on the street, slouched unhappily on couches and chairs. Whether they were mourning Little Rick, or some other loss, she could only guess.

"I already told the first cops," said the dispatcher, whose name was Eduardo, "we catch him first, we cut his balls off."

Kathy Dee glanced past him. Of the bandaged men in the back room, two had their arms in slings, one wore an eye patch and another was holding a hospital cane.

"Whose balls?" she asked.

Lips like a valentine, Eduardo was thinking. Then her smile got chilly and her eyes took on a steely glint that Eduardo associated with emergency room nurses. Chillier still, and he remembered the nuns in the mission school.

"Whose balls?"

"I don't know, yet. Little Rick didn't have no enemy in the world. Nice guy, you know what I'm saying?"

Kathy, who shortly before had been toting up Little Rick's battle scars, asked whether if nice Little Rick hadn't been killed by an enemy, could he possibly have had an argument with a friend?

"Lady, I swear I don't know," said Eduardo, with an expression that suggested he was damned sure it wasn't a fight with a friend.

"What was he doing over on Riverside when his car was here?"

"I think he had a girl over there," Eduardo answered too quickly.

"Maybe he got a ride over with one of the other drivers?"

"No. He walked."

"*Walked?*" Kathy Dee repeated incredulously and Eduardo nearly extended his hand for her to rap it with a ruler. "Eduardo. In New York, rich people walk. Working people like you and me and Little Rick, we drive. Right?"

"Right," Eduardo agreed. He had never thought about it before, but nobody *he* knew walked. Women, children, and the homeless rode the subway. Men drove cars.

"So I'm asking you, why didn't Little Rick take his car?"

"I wish I could tell you."

"Call me when you can."

She bought the Commissioner a slice of white pizza and a salad for herself and drove downtown to One Police Plaza where they had lunch on his desk, after Deputy Inspector Foley reheated the pizza in his toaster oven. The Commissioner drank a diet Coke with his eight hundred calories of melted cheese. Kathy filled a glass from the tap.

"How can you drink that stuff?"

"New York City has the best municipal water in the world . . . So I looked in the back room. Six guys in Band-Aids and slings. Another out front."

"Gang war?"

"I didn't see any lookouts. They were all just sitting around. Very unhappy, but not like they're in a fight."

The Commissioner telephoned the Two-Oh, smiling broadly at the scene his long experience on the Job told him was taking place: a petrified desk sergeant frantically signaling the lieutenant to get the captain out of the john. "Any big fights last night?"

No fights. He dialed the Two-Four, the precinct directly uptown. A desperate-to-please lieutenant told him the captain was out, over on Riverside Drive, where some rich guy's greenhouse had been broken into.

What, the Commissioner inquired dangerously, was a precinct captain doing personally investigating a B and E? The answer was that one of the mayor's deputies had called to mention that the burgled homeowner contributed big bucks to the mayor's campaign chest, which wasn't exactly overflowing these days. "Should I patch you in to the captain, Mr. Commissioner, sir?"

The Commissioner made a mental note to chew out the captain for not alerting his office to the mayoral pressure. "Tell your captain I'm sending Officer Dee over for a look." He banged down the phone.

"Why?" asked Kathy Dee.

"Little Rick's colleagues are wrapped in Band-Aids. Little Rick's body was found on Riverside Drive. Some guy's greenhouse on Riverside Drive got busted into."

"How could anybody own a greenhouse on Riverside Drive?"

"Well, go and find out," snapped the Commissioner, grabbing a phone to yell at somebody.

Kathy found mansions on Riverside Drive above Ninety-sixth Street, honest-to-goodness mansions separated from their neighbors by driveways, gardens, and iron fences. Outside the burgled one, the captain of the Twenty-fourth Precinct was having a short snort in the privacy of a prowl car and complaining to his driver, "I need this shit? I got this bigwig's mansion burgled. Then the mayor calls. Now the Commissioner's moll is coming over—why you making faces?"

"She's already here," his driver whispered through clenched teeth. Kathy Dee stuck her pretty little nose in the open window, and asked, "Captain Frye?"

Captain Frye's flask and jaw dropped simultaneously. "Oh, shit . . . Hello, Officer Dee. What's up?"

She smiled and the captain suddenly felt much better. A regular little sweetheart—kind of girl he'd always wanted for a daughter—lucky bastard commissioner. "May I look around?"

"Allow me." He got out of the car and led her to the front door. "Anything in particular you want to see?"

"The greenhouse."

"It's on the roof of the dining room, off the second floor."

"Was that the easiest way in?"

"They didn't break in, they broke out."

"I don't understand."

"They were already in the house. Apparently they used the garage door opener—probably boosted the remote control out of his car in some parking garage, copied the code, and slipped it back."

"So why didn't they go *out* the garage door?"

"A witness walking his dog sees them open the door, standing there holding the homeowner's stereos and TVs and computers, then shut it again. He calls the precinct and we dispatch a car. The blues open the garage and discover Crazy Eddie's going out of business sale. The mutts inside withdraw up the stairs, bust out of the greenhouse, climb down the back wall, and make their way through the surrounding gardens."

"Cutting themselves on the glass and tripping over things in the dark."

"Crime Scene Unit got a variety of blood types," he agreed cheerfully. "What's the Commissioner's interest in this—say hello, by the way, we worked together in Midtown North in '79—what's he—"

"I'll say hello," said Kathy Dee, with one last look around. She drove the couple of blocks to where Little Rick had been found face down on his back. Riverside Drive along here was divided in two, the main drag below, where most traffic passed, and a serpentine upper lane that serviced the mansions and apartment buildings.

Little Rick's final turf had been in the shadow of a bush that arced out of the strip park between the two roads. She stared at it a while, hoping to get more than she'd read in the Two-Four detective squad's reports. The Commissioner had taught her to try to imagine the victim's last thoughts. Some people die, surprised. Others know it's coming . . . What was he doing here? Had Eduardo the dispatcher told the truth? Was Little Rick visiting his girlfriend?

"Bullshit," growled the Commissioner when she bounced the thought off him. He was often irritable in the afternoon.

"Would you like some tea?"

"No—*now* where are you going?"

"I'm going to make some tea."

"Okay, I'll have one. Not that herb shit. Tea. Real tea."

"Yes, sir."

She came back from Inspector Foley's pantry with two steaming mugs. Commissioner Grove sniffed his suspiciously.

"Listen, young lady, something's missing."

"What's missing?"

"*Think.* You got six perps standing in an open garage door, who close it, drop their loot, and run upstairs and through a wall of glass. You got a livery service driver dead around the corner. You got his car safe back at the Bolivar Car Service. The dead driver knows the perps. They're in the same crew. What's missing?"

"The car."

"What car?"

"The getaway car."

"Maybe Little Rick's the wheelman. Where's the car?"

"Missing."

"Missing to whom?"

"The perps. They're standing there with the stuff they stole. And Little Rick doesn't come with the car. But the cops do. So they have to run away without the stuff they stole. So they're really pissed off and they kill Little Rick."

Kathy knew she was right when the mentor from hell asked his next question: "What else is missing?"

She thought hard. "I don't know. It's the getaway car."

"What else?"

"I don't know."

"Start with the car. Go talk to the guys in Band-Aids."

Kathy Dee hesitated. "What am *I* missing?"

"Sex."

"*What?*"

"It's just something I've noticed over the years," the Commissioner explained hastily, realizing that had popped out sounding a little different than he had meant it, or—judging by her offended expression—too much like he had meant it. "There's always sex somewhere in every human killing."

"But—"

"Get outta here," the Commissioner said. "For crissake, I got a police department to run. I can't spend the whole day teaching you to be a detective."

"But—"

"*Out!*"

Kathy Dee fled.

Deputy Inspector Foley, noticing the high color in her cheeks and missing her usual friendly smile, said to his clerk, "Wonder what he wanted her to do to him?" To which the clerk replied, "Clearly she didn't want to do it."

Inspector Foley winced, "Now we'll catch it." And seconds later, "*Foley, get in here!*" thundered through the walls.

The Commissioner hadn't yet made up his mind what to yell at Foley about, when he detected the shadow of a knowing smirk on the inspector's face. His own expression, already ominous, darkened.

"Deputy Inspector?"

"Yes, sir?"

"It wouldn't do that young lady's career much good if the wrong kind of rumors came out of this office about her and me."

"Rumors?" quaked Foley.

"*Would it?*"

"No, sir."

"See that they don't."

"But, sir? Rumors could start from other—"

"Because if I ever hear a goddamned rumor about her and me I'm going to know exactly where it started, Deputy Inspector Foley, and there are streets in this city where the beat cop is not wholly admired. Do you get my drift?"

*   *   *

Back at the Bolivar Car Service, Kathy Dee found Eduardo the dispatcher disconsolate. "Get the guy who offed Little Rick?" he asked.

"I thought you were going to cut his balls off."

Eduardo looked crestfallen. "We checked out everyone who had a beef with him. *Nada*. I don't know who did him. What about you?"

"What about the guys he left holding the bag in that mansion on Riverside Drive?"

"What mansion?"

"The one with the greenhouse."

Eduardo looked at her. "We talkin' man to man?"

Kathy said, "Yes. Man to man."

"I mean whatever might've happened at that certain mansion is diddly compared to Little Rick getting killed."

Kathy agreed. "Man to man, Eduardo, my boss thinks your crew killed Little Rick for stranding them."

"Your boss has his head up his ass. My guys grew up together. C'mon. My guys aren't animals. You think they're going to kill their own friend for a TV?"

Based on their criminal records, Kathy had few doubts that some of the bandaged men in the back room would kill for a TV under the right circumstances, such as the TV's owner resisting its being stolen. But—as she had tried to tell the Commissioner and didn't tell Eduardo—there was no blood on Little Rick, while the Bolivar Boys had been bleeding profusely, around the hour Little Rick's head was twisted off. On the other hand, of the crew she had seen, several were bigger than Little Rick, and the M.E. had told her to find a tall, powerful man.

"The fact is, Eduardo, Little Rick was supposed to be waiting someplace with a car. He didn't show. His friends had plenty of reason to be mad as hell—"

Eduardo started to repeat that his guys weren't animals, but she cut him off.

"—mad enough at that moment to do something to Little Rick they might feel bad about later."

"Little Rick was already dead."

"How do you know?"

"Because if he wasn't dead he'da been where he was supposed to be, outside a certain mansion with the motor running—if that's what was going down."

"No. One of your guys could have done him after, for not showing."

"I'm telling you he was dead already. When Little Rick is told to get a car, he comes with a car. Always. Like I go, 'Get the car.' Little Rick gets a car. Which is why when we catch this guy, I'm going to personally cut his balls off."

"Man to man," said Kathy Dee, "we'll arrest you for it." She stalked out, waded through the women and children on the sidewalk and the double-parked cabs. She felt herself crashing. It was seven and she'd been going since she brought the Commissioner the morning reports at eight.

Two Bolivar Boys were sitting on the hood of her car. One had his head swathed in surgical gauze. The other was scratching under his shirt at the heavy tape bandaging his ribs. Kathy opened her door. They just sat there, insolently watching her. In Spanish she said, forming the words slowly, "Please get off my car so I can drive away."

They exchanged looks and started laughing. The taped one clutched his ribs and winced.

About the only way to disturb Kathy Dee's placid nature was to laugh at her. Without thinking about it, she reached under her jacket toward her gun. They got off her car quickly, saying, "No problem, no problem."

Kathy got in, started up, then lowered her window.

"Hey?"

"Yeah?"

"What were you laughing for? All I said was get off my car."

They exchanged wary looks. "Is that what you said?"

"Wha'd you think I said?"

Both shrugged. The braver said, "You go, 'You wanna buy my car?' "

"I did?" She leafed through the phrasebook open on the seat beside her. "Oh, my . . . Hey, listen, you know Eduardo in there?"

Their faces closed up.

"Do you?"

"Yeah."

"If Eduardo ever asked you to get a car, what kind of car would you get for him?"

They looked relieved at the easy question. "Buick," said one.

"LTD," volunteered his friend.

"A four-door sedan?" she mused in Spanish.

They laughed, the taped one clutching his ribs, pleading, "Lady, you're killing me."

"Four-wheel drive?" his companion said. "What for, it ain't snowing."

The taped man bent double. "Stop! Stop!"

"Besides, you wheel around in a Jeep the cops think you're selling dope."

"You mean a big car."

"Four door. *Mucho grande. Mucho viejo.*"

She took pity on the taped one and drove a couple of blocks before she looked up *viejo. Mucho grande,* very big, she got. Very big, very *old.* Of course. Older sedans had the room for six Bolivar Boys and their loot.

When she called in, the Commissioner had left for a testimonial dinner at the Waldorf Astoria. She was hungry and feeling a little lonely. One of the problems with this "Commissioner's moll" arrangement was she spent most of her working hours without a real partner, and no teammates on a squad.

She drove over to Third Avenue in Midtown to an Irish joint cops hung out in, thinking to have a burger at the bar. A few people nodded, but no one invited her to join them and the only guy who sat down to talk was a married sergeant she didn't want to know.

Here was another problem. Her fellow officers didn't scorn her like an Internal Affairs pariah, but most avoided her, just to be on the safe side, off-duty as well as on.

"Eighty-six the burger."

Better to work than sit around bitching. She found a quiet pay phone and ordered up a list of vehicles stolen the night Little Rick died. Few owners of older cars bothered to report them stolen. Of big and old that night, there was only one, a Buick Electra, 1973, stolen from Mr. Jorge Jimenez, who lived on West 107th Street, a few blocks from where they found Rick's body.

At the Waldorf, in the Grand Ballroom, where three thousand high-flying Manhattanites had descended to dance and dine, the Commissioner figured he was having as much fun as a bear in a leg trap. They'd stuck him at the head table, flanked him with airheads in glitter and silk, and assembled a twelve-piece honkie band to rape Duke Ellington. He was debating whether a round from the .32 in his ankle holster would alert the waiter to his empty glass, or if he would be forced to wing the bastard with his .38, when suddenly his spirit soared: Here came Kathy Dee, cutting across the dance floor, scattering couples like a little blond bowling ball. He grinned with pleasure. She looked too pumped to care whether she looked out of place in her bomber jacket and jeans, though for his money there wasn't a broad in the joint who could touch her.

"Suppose," she whispered, swooping behind him, "suppose Little Rick got caught by the guy whose car he stole for the getaway."

"I *told* you something was missing."

"Yeah. Yeah."

The women were openly eavesdropping. Kathy leaned closer, her lips brushing his ear. "Guy named Jorge Jimenez on 107th."

"You ain't going to East Harlem."

"West. Right off Amsterdam. Three blocks from the greenhouse mansion."

The commissioner didn't like it; there were crackhouses on that block. But there was no way he could order her not to do the Job, so he joked, "Don't forget your gun. And take your pal what's-her-name from the Ninth with you."

"Darlene's pregnant."

"Take her anyway."

She telephoned Darlene from the Waldorf lobby. Darlene was home sick. Working the graveyard shift, she got her morning sickness in the evening. Kathy told her that her mother said that it was easier with the second child. Darlene went to throw up.

As tenements went, Jorge Jimenez's on West 107th was

model housing. It had aluminum storm windows, the front door locked, and the bells worked, after a fashion. Kathy got an electric clicking noise in reply and when she said, *"Policia,"* someone buzzed her in. A super was sweeping the stairs. The halls reeked of cooking, but did not stink. Wondering why stairs were always steeper than the Stairmaster in the Headquarters gym, Kathy knocked on the Jimenez's fourth-floor door.

A woman opened it on a chain, peered at her tin. She had shiny black hair streaming back in a bun, wide-set deep brown eyes, and a complexion almost as dark as the Commissioner's.

"Officer Dee," said Kathy. "I'd like to talk to Mr. Jorge Jimenez. May I come in?"

The woman backed into the apartment. She was strikingly beautiful, though oddly fearful, Kathy thought, for someone whose husband felt comfortable enough with the police to report a stolen car. When her children edged toward her, eyes big on Kathy, she knelt and enveloped them in her arms. They had been watching television on a huge old set that dominated the shabby living room. It was made of wood and imitation brass and had enormous cloth-covered speakers. Commissioner Grove had explained that poor people favored the big old cabinet models thieves couldn't carry out the window.

Between Kathy's English and fragmentary Spanish and Mrs. Jimenez's Spanish and fragmentary English, they established that Mr. Jimenez was at work. Mrs. Jimenez produced a tattered menu from a Hell's Kitchen saloon where, it appeared, Jorge Jimenez was a cook.

Kathy Dee knew the joint at the corner of Tenth and 57th, a block from John Jay College. A DEA guy she had dated had hung out there. She drove downtown fast, wondering if the guy was still around.

The joint was jumping. Night classes had broken; Roosevelt Hospital was nearby; and CBS television studios were across the street. Cops, nurses, and television technicians lined the bar three deep, and jammed the tables. She knew the owner by sight, pushed up to him at the end of the bar and flashed her tin. "Mr. Armstrong," she shouted over the roar of the crowd and the classical music blaring from the stereo, "I'm here to talk with one of your cooks, Jorge Jimenez."

Armstrong, bearded and almost as broad as he was tall, had a friendly face backed up by hard eyes. "Are you kidding?"

"I'm not kidding, Mr. Armstrong. Jorge's wife says he works here."

"I got a hundred hungry customers waiting for dinner. If I were to shout, 'There's a woman here going to arrest the cook,' they'd tear you limb from limb."

"Half your customers are cops. If I were to yell 'Officer needs assistance,' they would tear *you* limb from limb."

"Not if I yelled, 'When she's done with the cook she's going to arrest the bartender!'"

"We've got a problem," Kathy admitted.

"How about I buy you a drink? Things quiet down in an hour."

"Water," she said. "And I'll buy a medium burger."

"I got Asheville Spring and Adirondack Purge."

"Tap."

Armstrong went around the bar and drew it himself. "I've seen you here before, haven't I?"

"I'm taking Spanish at John Jay."

Armstrong shouted something in Spanish that she couldn't understand. Her reply puzzled him.

Her hamburger came. She put ketchup on it and money on the bar. Through the kitchen service slit she could see four cooks in short-sleeved white shirts, hard at work. "Which one is Jorge?"

"The huge smiling guy," said Armstrong, who was watching the room.

"He's not smiling." Jorge looked solemn as a high school principal—a high school principal with a short haircut, a baby face, and Schwarzenegger muscles.

"Something's bothering him."

"What?"

"He wouldn't tell me."

"Does he usually?"

"Jorge's worked for me for four years. Whenever I need another guy, he brings a cousin. What's the problem?"

"No problem. I'm following up his stolen car report."

"He got it back."

"He did?"

"Yeah. There it is." Armstrong nodded across Tenth Avenue where a nineteen-year-old Buick was parked under a street-light. It gleamed black except where it was rusty, and on the left front fender, which was red. Kathy kicked herself for missing it on the way in.

"He didn't cancel the stolen report."

"I suspect he figured that if reporting it stolen didn't get it back, then why bother. He got lucky, found it himself."

"Can you spare him now?"

"You mind talking to him in the cellar, stay out of the other guys' way?"

Armstrong led her into the back and down a flight of stairs into an underground prep kitchen with a couple of walk-in coolers, a chopping block, and an aluminum sink big enough to wash a Dalmatian. A skinny boy was sitting on an upturned milk carton, separating good lettuce leaves from bad. Armstrong went up to get Jorge. The boy gave Kathy a shy smile and went back to work. Overhead the restaurant roared like the ocean a couple of blocks from the beach.

She heard Jorge's heavy tread on the stairs. His shoulders were slumped and it occurred to her that nothing looked sadder than a cheerful person who wasn't smiling. It also occurred to her that she was not as invincible as she sometimes thought she was; having left Darlene at home she had placed herself in a potentially dangerous position in a cellar with a two-hundred-pound cook who might have twisted Little Rick's head off like a bottle cap.

"Stop right there, please."

Jorge's eyes got big.

Kathy glanced at the boy prepping vegetables, just in case he was coming to the defense of the man he owed his job and green card. There was graffiti on the wall beside him, written in neat block print: JORGE. DOCTOR. LAWYER. ENGINEER.

The Commissioner scratched and belched. His stomach rumbled. "You had lunch yet?"

"It's ten forty-five," Kathy replied through a mouth of red pins. She had erected a map of the West Side on an easel in front of his desk and was inserting pins to mark the Bolivar Car Service, the burgled mansion with the shattered greenhouse,

Jorge Jimenez's apartment, and the secluded stretch of Riverside Drive where Little Rick Garcia's body had been found.

"Getting near that time," the Commissioner ventured.

She stepped back, crossed her arms over her chest, to his disappointment, and said, "Here's how I read it. Jorge heads out to work and discovers that his treasured Buick is missing. The third car he's had stolen since he got a second job so he could afford a car. Mad as hell, he goes walking around the neighborhood looking for it. Here, on Riverside, he finds Little Rick waiting in it, motor running, two blocks from where he is supposed to pick up the Bolivar Boys and their loot. Jorge yanks Little Rick out of the car and breaks his neck."

"So Jorge hops in his own car and drives away?"

"Stranding the Bolivar Boys in the rich guy's garage."

"Bad night for the bad guys," the Commissioner chuckled. "Poor Jorge . . . Can you prove your case?"

"No witnesses."

"How about physical evidence? Any sign of Little Rick in Jorge's car? Prints, blood, hair, cigarette butts, beer can with his saliva?"

"Doubtful."

"Why?"

Kathy Dee shifted uncomfortably from one exquisite little foot to the other. The Commissioner's face darkened to the shade of a black hole about to devour a galaxy. "I said, *why?*"

"Jorge claims he found his car, abandoned, and that he drove it directly to a car wash by the Fordham Bridge."

"He *what?* That's a cold-blooded mutt move."

"He said it was soiled. When I pressed him he used the Spanish *violar.* Like violate or rape. He said he had to clean it up to make it his again. He said it smelled of the thief."

"Goddamn, you brought me another dogfight."

"I believe him."

"The mutt willfully destroyed evidence."

"Yes. But like a rape victim who has to take a bath."

"We're talking about a car here, not a woman's body."

"Jorge works sixty, seventy hours a week at two jobs, cooking in a bar, mopping floors in laundromats—the second job. The car's the only thing that makes him feel he can hold his head up like a man."

"He's got a wife and kids."

"He's very young. It's not enough. He sees drug dealers younger than him driving brand-new Jeeps. Believe me. He was violated."

"He's a stone killer."

"He's not. I saw his apartment. I saw his family. I saw what he wrote on the wall. I told you what he wrote."

"He shoulda wrote 'Mutt.' "

"I did *not* bring you a mutt. I brought you a decent ordinary human being who a mutt pushed too far."

Joe Grove sneered.

Kathy Dee snatched up the Unusual Occurrence reports and read aloud: "*Two* little boys killed in Harlem, probably molested first. *Four* drug dealers shot by the competition. *Two* bodega owners shot dead. And *three* drive-bys . . . Will the city be a better place with Jorge Jimenez behind bars?"

"You want to let him go?"

"I . . . I was just trying to say he's not a mutt, but maybe—"

"Let's not carry this human thing too far. I don't allow no God Squad on my force."

"Are you saying I missed something?" Kathy asked sullenly.

"Are you sure you didn't?"

"Like what?"

Joe averted his eyes. He had never seen her pout before. It did things to her lips that didn't bear thinking about. "Why not visit Little Rick's funeral?"

"Why?"

"See who shows and who don't."

The Ortiz Funeral Home and Pentecostal Church occupied side-by-side storefronts on 117th east of Amsterdam Avenue. Little Rick lay in a satin-lined coffin, his head on straight. His family filed by, little girls bewildered in their best dresses, solemn boys in confirmation suits. An old grandmother hugged herself and wailed. His mother and father were back in Bolivia, the funeral director told Kathy, who observed from behind a curtain.

The Bolivar Boys arrived, all scowls and sneers, and ushered the other mourners out. The coffin sat alone.

Eduardo the dispatcher came in, supporting a grieving woman on his arm. She was dressed in black, her face hidden by a veil of Spanish lace. Sobbing bitterly, she raised the veil to kiss Little Rick.

Kathy stepped through the curtain.

Eduardo's hand dropped into his pocket. "What are you doing here?"

"My question," said Kathy Dee. "What are you doing here, Mrs. Jimenez?"

Mrs. Jimenez whirled away. Kathy caught her arm. Eduardo grabbed Kathy's hair and Commissioner Joe Grove came through the door like an avalanche, and jammed a revolver into Eduardo's ear. "Let go of my officer, asshole."

"Watch it! He's got a gun in his pocket."

"Where it's going to stay unless he wants a wind tunnel where his brains ought to be."

"Chill, chill," cried Eduardo, raising his hands. "I was just helping Little Rick's lady!"

Mrs. Jimenez, whose arm Kathy still held, was trembling.

"Hey, she got a right to say good-bye," Eduardo said indignantly.

"Jorge know she's here?" asked Kathy.

"*Madre*," Mrs. Jimenez whispered at the sound of her husband's name. "He kill me."

The Commissioner frowned. "Sounds like 'Doctor, Lawyer, Engineer' has a temper, Irish."

"Sex," Kathy whispered.

"Told you sex was missing. Now here's what you do to wrap this up," he added in a low voice. "Go back to your notes and find out exactly who reported Jorge's car stolen. As for you, sir"—lifting Eduardo slightly off the floor—"on the off chance you've mislaid your pistol permit, perhaps I can offer you a ride downtown."

She got back to Headquarters first, brewed coffee, and poured him a cup as he came in. "Sorry I'm late. Some idiot from the *Times* thought me booking Eduardo would make a story for the Style section. Wha'd you get?"

"The car was reported stolen directly to the officers who responded to a domestic disturbance complaint at Jorge's apartment."

"Domestic disturbance?" The Commissioner looked very pleased with himself.

"Neighbors called 911. Mrs. Jimenez was screaming."

"Would you care to interpret these events?"

"I feel so stupid."

"You can always get by on your looks, Irish. How do you read it?"

"Jorge goes cruising in his car, looking for his wife. He catches her with Little Rick on Riverside Drive. She runs home. Little Rick climbs into Jorge's car, thinking to either smooth this over or intimidate him. Jorge breaks Little Rick's neck, drops his boy on the sidewalk, drives home, and tells Mrs. Jimenez that he has killed her lover. Her screams bring the blues, who've been called there in the past. The blues decide that Jorge looks like he's getting ready to kill somebody. They cuff him. But Mrs. Jimenez looks at her children, thinks, 'How can I send their father to jail?' and says to the blues, 'I was screaming because I was so upset our car was stolen again.' "

"Whoa," said the Commissioner. "Why would she say the car was stolen, knowing it meant more dealing with cops?"

Kathy said, "Panic. It's been a hell of an evening. But it's not a bad story, because it explains why Jorge's so upset, too. Anyway, the cops bought it."

The Commissioner nodded, "It would also explain any evidence of the killing found in the car."

"No," said Kathy. "That smart they're not. As soon as the cops leave their apartment it hits Jorge that she had really blown it with the car story, that now the cops will come back. So he took it to the car wash, just like he did the last time it was stolen."

"Why didn't he just report that he found it?"

"He didn't want to 'find' it too soon. He wanted to put time between Little Rick's death and his finding the car."

The Commissioner thought it through. "Okay, so we have a crime of passion by the husband and obstruction of justice by the wife. I like it. It's even more human than the car. I can relate to a guy who kills for a wife."

"But what happened to the Bolivar Boys' getaway car?"

"Best part. Little Rick went sinless to his Maker. Jorge got him before he had a chance to steal a car— Hey, Irish, don't look so blue."

"At least we were half-right," she said, with little conviction. "He killed for jealousy instead of a car."

"Still want to let him walk?"

"No, sir."

The Commissioner pulled some handcuffs from his desk. "Go pick him up."

"I don't deserve to make the arrest," said Kathy. "Give it to the Two-Four squad."

"That's mighty white of you, partner. But I didn't make Commissioner giving away collars and you won't either."

He saw her try her big smile, saw it didn't work.

"It's not my collar. *You* solved the case. I just ran around like I was your driver, or something."

"Or something," Joe said, tossing her the cuffs. "Go get him. Take backup. Plenty of it. And don't turn your back on that wife."

"Aren't you coming with me?"

"No, I got to make a call."

The prettiest little behind on the job went out the door. He sighed. Shaking his head, he flipped through his Rolodex, then telephoned a former protégé, now one of the bright young stars of the Detective Bureau. A sleepy voice answered on the first ring, cleared instantly at the familiar rumble of Joe's voice.

"Did I wake you? . . . Good. Listen, I'm sending you a smart kid. . . . How smart? Smarter than you. . . . I'll be taking a personal interest in her progress. Very personal. . . . No. Not like that." He tried to smile, but it didn't work. "More like a fatherly interest."

*Mary
Higgins
Clark*

PLUMBING
FOR WILLY

IF ALVIRAH MEEHAN HAD BEEN ABLE TO LOOK INTO A CRYSTAL BALL and watch the events of the next ten days unfold, she would have grabbed Willy by the hand and raced out of the green room. Instead she sat and chatted with the other guests of the Phil Donahue program. Today the subject was not sex orgies or battered husbands but people who had messed up their lives by winning big in the lottery.

The support group for lottery winners had been contacted by the Donahue show and now the worst-case guests had been chosen. Alvirah and Willy would be a counterpoint to the others, the interviewer told them. "Whatever she means by that," Alvirah commented to Willy after their initial interview.

For her appearance, Alvirah had had her hair freshly colored to the soft strawberry shade that softened her angular face. This morning Willy had told her that she looked exactly the same as she did when he'd first laid eyes on her at a Knights of

Columbus dance more than forty years ago. Baroness Min von Schreiber had flown into New York from the Cypress Point Spa in Pebble Beach to select Alvirah's outfit for the broadcast. "Be sure to mention that the first thing you did when you won the lottery was to come to the Spa," she cautioned Alvirah. "With this damn recession business is not so brisk."

Alvirah was wearing a pale blue silk suit with a white blouse and her signature sunburst pin. She wished she'd managed to lose the twenty pounds she'd regained when she and Willy went to Spain in August, but still Alvirah knew she looked very nice. Very nice for her, that was. She had no illusions that with her slightly jutting jaw and broad frame she'd ever be tapped to compete in the Mrs. America contest.

There were two other sets of guests; three co-workers in a pantyhose factory who'd shared a ten million dollar ticket six years ago. They'd decided their luck was so good that they should buy racehorses with their winnings and were now broke. Their future checks were owed to the banks and Uncle Sam. The other winners, a couple, had won sixteen million dollars, bought a hotel in Vermont, and were now slaving seven days a week trying to keep up with the overhead. Any leftover money was used to place classified ads trying to dump the hotel on someone else.

An assistant came to bring them into the studio.

Alvirah was used to being on television now. She knew enough to sit at a slight angle so she looked a little thinner. She didn't wear chunky jewelry that could rustle against the microphone. She kept her sentences short.

Willy, on the other hand, could never get used to being in the public eye. Even though Alvirah always assured him he was a grand-looking man and people did take him for Tip O'Neill, he was happiest with a ratchet in his hand fixing a leaking pipe. Willy was a born plumber.

Donahue began in his usual breezy, slightly incredulous voice. "Can you believe that after you win millions of dollars in the lottery you need a support group? Can you believe that you can be broke even though you have big fat checks *still coming in?*"

"Nah," the studio audience dutifully shrieked.

Alvirah remembered to tuck her stomach in then reached for

Willy's hands and entwined his fingers in hers. She didn't want him to look nervous on the television screen. A lot of their family and friends would be watching. Sister Cordelia, Willy's oldest sister, had invited a whole crowd of retired nuns to the convent to see the show.

Three men observing the program with avid interest were not Donahue's usual viewers. Sammy, Clarence and Tony had just been released from the maximum security prison near Albany where they'd been guests of the state for twelve years for their part in the armed robbery of a Brink's truck. Unfortunately for them they never got to spend their six hundred thousand dollar heist. The getaway car had blown a tire a block from the scene of the crime.

Now, having paid their debt to society, they were looking for a new way to get rich. The idea of kidnapping the relative of a lottery winner was Clarence's brainchild. That was why they were watching Donahue today from their seedy room in the shabby Lincoln Arms Hotel on Ninth Avenue and Fortieth Street. Tony at thirty-five was ten years younger than the others. Like his brother, Sammy, he was barrel-chested, with powerful arms. Small eyes disappeared into the folds of flesh from hooded lids. His thick dark hair was unkempt. He obeyed his brother blindly and his brother obeyed Clarence.

Clarence was a total contrast to the others. Small, wiry, and soft-voiced he emitted a chilling aura. With good reason people were instinctively afraid of him. Clarence had been born without a conscience, and a number of unsolved homicides would have been cleared from the books if he had talked in his sleep during his incarceration.

Sammy had never admitted to Clarence that Tony had been joyriding in the getaway car the night before the Brink's robbery and had run over a street full of glass. Tony would not have lived to express his regret that he hadn't checked the tires.

One of the lottery winners who'd invested in the horses was whining, "There wasn't enough money in the world to feed those nags." His partners nodded vigorously.

Sammy snorted, "Those jerks can't rub two nickels together." He reached to turn off the set.

"Wait a minute," Clarence snapped.

Alvirah was speaking. "We weren't used to money," she explained. "I mean, we lived a nice life. We had a three-room apartment in Flushing and still keep it just in case the state goes broke and tells us to take a flying leap for the rest of our checks. But I was a cleaning woman and Willy a plumber and we had to be careful."

"Plumbers make a fortune," Donahue protested.

"Not Willy," Alvirah smiled. "He spent at least half his time fixing things free at rectories and convents and for people who were hard up. You know how it is. It's so expensive to get sinks and toilets and tubs working and Willy felt that this was his way of making life easier for other people. He still does it."

"Well, surely you've had some fun with the money?" Donahue asked. "You're very well dressed."

Alvirah remembered to get in a plug for the Cypress Point Spa as she explained that, yes indeed, they had fun. They'd bought an apartment on Central Park South. They traveled a lot. They gave to charity. She wrote articles for the *New York Globe* and she'd been fortunate enough to solve some crimes along the way. She'd always wanted to be a detective. "Nevertheless," she concluded firmly, "in the five years since we've been winners we've saved half of every single check. And that money is all in the bank."

Clarence, followed by Sammy and Tony, joined in the vigorous applause of the studio audience. Clarence was smiling now, a thin, mirthless smile. "Two million bucks a year. Let's say almost half of that for taxes so that means they net a little over a million bucks a year and save half of that. They gotta have two million plus in the bank. That oughta keep us going for a while."

"We snatch her?" Tony asked pointing at the screen.

Clarence withered him with a glance. "No, you dope. Look at the two of them. He's hanging on to her like she's a life preserver. He'd fall apart and go running to the cops. We take *him*. She'll take orders and pay to get him back." He looked around. "I hope Willy enjoys staying with us."

Tony frowned. "We gotta keep him blindfolded. I don't want him picking me out of no lineup."

It was Sammy who sighed. "Tony, don't worry about it. The

minute we get the money, Willy Meehan will be looking for leaks in the Hudson River."

Two weeks later, Alvirah was having her hair done at Louis Vincent, the salon around the corner from the Central Park South apartment. "Since the program was aired, I'm getting so many letters," she told Vincent. "Do you know I even got one from the President? He congratulated us on our wise handling of our finances. He said we were a perfect example of trickle-up prosperity. I wish he'd invited us to a White House dinner. I've always wanted to go to one of those. Well, maybe someday."

"Just make sure I do your hair," Vincent admonished as he gave a final touch to Alvirah's coiffure. "Are you having a manicure?"

Afterward Alvirah knew she should have listened to the queer feeling that suggested she get back to the apartment. She would have caught Willy before he rushed into the car with those men.

Half an hour later when the doorman saw her, he broke into a relieved smile. "Mrs. Meehan, it must have been a mistake. Your husband was so worried."

Incredulous, Alvirah listened as Jose told her that Willy had come running from the elevator, in tears. He'd yelled that Alvirah had had a heart attack under the dryer and had been rushed to Roosevelt Hospital.

"A guy was outside in a black Cadillac," Jose said. "He pulled into the driveway when I opened the door. The doctor sent his own car for Mr. Meehan."

"That sounds funny," Alvirah said slowly. "I'll get over to the hospital right away."

"I'll call a cab," the doorman told her. His phone rang. With an apologetic smile, he picked it up. "Two-eleven Central Park South." He listened, then, looking puzzled, said, "It's for you, Mrs. Meehan."

"Me?" Alvirah grabbed the phone and with a sinking heart heard a whispered voice say, "Alvirah, listen carefully. Tell the doorman your husband is fine. It was all a misunderstanding. He's going to meet you later. Then go upstairs to your apartment and wait for instructions."

Willy had been kidnapped. Alvirah knew it. Oh God, she thought. "That's fine," she managed to say. "Tell Willy I'll meet him in an hour."

"You're a very smart woman, Mrs. Meehan," the voice whispered.

There was a click in her ear. Alvirah turned to Jose. "Complete mistake of course. Poor Willy." She tried to laugh. "Ah . . . ha . . . ha . . ."

Jose beamed. "In Puerto Rico I never once hear about doctor sending his car."

The apartment was on the twenty-second floor and had a terrace overlooking Central Park. Usually Alvirah smiled the minute she opened the door. The apartment was so pretty, and if she said so herself, she had an eye for furniture. All those years of cleaning other people's houses had been an education in interior design.

But today she took no comfort in the matching ivory couch and loveseat, Willy's deep comfortable chair with its own ottoman, the crimson red and royal blue oriental carpet, the black lacquered table and chairs in the dining area, the late afternoon sun that danced across the blanket of autumn leaves in the park.

What good was any of it if anything happened to Willy? With all her heart, Alvirah fiercely wished they'd never won the lottery and were back in their Flushing apartment over Orazio Romano's tailor shop. It was at this time she'd be coming home from cleaning Mrs. O'Keefe's house and joking to Willy that Mrs. O'Keefe had been vaccinated with a Victrola needle. "Willy, she never shuts up. Even shouts over the vacuum. It's a good thing she isn't messy. I'd never get the work done."

The phone rang. Alvirah rushed to pick up the extension in the living room then changed her mind and in stumbling haste ran into the bedroom. The recording machine was there. She pushed the record button as she picked up the phone.

It was the same whispery voice. "Alvirah?"

"Yes. Where's Willy? Whatever you do, don't hurt him." She could hear background sounds like planes taking off. Was Willy at an airport?

"We won't hurt him as long as we get the money and as long as you don't call the cops. You *didn't* call them, did you?"

"No. I want to talk to Willy."

"In a minute. How much money have you got in the bank?"

"Something over two million dollars."

"You're an honest woman, Alvirah. That's just about what we figured. If you want Willy back you'd better start making some withdrawals."

"You can have it all."

There was a low chuckle. "I like you, Alvirah. Two million is fine. Take it out in cash. Don't give a hint that anything is wrong. No marked money, baby. And don't go to the cops. We'll be watching you."

The airport sounds became almost deafening. "I can't hear you," Alvirah said desperately. "And I'm not giving you one cent until I'm sure that Willy is still alive."

"Talk to him."

A minute later a sheepish voice said, "Hi, honey."

Relief, total and overwhelming, flooded Alvirah. Her ever-resourceful brain, which had been inactive since Jose told her about Willy getting in the "doctor's car," resumed its normal steel-trap efficiency.

"Honey," she yelled so that his abductors could hear, "tell those guys to take good care of you. Otherwise they won't get a plug nickel."

Willy's hands were tied together. So were his feet. He watched as the boss, Clarence, put his thumb on the handset and the connection broke. "That's quite a woman you have, Willy," Clarence said. Then Clarence turned off the machine that simulated airport background.

Willy felt like a jerk. If Alvirah had really had a heart attack, Louis or Vincent would have called him from the salon. He should have known that. What a dope he was. He looked around. This was some crummy dump. When he got in the car the guy who was hiding in the backseat put a gun in his neck. "Try to make trouble and I blow you away." The gun was jostling against him when they hustled him through the lobby, up the rickety elevator of this crummy joint. It was only a block from the Lincoln Tunnel. The windows were closed tight, but even so the exhaust fumes from the buses and trucks and cars were overwhelming. You could practically see them.

Willy had sized up Tony and Sammy fast. Not too much upstairs. He might be able to give them the slip somehow. But when Clarence came in, announcing that he'd warned Alvirah to let the doorman think everything was hunky-dory, Willy felt his first real fear. Clarence reminded him of Nutsy, a guy he'd known as a kid. Nutsy used to shoot his BB gun into birds' nests.

It was obvious Clarence was the boss. He called Alvirah and talked to her about the ransom. He made the decision to put Willy on the phone. Now he said, "Okay, put him back in the closet."

"Hey, wait a minute," Willy protested. "I'm starving."

"We're gonna order hamburgers and french fries," Sammy told him as he slipped a gag over Willy's mouth. "We'll letcha eat."

Tony trussed Willy's feet and legs in a spiral sequence of cord and knots and shoved him into the narrow closet. The door did not seal against the frame and Willy could hear the low-toned conversation. "Two million bucks means she has to go to twenty banks. She's too smart to leave more than a hundred thou in any of them. That's how much is insured. Figuring the forms she has to fill out and the bank, counting the money, give her three, four days to get it."

"She'll need four," Clarence said. "We get the money by Friday night. We tell her we're gonna count it and then she can pick up Willy." He laughed. "Then we send her a map with a big X to show where to start dredging."

Alvirah sat for hours in Willy's chair, staring unseeingly as the late afternoon sun sent slanting shadows over Central Park. The last lingering rays disappeared. She reached to turn on the lamp and got up slowly. It was no use thinking of all the good times she and Willy had had these forty years or that just this morning they were going through brochures to decide on whether to take a camel trip through India or a balloon safari in western Africa.

I'm going to get him back, she decided, her jaw jutting out a little more aggressively. The first thing she had to do was to make a cup of tea. The next was to get out all the bankbooks and lay a plan for going from one bank to another and withdrawing cash.

The banks were scattered all over Manhattan and Queens. One-hundred-thousand-dollar deposits in each of them and, of course, accumulated interest, which they took out at the end of the year and used to start a new account. "No double the money schemes for us," they'd agreed. In the bank. Insured. Period. When someone had tried to talk them into buying zero bonds that paid off in ten or fifteen years, Alvirah had said, "At our age we don't buy things that pay off in ten years."

She smiled, remembering that Willy had chimed in, "And we don't buy green bananas either."

Alvirah swallowed a giant lump in her throat as she sipped the tea and decided that tomorrow morning she'd start on Fifty-seventh Street at Chase Manhattan, go across the street to Chemical, work her way along Park Avenue starting at Citibank and then hit Wall Street.

It was a long night lying awake wondering if Willy was okay. I'm going to make them let me talk to him every night until I get all the money, she promised herself. That way they won't hurt him till I figure something out.

At dawn she was becoming tempted to call the police. By the time she got up, at seven, she'd decided against it. These people might have a spy in the building who would report if there was a lot of activity in the apartment. She couldn't take a chance.

Willy spent the night in the closet. They loosened the ropes enough for him to stretch out a little. But they didn't give him a blanket or pillow and his head was resting on someone's shoe. There was no way to push it aside. There was too much junk in the closet. When he dozed off occasionally he dreamt that his neck was embedded on the side of Mount Rushmore directly below the sculpture of Teddy Roosevelt's face.

The banks didn't open till nine. By eight-thirty, Alvirah, in a burst of pressure-cooker energy, had cleaned the already clean apartment. Her bankbooks were in her voluminous shoulder bag. She had dug from the closet a frankfurter-shaped plastic carry-all, the one remnant on Central Park South of the days when she and Willy spent their vacations taking Greyhound tours to the Catskills.

The October morning was crisp and Alvirah was wearing a light green suit that she'd bought when she was on one of her diets. The skirt wouldn't close, but a large pin solved that problem. Automatically she fastened her sunburst pin with the concealed recorder on the lapel.

It was still too early to leave. Trying to keep up the positive thinking that everything would be hunky-dory as soon as the money was paid, Alvirah reheated the kettle and turned on the CBS morning news.

For once the headlines were fairly mundane. There was no bigshot Mafia guy on trial. No fatal attraction homicide. Nobody had been arrested for selling phony junk bonds.

Alvirah sipped her tea and was about to hit the OFF button when the newscaster announced that as of today, New Yorkers could use the device that recorded the phone number of incoming callers within the 212 area code.

It took a minute for her to realize what that meant. Then Alvirah jumped up and ran to the utility closet. Among the other electronic devices that she and Willy delighted in taking home from Hammacher Schlemmer was the recording machine that listed incoming phone numbers. They'd bought it not realizing it was useless in New York.

Dear Lord and his Blessed Mother, she prayed as she ripped the box open, pulled out the recorder and with trembling fingers substituted it for the answering machine in the bedroom. *Let them be keeping Willy in New York. Let them call from wherever they're hiding him.*

She remembered to record an announcement. "You have reached the home of Alvirah and Willy Meehan. At the beep please leave a message. We'll get back to you real soon." She played it back. Her voice sounded different, worried, full of stress.

She forced herself to remember that she had won the dramatic medal in the sixth-grade play at St. Francis Xavier School in the Bronx. Be an actress, she told herself firmly. She took a deep breath and began again: "Hell-lo. You have reached the home . . ."

That's more like it, she decided when she listened to the new version. Then, clutching her shoulder bag, Alvirah headed for Chase Manhattan Bank to begin to put together Willy's ransom money.

I'm gonna go nuts, Willy thought as he tried to flex arms that somehow managed to be both numb and aching. His legs were still firmly trussed together. He'd given up on them. At eight-thirty he heard a faint rapping. Probably what passed for room service in this dump. They brought up lousy food on paper plates. At least that was the way the hamburgers had been delivered last night. Even so, the thought of a cup of coffee and a piece of toast set Willy's mouth to watering.

A moment later the closet door opened. Sammy and Tony were staring down at him. Sammy held the gun while Tony released Willy's gag. "Didja have a good night's sleep?" Tony's unlovely smile revealed a broken eyetooth.

Willy longed to have his hands free for just two minutes. They itched to give Tony a matching set of eyeteeth. "Slept like a baby," he lied. He nodded in the direction of the bathroom. "How about it?"

"What?" Tony blinked, his rubbery face drooping into puzzlement.

"He needs to go to the head," Clarence said. He crossed the narrow room and bent over Willy. "See that gun?" He pointed to it. "It has a silencer. You try anything funny and it's all over. Sammy has a very nervous trigger finger. Then we'll all be mad because you gave us so much trouble. And we'll have to take it out on your wife. Get it?"

Willy was absolutely certain that Clarence meant it. Tony might be dopey. Sammy might have a trigger finger but he wouldn't do anything without getting the okay from Clarence. And Clarence was a killer. He tried to sound calm. "I get it."

Somehow he managed to hobble to the bathroom. Tony loosened his hands enough that he could splash some water in his face. Willy looked around in disgust. The tile was broken and for sure it hadn't been cleaned in years. Flecks of rust-corroded enamel covered the tub and sink. Worst of all was the constant dripping from the water tank, faucets, and shower head. "Sounds like Niagara Falls in here," Willy commented to Tony, who was standing at the door.

Tony shoved him over to where Sammy and Clarence were sitting at a rickety card table, which was piled with containers of coffee and objects that resembled abandoned Egg McMuffins. Clarence nodded to the folding chair next to Sammy. "Sit there." Then he whirled. "Shut that damn door," he ordered Tony. "That stinking dripping is driving me nuts. Kept me awake half the night."

A thought came to Willy. He tried to sound casual. "I guess we'll be here a couple of days. If you pick up a few tools for me I can fix that for you." He reached for a container. "I'm the best plumber you ever kidnapped."

Alvirah learned that it was much easier to put money in a bank than to get it out. When she presented her withdrawal slip at Chase Manhattan, the teller's eyes bulged. Then he asked her to step over to an assistant manager's desk.

Fifteen minutes later Alvirah was still adamantly insisting that, no, she wasn't unhappy with the service. Yes, she was sure she wanted the money in cash. Yes, she understood what a certified check was. Finally she demanded emphatically, "Is it my money or isn't it?"

"Of course. Of course." They would have to ask her to fill out some forms—government regulations for cash withdrawals of over ten thousand dollars.

Then they had to count the money. Eyes popped when Alvirah told them she wanted five hundred hundred-dollar bills and one thousand fifty-dollar bills. That took a lot of counting.

It was nearly noon when Alvirah hailed a cab to cover the three blocks to the apartment, dump the money in a dresser drawer, and start out again for the Chemical Bank on Eighth Avenue.

By the end of the day she'd managed to get only three hundred thousand of the two million she needed. Then she sat in the apartment staring at the phone. There *was* a way to move quicker. In the morning she'd call the rest of the banks and tell them to expect her withdrawals. Start counting now, fellows.

At six-thirty the phone rang. Alvirah grabbed it as a phone number appeared on the surface of the recording machine. A familiar number. Alvirah realized the caller was the formidable Sister Cordelia.

Willy had seven sisters. Six of them had gone in the convent. The seventh, now deceased, was the mother of Brian, the playwright Alvirah and Willy loved as a son. Brian was in London now. Alvirah would have turned to him for help if he'd been in New York.

But she wasn't about to tell Cordelia about Willy's abduction. Cordelia would have the White House on the phone demanding that the President dispatch the standing army to rescue her brother.

Cordelia sounded a little peeved. "Alvirah, Willy was supposed to come over this afternoon. One of the old girls we visit needs to have her toilet fixed. It's not like him to forget. Let me talk to him."

Alvirah laughed that same he-har-har laugh that sounded even to her ears like the canned stuff you hear on lousy television shows. "Cordelia, it must have gone out of his mind," she said. "Willy is . . . he's . . ." She had a burst of inspiration. "Willy's in Washington to testify about the cheapest way to fix plumbing in the tenements the government is restoring. You know how he can do miracles to make things work. The President read that Willy is a genius at that and sent for him."

"The President!" Cordelia's incredulous tone made Alvirah wish she'd named Senator Moynihan or maybe some congressman. I never lie, she fretted. I don't know how.

"Willy would never go to Washington without you," Cordelia snorted.

"They sent a car for him." Well, at least that's true, Alvirah thought.

She heard the *hrrump* on the other end of the line. Cordelia was nobody's fool. "Well, when he gets back, tell him to get right over here."

Two minutes later the phone rang again. This time the number that came up was not familiar. It's THEM, Alvirah thought. She realized her hand was shaking. Forcing herself to think of the sixth-grade dramatic medal, she reached for the receiver.

Her hello was hardy and confident.

"We hope you've been banking, Mrs. Meehan."

"Yes, I have. Put Willy on."

"You can talk to him in a minute. We want the money by Friday night."

"Friday night! It's Tuesday now. That only gives me three days. It takes a long time to get all that together."

"*Do it.* Say hello to Willy."

"Hi, honey." Willy's voice sounded subdued. Then he said, "Hey, let me talk."

Alvirah heard the sound of the receiver dropping. "Okay, Alvirah," the whispery voice said. "We're not going to call you again until Friday night at seven o'clock. We'll let you talk to Willy then and we'll tell you where to meet us. Remember, any funny business and in the future you'll have to pay to have your plumbing fixed. Willy won't be around to take care of it."

The receiver clicked in her ear. *Willy. Willy.* Her hand still gripping the phone, Alvirah stared at the number listed on the machine: 555-7000. Should she call it back? But suppose one of them answered. They'd know she was tracing them. Instead she called the *Globe*. As she expected, her editor, Jim, was still at his desk. She explained what she needed.

"Sure, I can get it for you, Alvirah. You sound kind of mysterious. Are you working on a case you can write up for us?"

"I'm not sure yet."

Ten minutes later he called back. "Hey, Alvirah, that's some dump you're looking up. It's the Lincoln Arms Hotel on Ninth Avenue, near the Tunnel. It's one step down from a flop house."

The Lincoln Arms Hotel. Alvirah managed to thank Jim before she slammed down the phone and headed out the door.

Just in case she *was* being watched she left the apartment house through the garage and hailed a cab. She started to tell the driver to take her to the hotel, then thought better of it. Suppose one of Willy's kidnappers spotted her? Instead she had him drop her at the bus terminal. That was only a block away from the Lincoln Tunnel.

Her kerchief covering her head, her coat collar turned up, Alvirah walked past the Lincoln Arms Hotel. Dismayed, she realized it was a pretty big place. She glanced up at the windows. Was Willy behind one of them? The building looked as though it had been built before the Civil War, but it was at least ten or twelve stories high. How could she ever find him in this place? Once again she wondered if she should call the cops and then remembered again the time some wife did call and the cops were spotted at the ransom drop and the kidnappers sped away. They found the body three weeks later.

Alvirah stood in the shadows at the side of the hotel and prayed to St. Jude, the saint of the impossible. And then she spotted it. A sign in the window. HELP WANTED. Four to twelve midnight shift. Room service? She *had* to get that job, but not looking like this.

Ignoring the trucks and cars and buses that were barreling toward the tunnel entrance, Alvirah dashed into the street, grabbed a cab, and snapped the address of the apartment in Flushing. Her brain was working overtime.

The old apartment had been their home for forty years and looked exactly the same as it had the day they'd won the lottery. The dark gray overstuffed velour couch and matching chair, the green and orange rug the lady she used to clean for on Tuesdays had been throwing out, the mahogany veneer bedroom set that had been Willy's mother's bridal furniture.

In the closet were all the clothes she'd worn in those days. Splashy print dresses from Alexander's. Polyester slacks and sweatshirts, sneakers and high-heeled shoes purchased at outlets. In the mirror cabinet of the bathroom she found the henna rinse that made her hair the color of the rising sun on the Japanese flag.

An hour later there was no vestige left of the gentrified lottery winner. Bright red hair wisped around a face now startling with the makeup she used to love before Baroness Min taught her that less is better. Her old lipstick exactly matched her flaming hair. Her eyes were emblazoned in purple shadow. Dungarees too tight across the seat, ankles hidden by thick socks and stuffed into well-worn sneakers, a fleece-lined sweatshirt with the skyline of Manhattan emblazoned across the back finished the transformation.

Alvirah surveyed the overall result with satisfaction. I look like someone who'd apply for a job in that crummy hotel, she decided. Reluctantly she left her sunburst pin in a drawer. It just didn't look right on the sweatshirt.

When she pulled on her old all-weather coat she remembered to switch her money and keys to the voluminous black and green totebag that she'd always carried to her cleaning jobs.

Forty minutes later she was in the Lincoln Arms Hotel. The grimy lobby consisted of a battered desk in front of a wall of mailboxes and four black naugahyde chairs in advanced stages of disrepair. The stained brown carpet was covered with gaping holes that revealed ancient linoleum flooring.

Never mind room service, they ought to look for a cleaning woman, Alvirah thought as she approached the desk.

The clerk, sallow complexioned, bleary-eyed, looked up.

"Whaddaya want?"

"A job. I'm a good waitress."

Something that was more sneer than smile moved the clerk's lips. "You don't need to be good, just fast. Hold old are ya?"

"Fifty," Alvirah lied.

"You're fifty. I'm twelve. Go home."

"I need a job," Alvirah persisted, her heart pounding. She could feel Willy's presence. She'd have taken an oath that he was hidden somewhere in this hotel. "Give me a chance. I'll work free for three or four days. If I'm not the best worker you ever had by, let's say Saturday, you can fire me."

The clerk shrugged. "So whadda I got to lose? Be here tomorrow at four sharp. Whaddaya say your name was?"

"Tessie," Alvirah said firmly. "Tessie Magink."

Wednesday morning Willy could sense the tension tightening between his captors. Clarence flatly refused to allow Sammy to step outside the room. When Sammy complained, Clarence snapped, "After twelve years in a cell you shouldn't have no trouble staying put."

There was no sign of a chambermaid beating down the door to clean the room. But Willy decided it probably hadn't been cleaned in a year anyhow. The three cot-like beds were lined up together, heads against the bathroom wall. A narrow dresser covered with peeling sheets of Contact, a black and white television, and a round table with four chairs completed the decor.

On Tuesday night Willy had persuaded his captors to allow him to sleep on the bathroom floor. It was bigger than the closet and, as he pointed out, stretched out that extra bit would make it possible for him to be able to walk when they exchanged him for the ransom. He did not miss the glances they traded at the suggestion. They had no intention of letting him go free to talk about them. That meant he had about forty-eight hours to figure out a way of being rescued from this fleabag.

At three in the morning when he'd heard Sammy and Tony snoring in harmony and Clarence's irritated but regular gasps, Willie had managed to sit up, get to his feet, and hop over to the toilet. The rope that tethered him to the bathtub faucet allowed him just enough room to touch the lid of the water tank. With his bound hands he lifted it, laid it on the sink, and reached into the grimy, rust-coated water of the tank. The result was that a few minutes later the dripping had become louder, more frequent and more insistent.

That was why Clarence had awakened to the distressing sound of constantly bubbling water. Willy smiled a grim, inner smile as Clarence barked, "I'm gonna go nuts. Sounds like a camel peeing."

When the room service breakfast was being delivered Willy was again securely tied and gagged in the closet this time with Sammy's gun at his temple. From the hall outside the room, Willy could hear the faint croak of the obviously old man who was apparently the sole room service employee. It was useless to even think about attracting his attention.

That afternoon Clarence began stuffing towels around the bathroom door, but nothing could block out the sound of running water. "I'm getting one of my bad headaches," he snarled, settling down on the unmade bed. A few minutes later Tony began to whistle. Sammy shut him up immediately. Willy heard him whisper, "When Clarence gets one of his headaches, watch out."

Tony was clearly bored. His ferret eyes glazed over as he sat watching television, the sound barely turned on. Willy sat next to him, tied to the chair, the gag loosened enough that he could talk through almost closed lips.

At the table, Sammy played endless games of solitaire. In late afternoon, Tony got bored with the television and snapped it off. "You got any kids?" he asked Willy.

Willy knew that if he had any hope of getting out of this dump alive, Tony would be his ticket. Trying to ignore the combination of cramps and numbness in his arms and legs, he told Tony that he and Alvirah had never been blessed with kids, but they thought of his nephew, Brian, as their own child especially since Brian's mother who was Willy's sister had been called to her eternal reward. "I have six other sisters," he explained. "They're all nuns. Cordelia is the oldest. She's sixty-eight going on twenty-one."

Tony's jaw dropped. "No foolin'. When I was a kid and kind of on the streets and picking up a few bucks separating women from their pocketbooks, if you know what I mean, I never once hit on a nun even when they were heading for the supermarket meaning they were carrying cash. When I had a good hit I even left a coupla bucks in the convent mailbox, sort of an expression of gratitude."

Willy tried to look impressed at Tony's largess.

"Will you shut up?" Clarence barked from the bed. "My head's splitting."

Willy breathed a silent prayer as he said, "You know I could fix that leak if I just had a monkey wrench and a screwdriver."

If he could just get his hands on that tank, he thought. He could flood the joint. They couldn't very well shoot him if people were rushing in to stop the cascade of water he could unloose.

Sister Cordelia knew something was wrong. Much as she loved Willy she could not imagine the President sending for him in a private car. Something else; Alvirah was always so open you could read her like the headline of the *New York Post*. But when Cordelia tried to phone Alvirah Wednesday morning there was no answer. Then, when she did reach her at three-thirty, Alvirah sounded out of breath. She was just running out, she explained, but didn't say where. Of course,

Willy was fine. Why wouldn't he be? He'd be home by the weekend.

The convent was an apartment in an old building on Amsterdam Avenue and 110th Street. Sister Cordelia lived there with four elderly sisters and the one novice, twenty-seven-year-old Sister Maeve Marie who had been a police-woman for three years before realizing she had a vocation.

When Cordelia hung up after speaking to Alvirah she sat down heavily on a sturdy kitchen chair. "Maeve," she said, "something is wrong with Willy. I feel it in my bones."

The phone rang again. It was Arturo Morales, the manager of the bank in Flushing around the corner from Willy and Alvirah's old apartment.

"Sister," he began, sounding distressed, "I hate to bother you, but I'm worried."

Cordelia's heart sank as Arturo explained that Alvirah had tried to withdraw one hundred thousand dollars from the bank. They were able to give her only twenty but had promised to have the rest Friday morning. She absolutely needed it by then.

Cordelia thanked him for the information, promised never to hint that he'd violated bank confidentiality, hung up and snapped to Maeve Marie, "Come on. We're going to see Alvirah."

Alvirah reported to the Lincoln Arms Hotel promptly at four o'clock. She'd changed her clothes in the Port Authority. Now standing in front of the desk clerk she felt secure in her disguise. The clerk jerked his head to indicate that she was to go down the corridor to the door marked STAY OUT.

It led to the kitchen. The chef, a bony seventy-year-old who bore a startling resemblance to the cowboy star of the forties Gabby Hayes, was preparing hamburgers. Clouds of smoke rose from the spatters of grease on the grill. He looked up. "You Tessie?"

Alvirah nodded.

"Okay. I'm Hank. Start delivering."

There were no subtleties in the room service department. The kind of brown plastic tray that was found in hospital cafeterias, coarse napkins, plastic utensils, sample-sized mustard, ketchup, and relish.

Hank shoveled limp hamburgers onto buns. "Pour the coffee. Don't fill the cups too much. Dish out the french fries."

Alvirah obeyed. "How many rooms in this place?" she asked as she set up trays.

"Hundred."

"That many!"

Hank grinned, revealing tobacco-stained false teeth. "Only forty rented overnight. The by-the-hour trade ain't looking for room service."

Alvirah considered. Forty wasn't too bad. She figured there had to be at least two men involved in the kidnapping. One to drive the car, one to keep Willy from bopping him. Maybe even one more to make that first phone call. She needed to watch for big orders. At least it was a start.

She began delivering with Hank's firm reminder to collect on the spot. The hamburgers went to the bar, which was inhabited by a dozen or so rough-looking guys you wouldn't want to meet on a dark night. The second order she brought to the room clerk and hotel manager, who presided over the premises from an airless room behind the desk. Their heros were on the house. Her next tray, containing cornflakes and a double boilermaker was for a disheveled, bleary-eyed senior citizen. Alvirah was sure the cornflakes were an afterthought.

Next she was sent with a heavy tray to four men playing cards on the ninth floor. Another card game group on the seventh floor ordered pizzas. On the eighth floor she was met at the door by a husky guy who said, "Oh. You're new. I'll take it. When you knock on the door, don't bang. My brother got a bad headache." Behind him Alvirah could see a man lying on a bed, a cloth over his eyes. The persistent dripping sound from the bathroom reminded her overwhelmingly of Willy. He'd have that leak fixed in no time flat.

There was clearly no one else in the room and the guy at the door looked as though he could have cleaned the contents of the tray on his own. In the closet Willy could just about hear the cadence of a voice that made him ache to be back with Alvirah.

There were enough room service calls to keep her busy from six until about ten. From her own observations and from the explanations of Hank, who grew increasingly garrulous as he began to appreciate her efficiency, Alvirah got to understand the setup. There were ten floors of rooms, ten rooms to a floor. The first six floors were reserved for the hourly guests. The upper floor rooms were the largest, all with baths, and tended to be rented for at least a few days.

Over a plump hamburger that she cooked for him at ten o'clock, Hank told her that everybody registered under a false name. Everybody paid cash. "Like one guy who comes in to clean out his private mailboxes. He publishes dirty magazines. 'Nother guy sets up card games. Lots of fellows come in here and get a bag on when they're supposed to be on a business trip. That kind of stuff. Nothing bad. It's sort of like a private club."

Hank's head began to droop after he'd finished the last of his third glass of beer. A few minutes later he was asleep. Quietly Alvirah went to the table that served as a combination chopping board and desk. When she brought down the money after each order was delivered she'd been instructed to put it in the cigar box that served as cash register. The order slip with the amount was placed in the box next to it. Hank had explained that at midnight, room service ended and the desk clerk tallied up the money, compared it with the receipts, and put the cash in the safe, which was hidden in the bottom of the refrigerator. The order slips were then dropped into a cardboard box under the table. There was a massive jumble of them in place now.

Some would never be missed. Figuring that the top layers had to be the most recent records, Alvirah scooped up an armful and stuffed them in her voluminous handbag. She delivered three more orders to the bar between eleven and twelve. In between deliveries, unable to stand the grimy kitchen, she set about cleaning it up as a bemused Hank watched.

After a quick stop at the Port Authority to change into her good clothes, scrub the rouge and purple shadow from her face, and wrap a turban around her flaming hair, Alvirah stepped out of a cab at quarter of one. Ramon, the night doorman, said, "Sister Cordelia was here. She asked a lot of questions about where you were."

Cordelia was no dope, Alvirah thought with grudging praise.

But a plan was forming in her mind and Cordelia was part of it.

Even before she sank her tired body into the Jacuzzi that was bubbling with Cypress Point Spa oils, Alvirah sorted out the greasy order slips. Within the hour she had narrowed the possibilities. Four rooms consistently sent for large orders. She pushed away the gnawing fear that they were all occupied by card players or some other kind of gamblers and that Willy might be in Alaska right now. Her instinct had told her the minute she set foot in the hotel that he was nearby.

It was nearly three when she got into the double bed. Tired as she was it was impossible to get to sleep. Finally she pictured him there, settling in beside her. "Nighty-night, Willy, lovey," she said aloud and in her head heard him saying, "Sleep tight, honey."

On Thursday morning Clarence's eyes were crossing with the crushing ache that was splitting his head from ear to ear. Even Tony was careful not to cross him. He didn't reach for the television set but contented himself sitting next to Willy and in a hoarse whisper telling him the story of his life. He'd gotten up to age seven, the year he'd discovered how easy it was to shoplift in the candy store when Clarence barked from the bed, "You say you can fix that damn leak?"

Willy didn't want to seem too excited but the muscles in his throat squeezed together as he nodded vigorously.

"Whaddaya need?"

"A monkey wrench," Willy croaked through the gag. "A screwdriver. Wire."

"All right. Sammy, you heard him. Go out and get that stuff."

Sammy was playing solitaire again. "I'll send Tony."

Clarence bolted up. "I said YOU. That dopey brother of yours'll blab to the nearest guy where he's going, why he's going, who he's getting it for. Now go."

Sammy shivered at the tone, remembering how Tony had gone joyriding in the getaway car. "Sure, Clarence, sure," he said soothingly. "And listen, long as I'm out, why not bring in some Chinese food, huh? Could taste good for a change."

Clarence's scowl faded momentarily. "Yeah, okay. Get lotsa soy sauce."

Sister Cordelia arrived at seven o'clock on Thursday morning. Alvirah was prepared for her. She'd been up half an hour and was wearing Willy's plaid bathrobe, which had the faint scent of his shaving lotion and a pot of coffee on the stove. "What's up?" Cordelia asked abruptly.

Over coffee and Sara Lee crumbcake Alvirah explained. "Cordelia," she concluded, "I won't tell you I'm not scared because that would be a lie. I'm scared to death for Willy. But if someone is watching this place or maybe has a delivery boy keeping an eye out and it gets back that strange people were coming and going, they'll kill Willy. Cordelia, I swear to you he's in that hotel and I have a plan. Maeve still has her gun permit, doesn't she?"

"Yes." Sister Cordelia's piercing gray eyes bored into Alvirah's face.

"And she's still friends with the guys she sent to prison, isn't she?"

"Oh sure. They all love her. You know they give Willy a hand fixing pipes whenever he needs it and they take turns delivering meals to our shut-ins."

"That's what I mean. They look like the people who hang out in that place. I want three or four of them to check into the Lincoln Arms tonight. Let them get a card game going. That happens all the time. Tomorrow night at seven o'clock, I get the call where to leave the money. They know that I won't turn it over until I talk to Willy. They can't carry him out of there so I want Maeve's guys covering the exits. It's our only chance."

Cordelia stared grimly into space, then said, "Alvirah, Willy always told me to trust your sixth sense. I guess I'd better do it now."

The chow mein was a welcome relief from the hamburgers. After dinner, Clarence ordered Willy to go into the john and get rid of the dripping noise. Sammy accompanied him. Willy's heart sank when Sammy said, "I don't know how to fix nothing, but I know how not to fix it so don't get smart."

So much for my big plan, Willy thought. Well, maybe I can stall it till I figure something out. He began by chipping at the years of accumulated rust around the base of the tank.

Alvirah dropped off the suitcase with her last bank pickup at twenty to four, barely time enough to rush to the Port Authority, change, and report to the job. As she trotted through the Lincoln Arms lobby she noticed a sweet-faced nun in traditional habit holding out a basket and quietly moving from one to the other occupants of the bar. Everybody threw in a contribution. In the kitchen, Alvirah asked Hank about the nun.

"Oh her. Yeah. She spends it on the kids who live around here. Makes everybody feel good to toss her a buck or two. Kind of spiritual, you know what I mean?"

That night deliveries were not as brisk as the night before. Alvirah suggested to Hank that she sort out all the old slips in the order box.

"Why?" Hank looked astonished.

Alvirah tugged at the sweatshirt she was wearing today. It said, I SPENT THE NIGHT WITH BURT REYNOLDS. Willy had bought it as a gag when they went to Reynolds's theater in Florida. She tried to look mysterious. Why would anyone sort out useless slips? "You never know," she whispered.

The answer seemed to satisfy Hank.

She hid the already sorted slips under the pile she dumped on the table. She already knew what she was looking for. Consistent orders in quantity since Monday.

She narrowed it down to the same four rooms she'd selected at home.

At six o'clock it suddenly got busy. By eight-thirty she'd delivered to three of the four suspect rooms. Two were the ongoing card games. One was now a crap game. She had to admit that none of the players looked like kidnappers.

Room 802 did not phone for an order. Maybe the guy with the bad headache and his brother had checked out. At midnight a discouraged Alvirah was about to leave when Hank grumbled, "Working with you is easy. The new day guy quit and tomorrow they're gonna bring in the kid who fills in. He screws up all the orders."

Breathing a grateful prayer of thanks Alvirah immediately

volunteered to come in for the morning shift of seven to one as
well as her usual four to twelve. She reasoned that she could
still rush to the banks, which had promised to have cash
between twelve-fifteen and three.

"I'll be back at seven," she promised Hank.

"So will I," he complained. "The day cook quit, too."

On the way out Alvirah noticed some familiar faces hanging
around the bar. Louie, who'd served seven years for bankrob-
bery and had a black belt in karate; Petey, who'd been a
strongman for a pawnbroker and served four years for assault;
Lefty, whose specialty was hot cars.

True to their training, even though Alvirah was sure they'd
seen her, neither Louie, Petey, nor Lefty gave any sign of
knowing her.

Willy reduced the dripping to it's original annoying level
then an irritable Clarence shouted in for him to knock off the
hammering. "I can put up with that noise for another twenty-
four hours."

And then what, Willy wondered. There was one hope.
Sammy was bored with observing him fiddling around with the
water tank. Tomorrow Sammy would be more careless. That
night Willy insured the further need of his services by again
crawling over to the water tank and adjusting the drip-drip
level.

In the morning Sammy's eyes were feverish. Tony started
talking about an old girlfriend he planned to look up when they
got to the hideout in Queens and no one told him to keep his
mouth shut. Meaning, Willy thought, they're not worried about
me hearing them.

When breakfast was delivered, Willy, securely stashed in the
closet, jumped so suddenly that the gun in Sammy's hand
almost went off. This time he didn't hear just a cadence of a
voice that reminded him of Alvirah. It was her ringing tone
asking Herman if his brother's headache was any better.

A startled Sammy hissed in Willy's ear, "You crazy or
somethin?"

Alvirah was looking for him. Willy had to help her. He had
to get back into the bathroom, work on the water tank, and tap
the wrench to the tune of "Casey Would Waltz with the

Strawberry Blonde," the song they were playing when he first asked Alvirah to dance at the K of C hall over forty years ago.

He got his chance four hours later when, wrench and screwdriver in hand, a jittery Sammy beside him, at Clarence's furious command, he resumed his task of jointly fixing and sabotaging the water tank.

He was careful not to overdo. He reasonably told a protesting Sammy that he wasn't making that much noise, and anyhow, this place would probably love to have one decent john. Scratching his four-day growth of beard, squirming in his wrinkled clothing, Willy began to send off signals three minutes apart, tap/TAP/taaap/taaap/tap—"and the band played on."

Alvirah was delivering pizzas to 702 when she heard it. The tapping. Oh God, she prayed, oh God. She placed the tray on the uneven tabletop. The occupant of the room, a nice-looking fellow in his thirties, was coming off a binge. He pointed up. "Wouldn't that kill you? They're renovating or something. Take your pick. Sounds like Niagara Falls or New Year's Eve up there."

It has to be 802, Alvirah decided, thinking of the guy on the bed, the doorkeeper, the open bathroom. They must shove Willy in the closet when they order room service. Even though she was so excited her heart was thumping through the sweatshirt that read, DON'T BE A LITTERBUG, she took time to caution the drinker that booze would be his ruination.

There was a phone in the hallway by the bar. Hoping she wasn't being observed by the desk clerk, Alvirah made a hurried call to Cordelia. She finished by saying, "They'll be phoning me at seven o'clock. That's when we strike."

At quarter of seven that night, the occupants of the bar of the Lincoln Arms Hotel were awed at the sight of eight mostly elderly nuns, in traditional floor-length habit, veils, and wimples, entering the lobby softly humming a hymn about the river Jordan. The desk clerk jumped up and made a shooing motion toward the revolving door behind them. Alvirah watched, tray in arms, as Maeve, the appointed spokesman, stared down the desk clerk.

"We have the owner's permission to sing a concert on every floor and ask for donations."

"You got no such thing."

Her voice dropped to a whisper. "We have Mr. . . . 's permission."

The clerk's face paled. "You guys shut up and get out your loot," he yelled at the occupants of the bar. "These here sisters are gonna sing hymns for ya."

"No, we're starting upstairs," Maeve told him. "We'll complete the concert here."

Alvirah protectively brought up the rear as the bevy of nuns led by Cordelia entered the elevator singing, "Michael row your boat ashore. HALLELUJAH."

They went directly to the eighth floor and clustered in the hallway where Lefty, Petey and Louie were waiting. At exactly seven o'clock Alvirah knocked on the door. "Room service," she called.

"We didn't order," a voice snarled.

"Someone did and I've got to collect," she shouted firmly.

She heard scuffling. A door slammed. The closet. They were hiding Willy. The door opened a crack. A nervous Tony instructed, "Leave the tray outside. How much?"

Alvirah kept her foot firmly in the door as strains of "Michael, row your boat ashore," filled the corridor. The oldest nuns materialized behind Alvirah. Clarence had the phone in his hand. "Shut up out there," he shouted.

"Hey, that's no way to talk to the sisters," Tony protested. Reverently he stood aside as they drifted past him into the room.

Sister Maeve brought up the rear, her hands folded in the sleeves of her gown. In an instant, she circled behind Clarence, yanked her right hand out and held a gun against his temple. In the crisp tone that had made her a superb cop, she whispered, "Freeze, or you're dead."

Tony opened his mouth to yell a warning to Sammy but it was obliterated by several loud hallelujahs as Lefty karated him into unconsciousness. Lefty then insured Clarence's silence with a judicious rap on the neck that made him collapse beside Tony on the floor.

Louie and Petey herded the reluctant Sister Cordelia and her elderly flock into the safety of the hallway. It was time to rescue Willy. Lefty had his hand ready to strike. Sister Maeve had her gun pointed. Alvirah threw open the closet door as she bellowed, "Room service."

Sammy was standing next to Willy, his gun in Willy's neck. "Outside, all of you," he snarled. "Drop that gun, lady."

Maeve hesitated, then obeyed.

Sammy released the safety catch on the revolver.

He's trapped and he's desperate, Alvirah thought frantically. *He's going to kill my Willy.* She forced herself to sound calm. "I've got a car in front of the hotel," she told him. "There's two million dollars in it. Take Willy and me with you. You can check the money, drive away and then let us out somewhere." She turned to Lefty and Maeve. "Don't try to stop us or he'll hurt Willy. Get lost both of you." She held her breath and stared at Willy's captor willing herself to seem confident.

Sammy hesitated for an instant. Alvirah watched as he turned the gun to point it at the door. "It better be there, lady," he snapped. "Untie his feet."

Obediently she knelt down and yanked at the knots binding Willie's ankles. She peeked up as she undid the last one. The gun was still pointed at the door. Alvirah remembered how she used to put her shoulder under Mrs. O'Keefe's piano and hoist it up to straighten out the carpet. One, two, three. She shot up like an arrow, her shoulder whamming into Sammy's gun hand. He pulled the trigger as he dropped the gun. The bullet released flaking paint from the drooping ceiling.

Willy threw his hands around Sammy, bearhugging him until the others rushed back into the room.

As though in a dream, Alvirah watched Lefty, Petey and Louie free Willy from his ropes and use them to secure the abductors. She heard Maeve dial 911 and say, "This is Officer Maeve O'Reilly, I mean Sister Maeve Marie reporting a kidnapping, attempted murder and successful apprehension of the perpetrators."

Alvirah felt Willy's arms around her. "Hi, honey," he whispered.

She was so filled with joy she couldn't speak. They gazed at each other. She took in his bloodshot eyes, stubble of beard, and matted hair. He studied her garish makeup and Don't be a

Litterbug sweatshirt. "Honey, you're gorgeous," Willy said fervently. "I'm sorry if I look like one of the Smith Brothers."

Alvirah rubbed her face against his. The tears of relief that were welling in her throat vanished as she began to laugh. "Oh, Sweetie," she cried, "you'll always look like Tip O'Neill to me."